A SPECIES OF REVENGE

Marjorie Eccles

Chivers Press • G.K. Hall & Co.
Bath, England   Thorndike, Maine USA

This Large Print edition is published by Chivers Press, England, and by G.K. Hall & Co., USA.

Published in 1998 in the U.K. by arrangement with HarperCollins Publishers Ltd.

Published in 1998 in the U.S. by arrangement with St. Martin's Press, Inc.

U.K. Hardcover ISBN 0–7540–3425–9 (Chivers Large Print)
U.K. Softcover ISBN 0–7540–3426–7 (Camden Large Print)
U.S. Softcover ISBN 0–7838–0288–9 (Nightingale Series Edition)

The text of this Large Print edition is unabridged.
Other aspects of the book may vary from the original edition.

Set in 16 pt. New Times Roman.

Printed in Great Britain on acid-free paper.

British Library Cataloguing in Publication Data available

Library of Congress Cataloging-in-Publication Data

Eccles, Marjorie.
    A species of revenge / Marjorie Eccles.
        p. cm.
    ISBN 0–7838–0288–9 (lg. print : sc : alk. paper)
    1. Large type books. I. Title.
    [PR6055.C33S54   1998]
    823'.914—dc21   98–7838

PART ONE

The house had a bad feeling again.

It was an atmosphere hard to describe. It hung on the air in spider's webs, invisible until you felt it clinging to your face; or it waited for you behind closed doors, and as you entered a room it curled to the ceiling, thick as smoke. It was unclean, like a fog seeping in around the edges of the windowpanes . . .

But no, it didn't come from outside.

It came from the unspoken tensions of the occupants, from within, from emotions and resentments bottled up for years and about to erupt again like some evil genie. It was there in the silences and the covert glances, in the sum of what was known, and remembered.

*   *   *

Patti Ryman is whistling as she pushes her bike to the summit of the hill, ready to deliver her newspapers on Saturday morning.

'A whistling woman and a crowing hen, Will bring the devil from his den,' *her granddad used to say. Patti grins. She isn't scared of the devil because she knows he doesn't exist. It isn't that which makes her hurry to get the deliveries to the two old houses over and done with. First, to Edwina Lodge, with its familiar 'For Sale' notice still in the garden but now with a red 'SOLD' sticker plastered across it, and the* Guardian *ordered to start on Monday. Having delivered the other papers there, she leaves her bike against the*

3

wall near the shrubbery inside the gates, and goes on to the next house, Simla, with the Independent *for Miss Kendrick and* The Times *for her brother, being careful not to tear these as they're pushed through the letter-box: Miss Kendrick teaches maths at Patti's school, she'll be her form tutor when the new school year starts in a few days' time, and Patti is more afraid of her than any old devil who may be hanging around. The brother, she's never seen, only heard of, so he doesn't bother her.*

No, it's something more than either Miss Kendrick or the devil which causes her to hurry through the dark shrubs and trees surrounding both houses, that makes her want to look back over her shoulder, as if something nasty is lurking in the undergrowth, that starts her heart jumping into her mouth.

She has every cause to be uneasy, though not just now.

She turns with relief into Ellington Close, the cul-de-sac of modern houses separating the two bigger ones, although, for a different reason, she never feels entirely comfortable there, either.

CHAPTER ONE

It could have been a surprise to nobody, thought Sarah Wilmot, a few hours later, gazing round the kitchen with disbelief, that the house had remained unsold for so long, and it was typical of her brother-in-law's state of mind that he should have been the sucker to buy it. Though 'sucker' wasn't a word that normally sprang to mind to describe Dermot.

Bought it he had, however. As if by taking a new job in a new place, by leaving the bright, modern new-town house and saddling himself with this Victorian monstrosity, by burying himself here in this backwater on the edge of the Black Country, he could make himself sufficiently miserable to forget what had happened. But it was barely three months since Lisa had died, and no one had yet got over the shock, least of all Dermot.

Except, to some extent, the children. Children were resilient. They couldn't sustain misery and grief forever—and who would want them to? Bereft and bewildered at first, they were gradually learning to come to terms with the situation. Playing outside now, oblivious of the sultry heat, discovering the new garden, two brown-haired little girls, Lucy leading as usual, red-cheeked in her excitement, Allie quieter, stopping occasionally to stand and stare, to take it all in. Lucy was all Dermot's daughter, in looks, charm and temperament, at nearly ten, an energetic and confident child. But Allie?

Younger than Lucy by eighteen months, she was a different matter altogether. She'd accepted news of the move meekly, unlike Lucy, who'd kicked up a fuss about leaving her school-friends and Granny and Grandpa, but had soon changed her mind when the idea of a new school and new friends was presented to her, and had then hardly been able to wait until they moved in. With Allie, it was hard to tell.

Now, in some indefinable way, she already looked more at home in the garden than Lucy did, as if she belonged there, standing underneath the pear tree, with the hot breeze of a threatening thunderstorm blowing her cotton dress against her thin, tense body.

The garden was decidedly the nicest thing about Edwina Lodge. Secluded and large, running down into thick, long grass at its end, spiked with foxgloves and overhung with big trees from the small wood beyond. The trees were heavy-leafed and lax with the heat of late summer, the garden overgrown, apart from a small tended area adjacent to the house, but all of a piece: a pear tree simply asking for a swing to hang from it, a broken-down pergola burdened with a rampant rose, tile-edged, blue-brick paths, a vegetable garden. Large enough to grow their own vegetables, said

6

Dermot, airily optimistic, he who'd never done more than push a reluctant lawn mower on Sunday mornings—when he was there—in Milton Keynes. Sarah visualized tidy rows of peas and beans. Courgettes, herbs, lettuces and salad onions. Maybe some rocket . . .

No chance! The arrangement was that she wouldn't be here any longer than it took to do her duty. Then back to her job in London, and concerts, exhibitions, theatres, shops, sophisticated dinners *à deux*. Simon. Dark-haired; guardsman-tall, immaculate, urbane. More than comfortably off. Everything a girl could want, in fact. She was very lucky, it went without saying.

She ran a hand through the short swing of thick, sun-streaked brown hair and went back with determination to her lists.

Ominously long, those lists, but it was a matter of principle that she should do as much as she could in the couple of weeks or so she was scheduled to stay: just until the girls had settled into school, getting the house shipshape, and finding for Dermot a housekeeper who would be willing to face up to the horrors of the house and, more specifically, the kitchen. The Aga was the most up-to-date piece of equipment there and was unquestionably prewar, second if not first. Sarah made a face at it, refused to contemplate the geyser over the sink and the pipe-festooned corners, abandoned it and took herself to the drawing room, via the dark and echoing hall which, with its cold, Minton-tiled floor and depressing stained glass, was no better.

Given time, money, know-how—none of which Dermot had—something might be done with the drawing room. The *pièce de résistance* of 'this valuable part-investment property' as the house agents' blurb had it—the investment being that part of the house already split up into three self-contained flats and which was, theoretically, to finance the whole. Huge and high-ceilinged, with elaborate plasterwork and a heavy, ornate black marble fireplace, the drawing room was solid and handsome, needing little more than a lick of paint and new wallpaper—but Dermot would need to think seriously about new furniture. Lisa's light, pretty things would fit in here no better than Lisa herself would have done. Only too easily could Sarah imagine her sister's reactions to the very idea of living here at all: turning her eyes up comically at the notion of such a place as home, at its size, at the cavernous kitchen and the dark, narrow staircases, of which there were two, plus the ones to the attics and cellars. Death traps, all of them.

And yet, heavily pregnant, tripping over the loose belt of her dressing gown, Lisa had lost her footing on the upper treads of the wide, well-lit, open staircase in their modern house in Milton Keynes, fallen from top to bottom and broken her neck.

Another of those swift, futile moments of pain and anger at the unnecessary waste, the misery of it, touched Sarah with a cold finger. She hugged herself, despite the heat.

A clock somewhere chimed a distant, silvery four. Dermot had been gone three-quarters of an hour, inspecting the flats with Mrs Burgoyne, receiving last-minute instructions. Dermot, a landlord!

'Don't be spiky, Sarah,' he'd said, not appreciative of opposition at any time, particularly not now. 'Mrs Burgoyne's convinced me the flats are a worthwhile proposition, and very little trouble.'

It had seemed to Sarah, and her parents too, that the whole enterprise was fraught with trouble, and this was one of the reasons why she'd volunteered to help Dermot over the settling-in period—although he might have cause to rethink his good luck, she thought, a quick bubble of laughter sending the shivers packing, given that housekeeping wasn't exactly one of her more conspicuous talents. But if she hadn't volunteered, her mother would certainly have felt compelled to do so, foregoing the cruise which Sarah's father had booked to mark his retirement, and to which they'd looked forward for years. A holiday which her mother so desperately needed, after the shock and heartbreak and subsequent upheaval of Lisa's death.

Sarah's whole warm, generous nature had

9

rebelled at such needless sacrifice, and she'd said, impulsively, 'I'll go,' earning both Dermot's and her father's gratitude. And, unfortunately, Simon's disapproval.

'The whole scheme's preposterous—and what am I going to do without you? In the office, not to mention otherwise?'

Sarah told herself that this apparent self-interest hid his real concern, and the 'otherwise' pleased her, but she stuck to her guns, reminding him that Devora Vine had supposedly been trained to take over in an emergency—and had been breathlessly waiting for just such an opportunity to prove she could—though she thought this last better not said, unwise to put thoughts into his head about the crush the Divine Devora had on him.

Simon owned and ran a glossy art and antiques magazine, a rather chichi, expensive quarterly with a small but steady, even growing, circulation. Its success wasn't surprising; he worked hard and was extremely knowledgeable in the field, having grown up with a silver spoon in his mouth, surrounded by the sort of things he wrote about.

She promised to stay no more than a few weeks, until the children were settled into school. They'd only be apart for two or three weekends, four at most.

'Or you could come up here and stay,' she'd suggested.

'I could.' His tone implied that the possibility

10

was remote. As if Lavenstock were Alaska or Australia, and not barely an hour and a half from London by InterCity. 'Well, maybe,' he added after some consideration, and she'd chalked up a small victory, seeing the smile he allowed himself. 'You know I can deny you nothing, my lovely.'

An exaggeration, on both counts, that she let pass. She'd been his personal assistant on the magazine for four years, and the possibility of a directorship was in the air, though an association of a different kind was more what he had in mind. Sarah suspected he was using the one as a carrot for the other, to try and make her see the sense of becoming Mrs Simon Asshe. Well, it was time she settled down, everyone thought so, including Sarah. Thirty-five was on the horizon. So why the hesitation?

'I can see you're set on going,' Simon had finally admitted, seeing the predicament and reluctantly conceding the reasons for her offer, 'so it's no use my trying to dissuade you. You must do what you have to—only don't make it too long, out there in the sticks. I fear Dermot could only too easily become used to you as an unpaid housekeeper.'

Sarah might have feared this, too, had she not already been well-armed against Dermot's admitted tendency to make use of people, especially his womenfolk: first, of his pretty Irish mother who, being as adept as he was at withdrawing from an unsatisfactory situation

11

and with no intention of being burdened with motherless grandchildren, had circumspectly taken herself off to live permanently in Marbella; and thereafter of Mrs Wilmot, his mother-in-law. He was on the surface easy-going and optimistic, full of good ideas, which other people unfortunately tended to get landed with—though he was generally thought well-meaning and was therefore forgiven, until patience wore thin. He had reason to be grateful to a great many people, though in the end, underneath the lazy, blue-eyed, inherited Celtic charm, Dermot was quite capable of looking after his own affairs. The Voss side of his nature, from his German father, perhaps. When you thought about that, it wasn't really all that astonishing that he'd taken this unprecedented step, made the decision to do it off his own bat, and carried it through all of a rush, against all the opposition. And surely understandable that he should be so devastated by Lisa's untimely end that he could no longer bear to stay in the place where they'd been so happy together.

She could hear the children's voices, clear on the heavy air as they played, blissfully unaware of the changes that lay ahead of them. Nothing would ever be the same for them again. Life with a daddy whom they'd hitherto only infrequently seen, apart from flying visits home, one who wasn't going to find such a drastic change in his lifestyle easy, either. And, in between, being looked after by a strange housekeeper.

Dermot had been a TV cameraman, our man in whatever trouble spots of the world demanded his presence, alighting in England only long enough to spoil the girls outrageously before leaving on yet another assignment. It had been an unsatisfactory sort of family life, though Lisa, loyal and good, had never complained. Well, Dermot had now been thrust into the realities and responsibilities of parenthood with a vengeance and, to do him justice, he'd faced up squarely to what had to be done, wangled himself out of his contract with the BBC and found himself a job working with a corporate film and video company. But how long would this satisfy him, after the excitements and dangers of his previous job?

Footsteps at last sounded on the stairs, Dermot with Mrs Burgoyne. The erstwhile owner of the house, she was a tiny, white-haired old lady with a soft pink and white, powdery skin and eyes like an electric drill. 'No trouble at all, the tenants,' she was repeating her assurances as they came into the drawing room with even Dermot, who was only just above middle height, appearing to tower over her. 'Because, of course, I've always made sure, as you must, I warn you, Mr Voss, to take only the *right* sort of person in to Edwina Lodge.' And she went on to detail, for Sarah's information, what Dermot already knew about his tenants.

The house was split more or less right down the middle, one half for the owners, one for the tenants. Upstairs, on the first floor, lived Mr Pitt, a librarian. Below him was the Baverstocks' flat—he was employed in the borough accounts department, and she ran a wholefood shop in Folgate Street. Unexceptionable, all of them.

And the attic-floor flat, inquired Sarah, the one where the huge window had been built out over the roof? The eyesore, she added to herself, the incongruity stuck like a blister to the side of the property, doing its bit to add to the ugliness of the house. There was a slight pause. Oh, that was Mr Fitzallan's furnished flat. The window had been added many years ago, by a previous owner of Edwina Lodge, simply for the view, which was magnificent. On a clear day you could see the Rotunda in Birmingham.

'And that reminds me, Mr Voss,' Mrs Burgoyne went on swiftly, 'did you pull that door smartly to, as I told you? I didn't hear you, come to think of it, and if you didn't, it won't have closed properly. Mr Fitzallan won't be pleased to come home and find his front door wide open, I can tell you. It's these little things that count.'

Dermot, restless, chafing under the weight of all this instruction, running his hand through his black curls, smiled disarmingly and admitted ruefully that he couldn't remember.

'I'll go up and check,' Sarah offered, looking at her watch. 'You'd better get off, hadn't you, if you want to get Mrs Burgoyne to the station to catch her train?'

Dermot flashed her a relieved smile. 'I'll be about half an hour, then I'll take you and the children straight to the hotel—we're staying at the Saracen's Head for a couple of nights, Mrs Burgoyne. An early night for all of us seems indicated in view of what we've to face in the next few days.'

'Monday's when your furniture arrives, isn't it?' Mrs Burgoyne asked, eyeing Sarah, clearly not equating a short skirt and bare legs with someone capable of dealing with the removal, as though she would dearly have loved to superintend it personally to prevent anything going wrong. But finally, with a last sharp look round, though with what seemed to Sarah an ultimately unregretful eye, she departed with Dermot for the train which was to carry her to retirement in her south-coast bungalow.

Sarah checked that the children were still safely and happily occupied—Allie, for one, was dreamily accident prone, seeming destined to go through life permanently sticking-plastered somewhere about her person; a recently broken collar bone and a small chip off one of her permanent front teeth from a fall off her bicycle was present testimony to this.

She ran up the two flights of stairs to the

attic flat, to find its front door was, after all, closed. But when she leaned her hand against it, it gave against her weight, and swung open. Before giving it the required slam, natural curiosity made her step forward a few paces and take a look round the room. Mrs Burgoyne certainly hadn't spread herself here with regard to the furniture. The few cheap and unmistakably second-hand, unrelated pieces added nothing to the room's character, nondescript with all-over, porridge-coloured paint and a curtainless window. This wasn't, however, the big, ugly protruding window at the side, with its vaunted view. Evidently, this room in which she was standing was the first of two rooms, and the window in question was in the second one, through the opposite door. She felt a sudden urge to see it for herself, curious to know whether you really could see as far as the Birmingham Bull Ring . . .She walked across and tried the door handle.

'It's locked.'

She whipped round. A man stood in the doorway. Mr Fitzallan, I presume. She had a feeling he'd been standing there for some time, and she was distinctly put out to know that guilty colour had flown to her cheeks, to hear herself stumbling apologies like an adolescent schoolgirl. He had, after all, given his permission for the flat to be inspected. If not by her.

'I—didn't hear you coming up the stairs.'

16

He inclined his head, not deigning to reply to this fatuously obvious statement. Mrs Burgoyne's warning had conjured up an elderly fusspot, a cantankerous, intolerant person. Looking at him, she saw no reason to change her opinion, except in regard to age. In his mid-forties, maybe, over six foot, wide-shouldered with tousled dark hair, wearing a beautiful slate-blue silk shirt and an unstructured suit in cream linen, polished loafers. Casually cool and elegant in a loose-limbed way, making her aware of every crease and crumple collected on the hot, sweaty journey here.

Boardroom and top management, every inch of him—and living *here*?

Sarah looked into a face as dark as the thunderheads piling up outside, saw a square jaw, a strong nose, felt a sense of harsh purpose. Their eyes met and held, hers wide and brown, his a brilliant and unexpected grey under lowering brows. For an instant, she thought she saw a hint of trouble behind them, in the lines of pain drawn down towards the mouth, but quickly decided it was simply general disagreableness.

'I'm sorry, I don't usually trespass without invitation,' she admitted, his lack of response to her warm smile transferring itself to her and making her unusually stilted. 'I was curious about that big window . . . Mrs Burgoyne says you can see the Rotunda from it. I saw it from the garden, the window, I mean.'

17

He stood aside for her to pass. 'It's hard to miss, Mrs Voss.' He didn't offer to show her the view.

'Good heavens, I'm not Mrs Voss! I'm just living with Dermot for the time being.' Realizing what she'd said, Sarah laughed and an explanation was on the tip of her tongue when the expression of either acute disinterest or disapproval, the one raised eyebrow, brought her to a halt. Her smiled died. No sense of humour, either. A spark of antagonism cracked across the space between them.

'I'm very sorry,' she repeated, and turned to go. There was nothing for it other than that, a dignified exit and as graceful an apology as she could muster. He made no attempt to detain her, and she escaped.

And hoped, as she fled down the stairs, that his elegant silk tie might choke him on a sweltering day like this, and thought the other tenants were certainly going to be interesting to meet, if this was Mrs Burgoyne's idea of 'the right sort of person'.

*   *   *

She'd just filled the kettle ready to make tea the moment Dermot got back—the girls would love a picnic out in the garden, sandwiches and Granny's jam tarts, never mind the wasps or the possibility of thunderstorms—when there was a knock on the back door. The woman who

18

stood there was plump and pleasant, in her early forties, her hair done in a top-heavy mop of curls over her forehead, otherwise shorn into a short back and sides, like a man's. She introduced herself as Doreen Bailey.

'Oh, do come in and sit down; Mrs Burgoyne mentioned your name.' Not intending to make the same mistake twice, Sarah this time made it clear who she was.

Mrs Bailey smiled and settled her ample figure with the ease of familiarity on to the ugly fifties vinyl-covered banquette seat which someone had once mistakenly fitted in a half-hearted attempt to modernize the kitchen. Sarah rummaged in the picnic basket. 'I'm just about to make some tea, if I can sort some cups out. Hope you don't mind plastic.'

'Better than Mrs B's cast-offs, I'll bet. She said she'd leave one or two mugs and plates for you to use while your stuff was being unpacked, but I should use your own—anything *she* hasn't taken, it won't be worth much, I can tell you. She'd cut a currant in two, that one.' She laughed and got up to open a cupboard next to the sink, sniffing. 'As I thought! Chipped, *and* cracked, what cheek! Only fit for the dustbin. She tell you I'd be willing to come and help out with the cleaning a couple of mornings a week?' she continued, without pause. 'I work afternoons at the checkout down at Safeway's, but I've come to Edwina Lodge twice a week, mornings, getting on for twelve years. I'd be

19

willing to carry on, if that's all right with you.'

Sarah said, perhaps unwisely on such short acquaintance, but she'd taken one of her immediate likings to Mrs Bailey, 'I'm sure Dermot would be delighted if you could manage it.'

Mrs Bailey gave a satisfied nod and, having drawn breath, went on, 'I do for Miss Kendrick and her brother as well—they live at Simla, next house along. Makes a change from the supermarket—I feel like a battery hen there, sometimes, and the housework gives me a bit of exercise, besides helping with the mortgage. I was determined we should go for one of the houses in the Close when they went up, but it's a struggle, sometimes.'

Sarah assumed she was referring to the cul-de-sac of newish houses which lay between this house and the next one in Albert Road, the one she'd called Simla. 'Ellington Close, you mean? That's convenient.'

'That's right. They pulled a big old house down and built our houses on the site. Heath Mount, the house was called—the Kendricks had lived there all their lives, their great-grandfather or some such built it, but you know what it's like trying to keep places like that going. They sold it in the end and moved into Simla. Bit of a comedown for them, but I shouldn't waste your breath feeling sorry for them, they couldn't have done so bad out of the deal, my Bob says, and he's in the building trade, painter and decorator, so he should know. Two sugars, m'duck, I know I shouldn't but I use a lot of energy.'

'What are they like?' asked Sarah, grabbing the opportunity to speak as Mrs Bailey paused to take possession of her tea.

'The Kendricks? All right. Bit on the snooty side. Clever, highbrow, you know. College types—Cambridge, I think it was. He writes books. And of course there's Mrs Loxley, the other sister.'

'What sort of books does he write?'

Mrs Bailey was vague. 'About art, and that sort of stuff. His study's full of pictures, not that I'm allowed in there, except to take him his coffee when his sister's not there. She teaches maths at the Princess Mary—the girls are all terrified of her, but they respect her, if you know what I mean. She's strict, but fair—got my niece through her maths GCSEs, and that's saying something! Patti's a lovely girl, and bright with it, but not when it comes to figures.'

Doreen Bailey's flow of chat was interrupted by the arrival of Dermot, Lucy hanging on his arm, Allie a step behind. 'Do I smell tea?' he demanded, smiling engagingly at the older woman who, in turn, was gazing admiringly at the handsome man with the tanned skin and the smiling blue eyes that exactly matched his open-necked shirt.

Damn, thought Sarah, who'd sensed a rich vein of information waiting to be tapped in Mrs

Bailey, now I shall have to wait to find out more about the tenants—though the obnoxious Mr Fitzallan could go and jump in the lake for all the interest she had in him.

CHAPTER TWO

St Nicholas's church, Lavenstock, was tolling its single melancholy note for eight o'clock communion as Harry Nevitt arrived at his council-owned allotment the next morning. The thunderstorms of the previous day had cleared the air, and it was a little cooler, though there was promise of returning heat later on. Meanwhile, the morning sparkled. Everything appeared clean and new-washed. Ruby beetroot leaves gleamed, celery stood erect and waved its bright green fronds, cabbages were diamond-studded. The earth was warm and damp and Harry was anxious to get cracking with the hoe, put paid to the weeds that would have come out in full marching order.

He considered himself lucky that his allotment was in one of the prime positions, in a coveted spot which not only had the best of the sun but also allowed him to park his car nearby, since it ran alongside the narrow dirt road that cut through the middle of the site. He'd worked it for twenty-odd years, getting the soil into good heart and growing prize-winning onions and chrysanthemums, and now he was retired, and a widower, he happily spent most of his day here. He lacked nothing: tea-making facilities and a radio, his daily paper and a deck chair in the little green hut where he kept his tools and his garden supplies. Even a much-disparaged mobile phone which his daughter insisted on him carrying around. Today, he'd also brought writing materials; he was working on yet another petition to the council to do something about repairing the road behind his allotment.

The state of it after the heavy rain proved his point. He'd had to park his car as near as he could get, which wasn't near enough. Swearing at the potholes in the surface, and because the half-hundredweight polythene bag of fertilizer he'd picked up at the allotment store—where they bought in bulk for economy—was slippery and awkward, and heavy for a seventy-four-year-old, he made his way clumsily towards the hut. He wasn't as nippy on his pins as he had been, and it was a wonder he didn't trip over the prone form and join it where it lay right across his path.

''Ere,' said Harry. 'What d'you think you're playing at?'

He wasn't an imaginative man, but it didn't take him long to realize this wasn't just a drunk still sleeping it off after a Saturday-night binge, nor was it a tramp, that the man was lying with his head in one of the rain-filled potholes and certainly wasn't going to stand up and apologize for getting in Harry's way. He looked pretty dead to Harry, and he'd seen a few corpses during his war service, but he put down his fertilizer sack and tentatively took hold of the outflung wrist. Then he picked up the bag again and carefully deposited it in his hut before getting out the despised phone and punching in 999.

The church bell stopped tolling just as the Town Hall clock began to strike eight.

* * *

'Dead for roughly twelve hours, probably less, that's as near as I can tell you at the moment. And *that,*' pronounced the pathologist, pointing to the shallow puddle of clay-coloured water, 'is almost certainly what killed him.'

The body had already been photographed *in situ,* and the video cameramen and the SOCO team were now busy on the surrounding area. The police surgeon, automatically summoned to what was an unexplained death and having done his duty of pronouncing an obviously dead body officially dead, but seeing grounds for suspicion, had given his opinion that his eminent colleague, the Home Office pathologist, Professor Timpson-Ludgate, who fortunately lived in the area, should be called in. He was now working on the body, speaking into a small tape recorder hung around his neck as he worked, a photographer in attendance to take close-ups at his instructions.

Familiarly known throughout the police as T-L, the pathologist glanced up at the detective inspector from his kneeling position, his bulk obscuring the body. 'He's been roughed up more than a bit, but I can tell you he died from drowning, unless I'm very much mistaken.'

Abigail Moon nodded. She knew it was perfectly possible to drown in two inches of water. 'Drunk?'

'No smell of drink on him, no vomit. Tell you better when I've opened him up.' He lifted the recorder from round his neck. 'He's all yours, meanwhile, and the best of British. Not a pretty sight, I'm afraid.'

The professor was a big, jovial man of Falstaffian appearance, a bit of a throwback, Abigail thought him, quite aware that under the nod to equality he privately thought feminism had gone too far, still had quaint, old-fashioned notions that women should be at home having babies and looking after their menfolk, rather than doing hard, difficult and often distasteful jobs. He gave her a quizzical glance as he spoke but he should have known her well enough by now to know that she wasn't about to have the vapours at the sight of a dead body. Not even ones much more horrible than this was likely to be. It didn't mean she didn't mind. Only that she'd trained herself to look, without actually *looking*. She'd already seen this one, anyway, when she'd first arrived at the scene.

'He'd been fighting, you say?'

'Well, these aren't love bites he's got. There's bruising to the jaw and cheekbone, a cut lip and a black eye, consistent with the sort of injuries you might expect from fighting, though they're superficial, and if he hit back there's no bruising or broken skin on his knuckles to show it.'

The morning was warming up by the minute. Abigail pushed her heavy bronze hair behind her ears and frowned. 'If he didn't fall down drunk, how did he drown? Running away from a fight, fell, knocked himself unconscious? He must have been unconscious or he'd have rolled away.'

The pathologist peeled off his gloves and levered himself to his feet, not without difficulty. He was carrying more weight than he should and knew it, but like most doctors, he didn't always follow his own advice. 'But there's this, too, which is what interests me more than anything.' Saving the best for last, he turned the body slightly and indicated a nasty-looking wound on the back of the head. 'I'll reserve judgement until I can take a closer look at him, but off the record, there's not much doubt it would at least be the cause of him losing consciousness.'

'So some other person was definitely involved, then?'

26

'Since the wound's on the back of the head, yes. Unless, of course, he fell, then rolled over before he lost consciousness. Remote, but possible. And in the absence of anything obvious he could have fallen against...' He shrugged his big shoulders. 'No point in speculating. The PM will resolve which it was, fall or a blow. In the meantime, it looks as though we're into your department, Inspector. Find me a rock or something similar, that fits the injury, preferably one with blood and hairs on it.'

'Could the same fall—supposing he did fall—account for his other injuries?'

'Not a chance. Take it from me, he'd been in some sort of rough-house. I'll do the PM as soon as possible, since I know you're impatient for a result. Not today—maybe tomorrow.' He made it sound like a favour. 'No one would think it, but we are allowed to have social commitments,' he added, squinting with disfavour down at his ruined, light-coloured trousers.

You and who else? thought Abigail, seeing her own day disappearing, fast, down the drain.

'I'm snowed under with bodies just now,' the professor saw fit to add, explaining with a lugubrious smile, 'Why they all seem to come at once, I don't know, you tell me, but they're dying like flies at the moment. Must be something in the water.'

'I'll take care to stick to the bottled sort,'

Abigail said as he finally departed, picking his way back between the puddles to where he'd left his distinctive vintage Rover. Water might be all she'd get the chance of that day. She was officially off duty and had planned a grand slam on the domestic chores, the afternoon working in her garden, and a deliciously relaxed evening with Ben Appleyard, intending to astonish him with the virtuosity of her cooking and a bottle of wine. Alas! As a newspaperman, editor of the local newspaper, he understood and forgave these sort of emergencies better than most men would, but even his apparently inexhaustible patience must have its limits. This wasn't the place to examine what those limits were, however. She gave the SOCOs the nod that it was their turn with the body. Cameras began flashing again and ex-Sergeant Dexter came forward and began his task with his usual thoroughness and practicality. The Scenes-of-Crime department had recently been civilianized, but Dexter had liked his job so much he had quit the Force in order to carry on. She was glad he was the one to be assigned to this case; he was moody, sometimes, could be taciturn if he was that way inclined, but he was knowledgeable, unflappable and meticulous to a degree. If Dave Dexter didn't find evidence, it usually wasn't there.

While he was occupied with searching for anything foreign to the scene, collecting trace evidence—hairs, fibres and dust samples from the victim's clothing in addition to those already taken from the surrounding area—bottling water samples from the puddle, she used the time to talk to the elderly man who'd found the body. He was sitting on an upended bale of peat inside his hut, a tall, thin man, smoking, drinking a mug of tea and looking blankly out over the neat rows of vegetables, the serried ranks of dahlias and chrysanthemums for cutting. If he was shaken, he wasn't showing it. All the same, the sort of discovery he'd made was a facer for anyone and he wasn't young any more. She went carefully with him.

'We're going to need an official statement from you, Mr Nevitt. I've a car coming to take you down to the station, but to give me something to be going on with, perhaps you could just tell me now how you found him— that is, if you feel up to it?'

He took another drag on his cigarette and assured her he was all right but there wasn't much more he could say, other than that he'd all but fallen over the body when he arrived at the allotment first thing. 'What I can tell you is, he wasn't there at half past eight last night. That were a heavy old thunderstorm we had around tea-time and I come down here, after, to see whether my chrysanths was still standing. What with one thing and another, I was here best part of an hour.'

'This road—is it used a lot? By people other than the allotment-holders, I mean?'

29

'It's a short cut through from Colley Street to the Leasowes.' He pronounced it 'Lezzers' in the time-honoured local way. 'That and the path at the back. We get a fair number of them joggers coming through, and kids on bikes and that, but the road's too bad for folks as don't have to, to risk their car suspensions. We've complained and complained to the council about it—what's the use of having a road if we can't use it?—but you might as well save your puff. They reckon there's no money for it, these days.'

Abigail nodded and looked around at the allotment holdings. It was a roughly triangular site, pointing down towards the river and the Riverside Community Centre on Stockwell Street. Along one side was Colley Street, a busy road that ran up through the town towards Holden Hill; along the other was the shorter street called the Leasowes, a much sought-after council-improved street of small, artisan-type houses. A narrow path ran along the base of the triangle at the back of the allotments, connecting the two streets, while running up from Stockwell Street and roughly bisecting the site was the unnamed, unmade-up road Harry Nevitt was complaining about.

'Hello, young Peter, thought you might be around somewhere,' the old man greeted DC Deeley, who'd arrived with the announcement that the car to take the old man down to the police station was ready, if Mr Nevitt was.

'Your mum were telling me you was a detective now.'

'Her allus did say I were destined for better things than a uniform, Harry,' Deeley answered, with a wink at Abigail, employing his broadest dialect.

'Oh ar. Dow let it go to your head, then.'

Built like a steamroller, cheerful, unflappable, Pete Deeley grinned and walked with the old man to the car and drove off with him.

'Right, Inspector. You can have another look at him now if you want, before we get him bagged up and taken away,' Dexter said.

'Nothing to identify him?'

'No wallet or credit cards, just his car keys and a handful of loose change in his trouser pocket—though the label on his pants says they were made in Germany, if that's any use to you ... not that it counts for a lot nowadays, last pair I bought was made in Sweden ... and his shirt and underpants are St Michael. I'll tell you where his shoes came from when we've dried them off in the lab and scraped the mud off.'

'Probably Taiwan,' Abigail said, ducking under the tape. Conscientiously, but without noticeable enthusiasm, she took a better view of the body. He was a youngish man—not yet forty, the pathologist had estimated, slightly built and of middle height, dark-haired and seen to be clean-shaven. Froth ballooned from his nose and mouth. The front of his clothing

31

was still caked with mud, but appeared to have been otherwise respectable.

'Not your usual yob that gets mixed up in a fight.'

The comment came from Sergeant Kite, who'd just arrived. The scene was now crowded with police, the allotments having been taped off and a uniformed PC detailed to keep away the disgruntled tenants as they arrived.

'T-L thinks he'd been in some sort of punch-up, Martin, for all that. If he was mugged, they've left him his ring and his watch.' She indicated the plain band on the wedding finger and the flat gold watch with the leather strap.

'In too much of a hurry, maybe. Just grabbed his wallet and scarpered.'

'I'm wondering if he had one with him. It was a muggy night, after the rain, too warm for a jacket. You men are at a disadvantage, no handbag, nowhere to put your wallet except your back pocket, but that's still buttoned up. And I can't see anybody stopping to do it up again if they'd just pinched a wallet from it. He'd loose change and car keys in his other pocket.'

Hitching her bag on to her shoulder, she thought about the keys, and the possibility that his car was somewhere near . . .

'We shan't get much from the immediate area around, I have to tell you,' Dexter was grumbling. 'Footprints or vehicle marks— forget it.'

The loose sharp stones, the potholes all over the place, would make this impossible, Abigail could see that. She repeated what the pathologist had said about the wound on the back of the victim's head possibly having been caused by a heavy stone.

'Keep an eye out for anything likely, Dave. And Martin,' she said to Kite. 'Get them knocking on doors.'

'We're not going to be popular.' Starting with Colley Street and the Leasowes, disturbing folks from their weekend lie-in this fine Sunday morning to find out whether anyone had heard a commotion last night. Would anyone have even remarked on it if they had, this end of Colley Street? Commotion was its normal condition, especially Friday and Saturday nights. 'We shall need more manpower—more uniforms from Reader,' he said.

Abigail pulled down her mouth. The chief inspector in charge of the uniformed branch wasn't exactly a pushover where his scarce resources were concerned. 'If he's awkward, shunt him over to me and I'll twist his arm. Meantime, all the pubs, not forgetting the Punch Bowl.'

'As if!'

'As if you could.' Saturday night without some sort of disturbance needing police intervention at the sleazy dive in Colley Street would indeed be a night to remember. 'But if we can find anyone who came along here after Mr

Nevitt left at half past eight, it'd help—maybe somebody took a short cut after closing time.'

'We'll be lucky! Anybody from the Punch, they wouldn't remember if they fell over an elephant.'

Abigail laughed. 'All the same . . . Right, I'll get back to the station now and report to the Super before he leaves.' Mayo would want a full briefing on what was happening before his departure for the Police Staff College, where he was leading a three-day seminar on the treatment of young offenders, and a start must be made on establishing the identity of the man, finding his car.

It was too early yet for anyone to have come forward to report him missing, but doubtless someone would, sooner or later. A thought enough to sober anyone: that on this bright and beautiful morning, among the dahlias and gladioli and all the fruitful produce of the earth, a young man, with all the expectancy of his life in front of him, should now lie mysteriously dead. While somewhere a wife, maybe children, waited for him.

CHAPTER THREE

There were sixteen houses in the Close that dipped down from the brow of the hill, sixteen where previously one had stood, that one having been Heath Mount, a Victorian edifice much bigger than Simla, or even Edwina Lodge. Most of the houses in Albert Road had been of that ilk, built at the time when the Industrial Revolution which had made Britain prosperous had been at its height and made its masters rich. Here on the edge of Lavenstock, their foundries, brickworks, claypits and glass kilns, chainworks and nail shops, had grown and spread out towards the great sprawl of Birmingham, and here they had built their splendid houses high on the ridge of Holden Hill, from whence they could look down on their creations and see that they were good. Imposing once, monuments to Victorian self-help, the houses had enjoyed their moment of glory but by now they'd had their day; most had been either split up into flats, taken over for business enterprises or pulled down and the land sold for development.

The houses that formed Ellington Close were mostly occupied by young families, childless couples and one or two retired people, though advertised as starter homes when they were built five years ago. It had begun to lose the raw look of a new housing development, to acquire some semblance of permanence, now that the flowering cherries were maturing and the rockeries flourishing . . . almost every garden had a rockery, a practical solution to gardens built on a slope. The houses were stepped down the hill in a rough crescent, away from Albert Road, in a pleasantly irregular pattern. The builder, or the architect who designed the site, had, to do him credit, used his imagination and had staggered them so that most of them had a magnificent view across workaday Holden Hill, down to the flat band of the canal in the bottom and the silvery dance of the river running parallel with it, right across Lavenstock and then up to the blue, tree-crowned hills which rose on the far side and looked out over three counties.

Everyone knew everyone else in the Close, although several of the houses had changed hands since they were built. They were three-bedroomed and detached—if only just—and in order to pack that number of houses on to a site of this size, they were dolls' houses, their dimensions minute. For two young people, to whom proximity is more important than space, this had a certain advantage, but when children arrived, the picture changed. Number thirteen had been on the market for almost as long as Edwina Lodge. The number wasn't regarded as a significant cause of their not being able to sell. It was generally thought that the occupants, Gail and Trevor Lawley, were asking too much, but what could they do when they owed more on their mortgage than the house was worth? Negative equity acquires a sharper edge when you find yourselves locked into it.

*   *   *

Monday morning, and Stanley Loates was, as usual, stationed at the front bay window of number seven, where he lived with his horrible old mother, when Patti Ryman entered the Close and began delivering her newspapers. She loathed him, the way he never smiled or came to the door to take the paper from her, just watched in that creepy way, day after day. She didn't give him the friendly wave she used to, not on your nelly! Not now she'd twigged he was only hoping for a look of her knickers as she bent down to push the delivery through number eight's letter-box. She yanked the newspaper bag further on to her shoulder. It was heavy, and she was tiny, but that didn't bother her. She was tough despite her size, as tough as any of the male oiks of her own age. She could cope. The money she got for this paper round was a joke, of course, but she hadn't yet been able to find a proper weekend job, and meanwhile it all helped, though her mum wasn't happy about it, you heard such stories. She'd have had a fit if she knew about Stanley Loates, but Patti hadn't mentioned the dirty old perv to her.

He was still standing there when she finished her round. It was all she could do not to knock on his door and tell him what she thought about him—but she didn't want to lose her job through his complaints. She decided it might be a very good idea to ask Mr Patel to put her on another round. Better still, tell her Aunt

Doreen, who also lived in the Close, what was going on, and let her deal with Stanley Loates.

Patti grinned. That'd fix him, all right!

*   *   *

Hope Kendrick heard the papers slide through the letter-box and land on the floor, but she was on her way to her brother's study with a tray and left them where they were.

She was careful to knock lightly before she entered the study. They'd always been meticulous about respecting each other's privacy, and Francis didn't like to be interrupted without warning when he was working.

'Coffee,' she announced, moving aside a pile of art magazines to find room for the tray on the table under the window. It was a dark, untidy room, where books took preference over human comfort, spilling off the shelves into hazardous piles on the floor, and where pictures of all kinds rubbed egalitarian shoulders in what space there was left.

Francis grunted, hunched over the work spread out on the big desk, and didn't immediately look up. It was barely half past eight but he liked his coffee early. He invariably rose at six, either to start work immediately, breakfastless, or to take one of his solitary walks, covering miles with his long strides before returning home to his desk.

As Hope put down the tray, it struck her with a pang how pronounced the academic stoop of his shoulders was becoming. He needed glasses now for close work. His head was bowed over the coloured prints and his hair was ruffled where he'd run his hands through it. She could see the slight thinning of his pate but resisted the temptation to smooth the floppy hair back over it. The back of his neck looked so vulnerable. It was difficult to remember, sometimes, that he was forty-six, no longer a little boy, though God knew he still needed looking after. Salutary to think that he was the same age as she was, her twin.

She poured two mugs of coffee. 'Want me to bring it over to you?' she asked, after a minute or two. The question was superfluous, more of a reminder to come and drink it before it grew cold, since he never drank or ate at his desk. Unnoticing and untidy about most other things, he was scrupulous where his work was concerned, and would never have risked spilling coffee over it.

He pushed his chair back, knocking over a leaning tower of books stacked on the floor beside it, and lounged over to sit by her at the chenille-covered table in front of the stone-mullioned window, open to a warm morning that promised another hot day. The roses that he loved and so carefully tended were in their second flush, and sent waves of perfume into the room. He leaned back and stuck out his long legs, clad in baggy cotton. He was thin and very tall, six foot three, and gangly. She was five foot ten herself, with the same sort of frame, although more tidily held together, and all her movements were, unlike his, quick and decisive. She had the same disregard for appearances; her hair, streaked with grey, was chopped off in an uncompromising bob, pushed back behind her ears, her face was innocent of make-up. She wore a faded cotton skirt and a man's shirt, though she'd omitted her usual big, enveloping sweater this morning in deference to the warm promise of the day. Her feet, in flat sandals, were almost as large as his. It was only her thick-lensed glasses that made any appreciable difference to their appearance.

He nodded towards a pile of manuscript on the table, fresh from the typist. 'Came this morning. That woman got a move on, for once.'

'Pleased with it?'

'As a first draft, it's not bad.'

In Francis-speak, this meant that he was. She picked the papers up, clipped together, neatly typed by Liz Fawcett, who was always quick and efficient, despite what Francis affected to believe, though they wouldn't remain in that state of perfection for long. The first of many drafts, it would be scribbled over and rewritten six or seven times before Francis was satisfied with the result. He was such a clear thinker, it always astonished Hope that he needed to work over his material to such an extent—but Francis was a complex character, never as straightforward as he seemed, slow to anger but formidable when roused. Suppressing this unprofitable line of thought, she peered through her spectacles in order to read the title on the cover sheet: 'The Cave and the Mountain: The importance of Symbolism in Mediaeval Iconography'. Francis was an authority on Byzantine art and had published several books on similar themes. Each one had made quiet ripples in the academic art world, but with this one she knew he was hoping to stir up more significant waves.

'They're moving into Edwina Lodge today,' she said, as she sipped her coffee. 'The new people.'

'Oh?'

He wasn't really interested. He cradled the coffee mug in his huge hands as he drank, in between each large gulp reaching out for a couple of his favourite jammy dodgers, scrunching them in his strong teeth, impatient to get back to work. His gaze strayed to the prints spread out on his desk. They were all of icons—madonnas, saints, the Christ. The reds and golds of the Greek icons glowed against the soft, pure colours of the Russian ones. *Our Lady of Vladimir* shone out in blue. There were two copies of the *Black Madonna of Czestochowa*. He went back to the desk and picked one up, studying it intently, back in his own world.

'A young couple,' Hope said.

And two little girls. She'd heard them calling out to each other as they played. Lucy and Allie (or some such) were their names, seemingly. She fervently wished there hadn't been children. Weren't they surrounded by too many of them already, in the Close? The summer holidays weren't quite over and you couldn't get away from them. We should have moved further away than just next door when the old house was sold, Hope thought, not for the first time—to the cottage, perhaps. But Francis hadn't wanted to move permanently to Shropshire, it was too far from the reference library in Birmingham and the availability of trains to London for him; it would have meant her finding another job in another school . . .

'I wonder at them—taking on all that responsibility,' she mused, her mind turning again to the new people. 'All right for the Burger, she was used to it, but young people like that, they don't usually take to that sort of thing . . . Imogen says we should ask them over for drinks.'

'What?' She had his attention now. An almost panic-stricken look crossed his face, to be replaced by the sort of stubbornness only Francis was capable of showing. 'Count me out. If Imogen wants them over, let her do the entertaining.'

'Francis, we can't. They're going to be our new neighbours, after all. We have to be civil to them; it needn't amount to anything more than that.'

'They'll ask us back. If they're young, they'll have parties, there'll be no end to it.'

'Francis—'

'You and Imogen do the necessary. She enjoys that sort of thing. You don't need me.'

He swung his chair round, dismissively held up the two Black Madonna prints, holding them side by side. 'Which do you prefer?'

'Not that one,' she said. She privately thought it rather vulgar, the way the beautiful simplicity of the original was obscured, 'dressed' as the Mother and Child were in their richly jewelled frames of robes and crowns. Adorned with hundreds of votive offerings in the form of rubies and other precious stones and hundreds of gold wedding rings, said to have been offered by pious couples.

'Ah, the Robe of Faithfulness,' Francis murmured. 'Both, I think, should be included.'

Hope let the subject of the new neighbours drop for the moment. She'd sowed the seeds, he'd have time to think about it before Imogen approached him, and though his agreement couldn't be guaranteed, Imogen was unlikely to meet with the outright refusal she'd have encountered if she'd had to mention it to him cold.

She would, of course, be expecting

opposition. Hope knew very well that Imogen was always prepared for that when confronting either of them with suggestions, admittedly not without cause. They rarely thought the same way. Sometimes Hope wondered how the three of them could have sprung from the same stock, so unlike were they. But, although everything the older twins were not, Imogen was unquestionably their sibling. She was their mother incarnate, in looks and in spirit, from the tips of her pretty, impatient feet to the crown of her shining dark hair (nature helped along by art, but Imogen was the last to let Hope's disapproval bother her). She not only had their mother's surprisingly practical, common-sense approach to life, but also their father, Roland's, undeniable charm, gambler and reprobate though he'd been, he who'd gone with the speed of light through the proceeds of the family business.

The money had originally been made through fireclay, rich deposits of which Great-great-grandfather Kendrick had discovered lay all around Holden Hill, waiting to be dug to make firebricks and furnaces. He'd made his pile by the time he died, leaving behind a legacy of ugly and dangerous clay-pits for future generations to deal with, and a comfortable lifestyle for the Kendrick descendants—who were numerous, since he'd had nine children. Most of them, however, despised the business, sold their shares profitably and became doctors, teachers, lawyers. One became a bishop and one—Roland, the grandson of the only son to carry on the business—a good-for-nothing. When he died, the debts he left were staggering. Their solicitor had told his children bluntly that they had no option but to get rid of Heath Mount. An opportunity to sell it for building development had just arisen and they'd be well advised to grab it with their three pairs of hands. He pointed out the advantages of living in a smaller, more manageable house, and sitting on a comfortable amount of money, having sold at the top of the market, instead of struggling with the upkeep of Heath Mount without the means to do so.

Sell Heath Mount? Pull it down? It was quite possible the elder Kendricks might never recover from the shock.

In the end, it had been Imogen who'd pushed them into the move. Left to themselves, the twins would have lived on in Heath Mount until it crumbled around their ears, shutting their eyes to the need for running repairs until it was too late. Francis with his head in the clouds over his Byzantine art and icons and Hope with her books and her senior maths syllabuses . . . did they exist on another planet, divorced from such humdrum things? Imogen demanded.

They tried to ignore her but she could be ruthless. She'd forced them to look at the situation fair and square, made them see that their only option was to do as Mr Crytch advised and move somewhere smaller. Francis had immediately assumed this to mean a custom-built bungalow or a luxury flat and had retreated into one of his haughty silences, refusing to discuss the matter. Hope had tried to be slightly more amenable but nevertheless managed to find some excuse to turn down every suggestion Imogen made. Imogen might never have succeeded in prising them out if Simla had not come on the market at about the same time, a face-saving solution, in that the vendor was almost as stubborn as they were, having inserted a proviso on the sale that the house should not be sold to a developer. It was smaller and better looked-after than Heath Mount, but of the same vintage, and it would mean they could live more or less in the same way they'd always been used to.

Well, that was Imo's version of the situation! Hope thought. Perhaps she wouldn't have been so keen on the idea herself if she'd known she'd be back living with them within five years, back from Brussels, her marriage to Tom Loxley, Euro MP, all but over. But five years ago she'd been comfortably off, and secure enough to claim only a modest sum out of the sale of Heath Mount, with the promise of a couple of rooms at the new house whenever she might need them on her visits home.

With her usual efficiency, she'd overseen the

move to Simla, insisting on having the plumbing at least updated and a new kitchen installed before they moved in. But Hope had scorned attempts to get them to abandon the old sagging armchairs, bookcases and sideboards like mausoleums, all of them familiar and less alarming than new things would have been. The old curtains had been made over somehow to fit the new windows, despite Imogen having actually sought the advice of an interior designer in the town. She might just as well have gone down to Lavenstock market and bought curtaining by the yard to machine up, for all the interest Hope could summon up. So that in the end, Simla, lacking only the Benares brass and elephant-foot coffee tables brought home from India by the general who'd first inhabited and named the house, looked much as Heath Mount had always done. And by now, even the new kitchen had acquired a decent lived-in air.

But still, Hope considered the price for freedom from financial worries was high; to be living in the middle of a housing development like the Close, with what seemed like more than its fair share of children, when they'd been used to space and privacy, was a lot to pay. Certainly, more than she'd bargained for.

*   *   *

'Mother would have sent round a note, asking

them to tea,' Imogen remarked, not without irony, still thinking about the new people at Edwina Lodge when Hope returned with the coffee things. 'On the lawn, perhaps, with cucumber sandwiches. I shall have to go and knock on the door like the Avon lady, since I don't know their name or telephone number. Oh, but of course, they'll have the same number as the Burger, won't they?'

'I'll warn you, Francis is being difficult,' Hope said.

Imogen raised expressive eyebrows. 'What's new?' She added, despite her promises to herself, before she could bite it off, 'Do rinse those mugs out and empty the pot, don't just leave them there,' which had patently been Hope's intention. Instead of saying, 'Wash them yourself, if you're so concerned,' as any other sister might have done, Hope washed and dried them with a meticulousness which, even if she hadn't meant it, was even more insulting. Imogen tried not to sigh.

They were just too damned exasperating for words, her brother and sister, too brainy and too superior to bother about mundane tasks until they assumed crisis proportions. She hadn't yet got over her fury, on her return from Brussels, at seeing the scruffy state of the kitchen she'd left newly refurbished. Hope had declared loftily that she'd got rid of Doreen Bailey, it was demeaning to both parties to pay someone to do menial work, which was all very

48

well, but not if you then shut your own eyes to it. It was only Doreen's good nature that allowed her to return. She was independent enough not to share Hope's views on what was demeaning, and she'd worked for the Kendricks, as well as Mrs Burgoyne, even before their father had died and the old house had been sold, so she knew what she was letting herself in for.

By now, the house was at least liveable in, and Imogen felt better for having asserted herself, banished the memory of that terrible old house. As a child, she had felt extinguished in the presence of her older brother and sister, in the shadow of their intellectual superiority, and frequently afraid of them. It hadn't been until she'd married Tom, in fact, and found that she could hold her own in his sophisticated world that she began to gain self-confidence.

It had been a mistake to think of Tom.

She hurriedly began with the list of neighbours and friends she might ask to the proposed welcome party, concentrating fiercely and pressing so hard with the ballpoint that it nearly tore through the cheap paper of the kitchen pad. She tried to ignore the nasty, lurching pain in the pit of her stomach. When was she going to be able to go through a single day without thinking about him?

Tom. A humorous, tolerant man. Threads of grey in his hair, small lines etched at the corners of his kind eyes. The look of utter

49

desolation when she told him she was leaving him. The words had come out of her mouth, unintended until given voice. Nothing, he'd repeated, his face bleak, the girl had meant nothing to him. Propinquity, an overconvivial evening, an adjacent hotel room, nothing else.

Nothing to him, perhaps, but everything to her.

She should have tried to shrug it off. Lots of men had their bit on the side, it was irrelevant, in some circles it almost seemed mandatory— their wives forgave them, in public at any rate. But she couldn't. Theirs hadn't been a relationship like that, it had been based on mutual trust, on knowing the other person through and through. It was this that had shattered her, the realization that she hadn't, in fact, known him at all. Was he, then, like every other man, not special as she'd always believed? She'd only his word that it had been no more than a one-night stand, that there'd been nothing of the sort before, and never would be again, she'd told herself, trying to make herself doubt him.

Why? she'd asked herself repeatedly. Why did he have to do it? Is there something wrong with me?

She'd scrutinized herself in every available mirror and found nothing physically wrong, apart from the usual female dissatisfactions with a body less than perfect. Glossy dark hair, discreetly and expensively hennaed, trim figure, tall but not, like Hope, enough to intimidate shorter men. Beautiful clothes that she'd learned how to wear.

Me, myself then. It must be I who am lacking.

Her own subsequent behaviour had helped nothing.

She closed her eyes. What are you doing now, Tom?

She saw him in her mind's eye in the elegant Brussels apartment, unlikely as it was that he'd be there at that time of day, listening to the opera recordings he loved: a world of music contained within softly coloured walls, pale spreads of carpet, cushioned chairs and sofas in jewel-coloured fabrics. Lamps that lit the gilt-framed Georgian mirrors, the deeply glowing pictures, the oil paintings that were his other passion in life. Nothing spared in the way of expense and taste. Nothing lacking, except a wife.

CHAPTER FOUR

Abigail Moon hurriedly splashed a watering can over the few tomato plants in growing bags outside the back door of her foursquare little house under the hill, briefly envying Harry Nevitt's spruce allotment as it had appeared on Sunday. Passionate as she'd become about gardening since acquiring her cottage, hers was necessarily of the low-maintenance variety— nothing so ambitious as growing vegetables, which needed more constant attention than she could give. The tomatoes were as far as she could go in that direction, and as for the rest, if it couldn't look after itself when necessary, it didn't get garden room here.

She loved her little plot to bits, though. Nonexistent when she'd taken it over, her knowledge of gardening at the same level, she'd learned as she went along, and though small, it had burgeoned into a restful place, lush with exuberant-greenery that hid twisting little paths and unexpected viewpoints to give an illusion of glamour to the flat fields and woods beyond.

Thinking about the allotment brought the dead man vividly to mind again as she left the country lane that led to the cottage, having been allowed through by her nearest neighbours' huge black dog, who guarded the entrance to the lane like Cerberus at the gates of Hades. It was four days since the man had been found, and still no positive identification, with the initial inquiries seeming to have reached a plateau. All available manpower had been deployed on the investigation, and throughout Sunday and Monday every inch of the area surrounding the spot where the unknown man had been found had been thoroughly searched. His car had been sought, without success. House-to-house inquiries had so far been fruitless. The media had been informed and brief announcements had appeared in the press and on local radio and television that the body of an unidentified man had been found behind the Colley Street allotments. As yet, this had brought forth no response from anyone who might have recognized him, though there was still time for this: there were bound to be some who'd missed tuning in or reading the papers.

But neither had there been any inquiries from relatives worried about loved ones, and that was more puzzling.

She arrived at Milford Road without getting snarled up in traffic, and parked in the station yard, noticing with a resigned grimace that the Super had, as usual, beaten her to it. His car was in its appointed place after his return from the staff college. After signing in, she checked with the night duty officer's occurrence book and found that nothing out of the ordinary had happened during the night, certainly nothing relevant to Sunday morning's body finding.

It was, however, only one of several investigations which needed her urgent attention. She was currently working on a spate of motor thefts which appeared to be more organized than the usual opportunist heists, there was a factory surveillance to be organized today with a depleted staff—Sergeant Carmody on leave on the Costa Brava and Kite due in court this morning. And she'd come in early to get her thoughts straightened out on a possible child-abuse case which had also landed on her desk, needing time alone to be able to think about the harrowing facts dispassionately—if anyone could be dispassionate about such a subject—before the busy day got under way and she was inundated with interruptions from all directions. With a cup of coffee at her elbow, she worked steadily on, regardless of people arriving in the CID room and the growing noise level outside her glass partition, and had collated enough material into a file to pass on to the Child Protection Unit by the time her telephone rang.

'Ready when you are, Abigail.'

Satisfied with what she'd achieved, she closed the file and went upstairs to Mayo's office. It was a daily routine that had developed, given time and opportunity, which was valuable to both of them. They'd worked closely together when Gil Mayo was a chief inspector, before he'd been made up to superintendent, and still maintained a brisk and friendly relationship which suited both of them. A big, forceful man who'd come up through the ranks, he didn't let it get under his skin that she was a graduate entrant who could well leave him behind within a few years.

She found him tinkering with the old clock he kept on the bookcase. Clocks were his hobby—the collecting, restoring, and timing thereof—and he preferred this unreliable old Victorian mantel clock with its comforting tick, needing daily tender loving care to keep it up to scratch, to the official one on the wall which kept perfect time and marked off its movements with an unnerving clunk.

The seminar had evidently gone well. He was cheerful and alert and got straight to the point. One thing you could always guarantee with Mayo, he didn't hang about. After a swift canter through the details of the rest of her cases, he said, 'Give me a rundown on what you've gathered on the Colley Street job so far. I don't like the way it appears to be shaping up—or not, as the case may be.'

'Not's the right word,' she said, taking the point that he'd already made himself familiar with what had been going on in that direction while he'd been away. But he listened attentively to what she had to tell him.

An active and practical man, he fitted into the chair of Super somewhat ambivalently, playing his new role to his own rules, more than he'd felt able to do in his previous job. Impatient of the amount of time needed for endless committees and policy meetings, he took every chance he could to play an active part whenever possible, to be in at the sharp end. It didn't worry Abigail, as long as he didn't interfere with her own responsibilities. He'd earned the reputation of being a good boss from those he outranked ... if you toed the line. If not . . . well, it wasn't often he let fly. He kept his powder dry until he needed it for his big guns, but when he did—take cover!

'Let's hear what you've got, all the same. Sit down and have some coffee. You look as though you could do with it.' He poured her a cup from the fresh pot which had just been brought in.

God, did she look that bad? Probably. She wondered if he remembered she'd had her day off cancelled on Sunday, with fat chance of being able to make it up, never mind take time off for an overdue hairstyling, which always made her feel a hag. She took a drink of coffee and vowed she'd make time to visit the hairdresser, somehow. She could take on board as much pressure as anybody, but she'd enough common sense to grab time off in lieu as soon as she could manage it. Which might, in the circumstances, unfortunately for her, be some time in coming, all things considered. Too bad. No use complaining. It went with the territory.

'We've had the PM report through,' she said. 'It's fairly conclusive.'

Asphyxial death due to drowning in water, was how Timpson-Ludgate had phrased it. The occipital fracture of the skull had resulted in loss of consciousness, whereby the victim, lying face downwards in the puddle, had subsequently drowned. Diatoms, or microscopic water algae, in the blood, proved conclusively that he was alive before the water entered his air passages. There were no *contre-coup* injuries to the brain to indicate that the fracture was due to his fall. Translated, this meant that he had been hit with, rather than fallen on to, some irregularly shaped, heavy object, possibly a stone. Had he fallen, the brain damage would have showed up on the opposite side to where the skull injury had been sustained, a seeming anomaly which occurred for some complex and not yet fully understood reason. A nice distinction, but important, since it proved conclusive evidence that his death was no accident.

'But the weapon hasn't turned up. We've combed the area, and found nothing. Plenty of stones, but none that obviously fit the bill. And nothing else that looks likely.'

'So we're talking murder. At the least manslaughter, a fight that got out of hand?'

'We've had no reports of any undue disturbances nearby, either in the Leasowes or Colley Street, apart from the usual Saturday-night rumpus at the Punch Bowl—bikers and some drunken louts celebrating United's win. Ending up with one youth in hospital, several others enjoying free lodging here for the night. We've ascertained it had nothing to do with our man.'

And in any case, she added, the Punch Bowl, or any other pub, was probably a nonstarter, since the medical evidence had revealed no traces of alcohol in the victim's system. 'The car keys are for a last year's BMW, but so far we haven't had any reports of one being abandoned. Kite's been on to the manufacturers . . . they've given him the model, and the retail outlets they were sent to—but it'll be a long job tracing it that way—could've changed hands several times since then. And of course, our man could have disturbed thieves or joyriders in the act and tackled them as they were taking it away.'

'Might be some connection with your motor thefts, is that what you're thinking? They've all been prestigious type cars so far.'

'I'm currently working on the theory, but I'm not optimistic, if it's part of the same scam. Respray, new numberplates and its chassis number ground off, you name it, and it'll be over the channel before you can blink.'

'On the other hand, the dead man's car may be tucked up tidily in his own garage. What about Missing Persons?'

'Not a hope. No one even remotely conforming to his description. And his prints aren't on the Index, either. He was wearing a wedding ring, which indicates the presence of a wife somewhere or other, but maybe she thinks she knows where he is.'

She hesitated. 'Among the loose change in his pocket were a couple of Belgian francs. Might have been left over from a recent holiday, of course, or it could just be that he actually is Belgian. We've put out the usual inquiries, on the offchance, but no luck there

58

either, yet. We might get some response from the fly-posters we're organizing. Heigh-ho.' She grinned suddenly. 'Well, we've had worse than this; it's early days, yet.'

'We've tried taxi drivers? Or bus conductors, if it comes to that, or if he came here by train from somewhere else? Just because he had his car keys in his pocket it doesn't necessarily mean he used his car on that occasion.'

'It's a reasonable assumption,' Abigail said.

'We seem to be running out of reasonable assumptions as far as he's concerned. Let's try the other kind, now.'

She'd learned to respect what some jaundiced people called Mayo's good luck, what some dared to call his intuition and he himself insisted was gut feeling. Whatever it was, he had an uncanny knack of being right.

She hoped he was wrong this time. What he was implying was the worst-case scenario. Unknown victim, unknown killer, with every chance of this remaining a case marked 'Closed'.

CHAPTER FIVE

'*Why* can't I have my ears pierced?' nagged Lucy.

She'd been at her new school for only two days but, typically, had already acquired a best friend named Jodie, who not only had her ears pierced but also, if what she'd told Lucy was to be believed, had her hair highlighted and possessed a pair of black patent-leather ankle boots which were the immediate and passionate object of Lucy's envy.

'When you're older, perhaps,' Sarah temporized.

'Why not *now?*'

'Because you'd have to wear sleepers if you did and your daddy doesn't think that suitable at your age—do you, Dermot?'

'Not really,' Dermot answered unconvincingly, and added weakly, 'We'll see,' thus storing up further trouble for himself.

Sarah poured herself a strong cup of coffee. 'Get on with your cornflakes, Lucy, or you'll be late for school.'

'Angel doesn't have her ears pierced,' said Allie.

There was a pause. 'Oh God,' Dermot said.

So Angel was back.

Angel, who'd lived and slept and played with Allie for months, her imaginary friend who'd then simply disappeared one day about six months ago, without explanation from Allie, greatly to everyone else's relief. Nobody was sorry that this smugly self-righteous child, aptly named from Allie's favourite story-book character, no longer formed part of the family, or was the unseen guest at the table, that Allie was at last able to do things without a prolonged discussion with her, something which irritated everyone else unbearably, especially her father. Sarah shot a warning glance at Dermot, who was showing every sign of his previous impatience with Allie over this. After a moment, with a shrug and a grunt, he subsided behind yesterday's newspaper.

Despite assurances that many children went through this stage, not to make too much of it, it would pass, Lisa had worried that the phantom child's presence was a sign of Allie's insecurity. Did her return signal some desperate need in Allie for comfort and reassurance? Sarah worried in her turn now. Was it a belated reaction to the loss of her mother? There'd been nightmares at first, sleepwalking, after Lisa had died, but she was sleeping peacefully through the nights now, just as Lucy had ceased to wail, 'I want my mummy, it's not *fair!*' every bedtime.

Sarah felt out of her depth, catapulted into family responsibilities she didn't feel fitted to cope with—and Dermot wasn't going to be much help over this, she could see. He was on edge and unapproachable, had been all week, ever since they'd moved in. His original enthusiasm for the whole project seemed to have evaporated. Reminding him that he'd brought it on himself—much as she'd have enjoyed doing so—would cut no ice with him; he'd pointed out only last night that the most stressful things which could happen to anyone were supposed to be divorce, bereavement and moving house—and he'd just suffered the last two.

But she knew it was mainly because this new venture was so far not coming up to his expectations, that this wasn't exactly the new life he'd envisaged when the idea of taking over Edwina Lodge had transferred itself from Mrs Burgoyne's mind to his own. The actuality, she suspected, had been enough to make him wonder if he hadn't been too easily seduced by her weasel words, by the brilliant idea of having his mortgage paid by the tenants' rents, plus a little over. Dermot-like, he hadn't actually thought it through, considered the responsibilities ensuing from living in a house that included three other units. Already, the tenant of the downstairs flat, Tina Baverstock, was becoming a major pain, buttonholing him like the Ancient Mariner on some pretext or other every time she saw him. The venture had, like so many of Dermot's notions, seemed like a good idea at the time, a sort of bohemian, extended-family situation where he'd imagined there would be plenty of social interaction, plus someone on hand when he needed to park his children.

But still, Sarah wouldn't have expected disillusionment to have set in so quickly. The honeymoon was over before it had begun.

Allie seemed oblivious to the tension her announcement had created. She was going on with her cereal, carefully scraping the dish clean, spooning up every drop of milk. Lucy, munching toast, showed no sign of being bothered that Angel was amongst them again, either. For all her elder-sister superiority, she'd never either laughed at, or questioned the existence of, Angel.

At the moment, in fact, Angel seemed to have had the last word on the subject of pierced ears. Lucy finished her breakfast without further nagging, though this didn't by any means signify that they'd heard the end of it. Lucy was nothing if not relentless.

As Dermot folded the newspaper, he glanced out of the window and gave a sudden choked exclamation. 'That bloody Baverstock woman! She was complaining to me yesterday about the paper girl leaving her bike here—I suppose that must be the girl—what's she going on at her again for? I *told* the woman it was all right!'

Before Sarah could answer, he'd rushed out. He was gone several minutes and when he came back, he had the morning's paper with him and was looking rather white around the mouth.

The telephone rang.

'I'll get it!' Lucy cried, jumping down from her chair.

'No!' Sarah said firmly, preparing to answer it herself. 'You get your things ready for school, if you've finished your breakfast.'

Lucy looked smug. 'I put them in my school bag *before* breakfast.'

'Well, *check*—and then help Allie.' Allie was capable of dawdling indefinitely over collecting two exercise books and some coloured pencils, and then forgetting something essential, and panicking.

Sarah's heart skipped when she heard the voice. Simon, showing all the signs of being prepared for a lengthy conversation, full of how he was missing her, when was she coming back to London . . .?

They spoke for several minutes and she looked anxiously at her watch as Simon began on what was evidently going to be a complicated saga, involving the Divine Devora. Well, of course, he would simply have no idea of what the morning scramble was like—the girls, in their new maroon blazers and little round grey hats, were now hopping on one foot, waiting for her to drive them to school.

'We'll be *late*,' Allie hissed, in a tizzy. To be late, the third day at their new school—! Not to be borne.

'Simon, I'm sorry, I'll have to ring you back. I have to drive the girls to school.'

A slight pause. 'I've a full day ahead of me, Sarah, that's why I rang now.'

'Oh, Lord, I'm sorry! It's just that—'

'I'll try again tonight—if you're sure you won't be too busy reading nursery rhymes and making cocoa,' he said stiffly.

64

'Not if you ring after seven thirty, I won't,' Sarah replied, equally cool, a little nettled by the sarcasm, wondering how she was going to tell him that she hadn't yet found anyone to run the house and look after the children, that Dermot wasn't making any effort himself in that direction, that she d have to stay on here at least another week.

*   *   *

Later that afternoon, James Fitzallan paced the floor of his comfortless attic flat, hands shoved deep in his pockets. It wasn't the place he called home, so the comfort or otherwise of it scarcely mattered. It served its purpose. Occasionally he stayed the night if circumstances warranted it, but its principal use to him was as a studio, and a place which had for several years accommodated his need to get away and be alone, when things had become intolerable. His impatient strides brought him to the big, protuberant window where he came to a halt, looking out, trying to fill his mind and his eyes with the sight of the changing clouds, the pearlescent sky, willing himself into the right mood. Easel and paint-brushes stood ready. It was no use. He couldn't seem to get started.

Skyscapes were what he painted. Nothing but treetops and sky, the same trees, differently hued in their due seasons, and skies that changed with the dawn and the sunset, with storm and wind and rain, with moonlight and sun, through spring and summer, to autumn and into winter. The immensity of the sky, and the clouds with their infinite mutations, the possibilities were endless.

He was no expert, no Constable. Nor fooled into thinking himself any more than a talented amateur, but painting had always released something in him that might otherwise have soured and curdled irreparably. Until recently. It was doing nothing for him now.

Down below in the garden, on the bumpy, weed-infested patch of grass that was the back lawn, the children, Lucy and Allie, played mock tennis with a motheaten ball and a couple of old racquets they'd discovered in the garden shed. They had, it seemed, cajoled the woman he now knew was their aunt, Sarah, to show them how to serve, which she was doing with more enthusiasm than skill, impatient with the bumps in the lawn that bounced the ball in the wrong direction, though she was evidently enjoying herself, from the way she laughed. He'd seen them often since they'd arrived here, spoken to them several times: the two small girls, Lucy and Allie, and this warm and vibrant woman, with her quick laugh and shining brown hair, like pulled toffee. Amends would have to be made for that first meeting, which had started them off wrong-footed. He'd found himself thinking of her, a lot, in odd moments,

66

since then. So far, she'd treated him with polite reserve whenever they happened to meet, though she didn't, despite her coolness towards him, look the sort to hold on to a grudge. She'd caught him at a bad moment, the worst possible one, after a difficult out-of-hours meeting called for Saturday morning and an unexpected quarrel with his normally mild-tempered and long-suffering father. It had been his own fault, Fitzallan admitted it. His father didn't lose his temper without a great deal of provocation. It had ended with his own apologies, no bones broken, but not liking himself very much, realizing how damned difficult to live with he'd become over the last years.

He couldn't tear himself away from the window. He hadn't been able to bring himself so much as to look at a child since it had happened, but now he indulged himself, watching the three energetic bodies in the garden, the brown limbs flashing. From this distance Sarah could have been an older sister. She wasn't pretty until she smiled, then she was enchanting. Allie had the same quality.

He'd never before painted a living figure, but the desire to do so was suddenly overwhelming—a kind of catharsis? He doubted whether he'd even ask for permission, he'd look such a bloody fool if it should turn out badly, as it might well do.

Sarah called a halt, declaring it was too hot for more, and all three of them flopped down in a laughing heap on to the grass. Fitzallan found the beginnings of a smile in himself, too. It felt to have been a very long time since he'd last smiled, and stranger still that he welcomed it. In the last few years he'd gone through his own private hell, but now he was suddenly sick of himself and what he'd become. He wanted to rejoin the human race.

*   *   *

Rodney Shepherd returned home with his wife from his holiday in the Canaries with a fine deep tan, several bottles of cheaply acquired wine in his baggage and a few extra pounds around his waistline which he could have done without. Despite this last, he was well pleased with life. He remarked to his wife, as they picked the Rover up from the long-stay car park at the airport in Birmingham and drove home, that their twenty-fifth wedding anniversary celebration holiday had been one to remember. They'd escaped both sunburn and travellers' trots, the hotel had been brilliant—two swimming pools—that foreign food hadn't been half bad, really, but it was great to be home and how about some good old fish and chips from Fryer Tuck's for supper—?

'What the hell does that fool think he's doing, parking there?' he demanded, braking hard after manoeuvring the car down the narrow entry and around the corner to the back of his premises.

Rodney was an electrical supplier, he and Moira lived in the flat above the shop in Colley Street, and the only parking space he had was in the tiny yard behind the shop. It was awkward enough to get into at the best of times, the access lane behind being so narrow, but now a dark-red car was carelessly parked just before the double gates, leaving several feet of its front end protruding across them.

'You'll not get the Rover in, Rod,' Moira said, unwisely.

'You see if I damn well won't,' answered Rodney, his bonhomie quickly evaporating, macho instincts taking its place.

'You'll scratch the paintwork.'

'Not mine, I won't. He gets an inch off his, tough! No way am I going knocking on doors halfway down to Lavenstock to find who it belongs to. Some buggers'll park anywhere for free.'

But it was the three gins he'd had on the aircraft talking. Rodney wouldn't have dreamed of damaging any car if he could help it, no matter whose it was, never mind a car like that. He'd more respect for a good paint job, and with some fancy manoeuvring, and a lot of swearing, he successfully squeezed his own car past, though he'd no space to turn into the yard, the access being to his premises only, and ending at the point where high chain-link fencing separated it from the supermarket car park next door.

*   *   *

'Professor Kendrick, Cambridge? Good Lord. Surprising world we live in!' declared Dermot that evening, once more having arrived home too late to see the girls before they went to bed. He wasn't used to what he called 'office hours' and had evidently made up for it by spending the intervening time somewhere convivial. 'Professor Kendrick!' he repeated. His eyes were bright with malicious amusement.

'I don't know about professor,' Sarah said, 'but yes, I think he *was* at Cambridge.'

'Then it's sure to be the same one. He was a lecturer there—we went out to do a story on some scandal he was connected with, years ago—though I only remember vaguely what it was.'

But there'd been nothing vague about Dermot's reaction to the name. He hadn't needed to think, and Sarah was sure he hadn't forgotten the circumstances, either. Dermot rarely forgot anything to do with his work. She wondered what his reasons were for keeping it to himself, but she didn't press him in view of what she might have to tell him later.

He said, with a pretence of casualness, 'Well, I shall probably know him when I see him—it's tomorrow we're bidden to this welcome shindig, isn't it? God, how suburban!'

70

'It's a way of getting to know people. I think it's very nice of the Kendricks to take the trouble to introduce us—well, you,' Sarah said primly and rather pointedly. Though it had been Imogen Loxley who'd first telephoned to issue the invitation, who'd responded with alacrity to Sarah's suggestion to come over and join her for coffee, who'd afterwards donned a borrowed overall to cover her elegant casual clothes, picked up a paintbrush and spent an hour helping Sarah finish off the woodwork in the breakfast room. And a very nice small sitting-dining room it was now, thought Sarah—the walls a warm apricot, the paintwork a sharp white, Lisa's collection of porcelain plates on the walls, the smell of a summer evening drifting through the open window.

'I can recommend you an interior decorator,' Imogen had said, after being shown round the rest of the house and empathizing immediately with the enormity of the problem.

'One who doesn't want paying?' Sarah had laughed.

'Well, no, but she'd advise you on wallpapers and curtains, if you bought them from her. I'll ask her along to meet you when you come over. She's Lois French, of Interiors, that shop at the corner of Butter Lane, just off the Cornmarket.'

'Oh, I've seen it! Much too grand for us.' But

Sarah looked forward to meeting the woman. Dermot could use all the help and advice he could get.

'It doesn't matter to me, of course,' she told him now, as a preliminary to approaching the subject of her departure, 'but you'll still be here when I'm gone. You can't live in a community and not be part of it.'

'I don't see why not,' Dermot shrugged, but Sarah knew it was only a token objection. He was too gregarious not to want to meet his neighbours, especially now that Francis Kendrick's name had cropped up and sparked his interest. Dermot had a certain capacity for mischief, and she sensed he was ripe for it. She devoutly hoped he'd have the sense not to make waves at the party, or at any other time.

The antiquated telephone shrilled distantly from the hall. 'That'll be Simon.' She went to answer it with a certain amount of foreboding. She'd never been a match for Simon when he was feeling aggrieved, and if he started being really persuasive, she might well give in. She was feeling decidedly fed up with acting as Dermot's dogsbody, with the whole crackpot set-up here. If it wasn't for the children ... well, if it wasn't for the children, she wouldn't be here at all.

By the time she got to it, the telephone had stopped, probably having been ringing for some time before they'd heard it and Simon having lost patience. She stood undecided, debating whether or not to ring him back, when there was a knock on the door, and when she opened it, there was the dark-browed Fitzallan on the step. He'd come downstairs from his attic eyrie to ask permission to have a bonfire in the garden, he informed her abruptly.

'A bonfire? There's a spot at the end of the garden that Dermot was using the other day, if you must—but I have to tell you I regard bonfires as extremely antisocial.'

He looked at her as he digested this, saying nothing for a while. 'Perhaps I should find some other way of disposing of my rubbish.'

'Perhaps you should.'

They stood looking at each other. He finally spoke. 'Look. Please don't be uptight with me. I apologize for the other day. I'd had a right old morning, unexpected meeting called, when all hell was let loose. No excuse, none whatever, but please—let's be friends.'

He obviously couldn't exactly bring himself to smile, but equally obviously, in his own way, he meant to charm, and she was at least appeased, despite herself. She always found it faintly ridiculous to take umbrage, anyway, and he seemed to be wanting to make amends for his behaviour on her first day here. 'What is it you want to burn, Mr Fitzallan?'

'Fitz. It's James Fitzallan, but Fitz is what everyone calls me. Come and see for yourself how much there is before you allow me to commit it to the flames—and incidentally, you

73

can take a look at that view—though I warn you, it's not all it's cracked up to be.'

She followed him upstairs and there was the famous view, from the famous window.

You *could* see the Rotunda, just—if you were pointed in the right direction and told what to look for. Otherwise, what you saw was a panoramic view of sky, and the tops of trees just below, and beyond them, between lights winking palely in the early evening, the seemingly endless, undulating landscape of houses, factories, blocks of high-rise flats and roads leading towards several blobs on the horizon, one of which he said was the Rotunda.

And behind her, on the walls of the room, a continuing cyclorama, in the paintings which covered them: the great sweep of skies and trees portrayed on the canvases hung, stacked and laid flat on the floor, all of them unframed.

'Do you do this for a living?'

'Good God, no! I'm not a professional, as you'll see only too well, if you look closely. I run a design consultancy. You could call this a hobby, if that's a word you'd use, though I wouldn't. Let's just say it's served its purpose.' She looked quickly for that flash of raw pain which had struck her before, but his face was closed. 'Obsessive as to subject matter,' he went on, 'but it's the only thing I can do. I'd like to try a human figure, but I'm not sure . . . At

74

any rate, I think I've painted myself out of this as a subject by now, hence the bonfire.'

She was shocked. 'You can't!'

His brilliant eyes lit with something which might possibly have been amusement as he followed her glance to the scores of canvases. 'As a painter, I'm a damned good designer. But maybe burning them is a trifle Draconian, what do you think? No—' He held up a warning hand. 'Don't answer that. I'd honestly rather not know.'

She wanted to laugh, having a suspicion that he'd never had any intention of putting all his work on the bonfire, it was simply a contorted way of arriving at an apology. 'It's no good asking me, anyway, I've no qualifications to judge. You should ask my—the man I work for,' she amended hastily. Bringing Simon into this was, she realized, the last thing she wanted to do, only she'd been thrown by James Fitzallan, his change of attitude. She'd written him off, but now, against all odds, she found she might be warming to him.

'What about you? What sort of work do you do?' he was asking. 'Sit down, if we can find you somewhere among all this, and I'll make some coffee while you tell me the story of your life.'

When she left half an hour later, she realized this was more or less what she'd done, while he'd skated the surface and she'd learned practically nothing about him.

CHAPTER SIX

Rodney Shepherd's mood couldn't be described as best pleased when he woke up the next morning to find the strange car still blocking his entry, when he was expecting customers and deliveries. He picked the telephone up and rang the police in a rage, ordering them to come and tow away this sodding BMW that was blocking his entry, or he wouldn't be responsible for the consequences.

The offending car was removed from behind his premises by the police with a speed which satisfied even Rodney.

The details having been input in to the National Computer, within minutes it was found to be registered to a Philip James Ensor, with an address in Solihull. The keys in the pocket of the man who had died at the Colley Street allotments were found to fit the car, and his prints corresponded with those all over the inside. A jacket was neatly folded on the back seat and his wallet was locked in the glove compartment. Jubilation all round at Milford Road Police Station was tempered by a telephone call Abigail made to his home which disclosed the presence of a wife who had thought he was still abroad on a business trip.

Lord.

'I've made an appointment with Mrs Ensor over at Solihull,' she told Mayo. 'I'm taking Martin Kite with me, OK?'

She was impatient to be off. She'd convinced herself that she'd done all that was possible, and felt that the trail had gone cold, and now here was the break she'd needed, out of the blue.

'That's it, you stick with it, now that you've got a lead,' Mayo advised crisply. 'Get over there as quickly as you can—the wife doesn't know yet?'

'Wish she did—but I didn't think it was the sort of thing to tell her over the telephone.' He nodded his understanding. Apart from breaking it gently, in a case like this, you had to take advantage of the situation to grasp anything that might give a possible clue as to why someone had taken Ensor's life.

*   *   *

'What kept us?' Abigail asked, inside half an hour later, as Kite eventually slowed down and began to thread his way competently through the built-up suburban areas on the outskirts of Birmingham. She'd have preferred to do the driving herself, but Kite was a Class One police driver, and proud of it, and she decided it wasn't worth trampling on his masculine ego this time. She relegated herself to navigating

77

from the map spread across her knees.

'No point in hanging around.' Kite's watchword. He should channel his energies into getting his inspector's exams, she thought. But Kite insisted he was happy where he was, and he was a damn good sergeant, very like Mayo, in that things moved when he was around. He ran his cases competently, without the need for flourishing trumpets.

It was a change, working with him, rather than the lugubrious Sergeant Carmody, who usually doubled up with her when she needed partnering. He was at present on leave, no doubt bored to death on the Costa Brava with his wife and his mother-in-law, counting the days until he got back to work.

'You're too used to plodding along with old Ted,' Kite said, picking up her thoughts. 'When's he due back? Another week? God, it'd bore me stiff, sitting around the poolside with the ma-in-law for company.'

'Don't suppose Ted's too happy. He'd swap the Costa Brava any day for what we've got on. Hang on, we're nearly there.'

Another turning, and they'd reached their destination, a smart house on one of the new estates that were spreading out and stretching ever nearer towards Stratford-upon-Avon.

Judith Ensor was a woman in her late twenties, slim, small, with a gorgeous figure and a cloud of dark hair, a heart-shaped face, big grey eyes fringed with thick lashes, which she was inclined to flutter. She had a very slight, but attractive, lisp. She was ready for work, her clothes and make-up immaculate. Had Abigail been asked to hazard a guess as to what that work was, she'd have plumped unhesitatingly for beauty counsellor, hairdresser, fashion consultant or some allied occupation, but she would have been wrong. Mrs Ensor worked at a car-component factory as an industrial nurse. She might well constitute an industrial hazard herself, if she walked through the factory looking like that.

She sat very still when she was told the news. Under the pearly make-up it was impossible to see whether she had paled, but her eyes looked slightly unfocused and her lips were stiff when she spoke.

'I knew something would happen one day.'

'Would you care to elaborate on that, Mrs Ensor?'

'What?' She blinked several times in rapid succession. The big grey eyes were lustrous with what might have been tears. 'Oh, oh just—his car, you know—he drove it so *fast.*'

'I don't think you can have understood. It wasn't a car accident, I'm afraid.'

Shock took people differently. It was possible she hadn't taken it in when Abigail had told her how her husband had died. But Abigail didn't have the impression she'd been thinking of a car accident when she made that initial response. A quick recovery, though, if it had been a slip of the tongue. Judith Ensor began to interest her.

'Is there a relative or anyone you'd like us to contact, to be with you?' Abigail asked. 'Your children?'

'We have no children.' It was stated matter-of-factly, but with enough neutrality to show that it might seriously matter, and Abigail again shifted her perspective of the woman. Clumsy of me, she chided herself, you could never tell, and I should've noticed this isn't a family home. The room they were sitting in was as immaculate as its owner's person, furnished like a colour supplement, with all the material possessions of a successful, childless couple. There were holiday souvenirs from abroad. A conservatory out of *House & Garden* added to the back. Mrs Ensor's own smart car was in the drive, this year's model. Yet there was something wrong, something empty about the set-up, and it wasn't only the lack of children.

'When did you last see your husband?' she asked. Judith Ensor sat back and crossed her pretty legs, shown off by the close-fitting short skirt she was wearing. Her expression hardened. Abigail, looking more closely, upwardly readjusted her assessment of her age by something like ten years.

'I saw him last a fortnight ago,' she said. 'He was supposed to be in Cologne, on business. I wasn't expecting him back until after the weekend.'

Philip Ensor, it turned out, had been the senior sales representative for a freight-forwarding firm based in Bletchley, a job which had necessitated him travelling all over the world on occasions, though his journeys were mainly restricted to Europe.

'It may have been business, then, that took him to Lavenstock last Saturday night?' Abigail asked, adding the name of the firm to her careful, methodical notes.

'Lavenstock?' It might have been on another planet and not simply a town in the next county. 'I don't know. What makes you think *I'd* have been told, anyway? As far as I was concerned, he was supposed to have been in *Cologne,* wasn't he?' The pretty hand with the immaculately lacquered nails was taut on the chair arm.

'Might he have been visiting someone there he knew?' Abigail suggested.

'Look, he didn't know anyone *here!* He wasn't the sort to socialize. We've lived here nearly a year and he scarcely knew the neighbours either side, he was away so much.' There was a bitterness in her voice she didn't trouble to hide now. 'That's why we moved here from Bletchley. With him away so much, at least here I'd be near Lew and Avis—that's my brother and his wife.'

Abigail's next question seemed by now unnecessary, but the answer couldn't be taken for granted. 'Forgive me, but were relations between you and your husband friendly?'

She laughed shortly. 'Is it that obvious?'

'So it's possible he went to Lavenstock to see another woman?'

'No.'

'You're sure?' She'd sounded absolutely dead certain, but Abigail pressed on. 'All the indications were that he'd been involved in a fight, just before his death. If he's been seeing someone else, Mrs Ensor, it could have been with a jealous husband.'

'He didn't go there to see another woman,' she repeated flatly.

'That sounds pretty categoric.'

'So it should; I haven't been married to Phil for fourteen years without knowing him that well. And another thing—he'd never get involved in a fight. Never.' Her mouth twisted, marring the symmetry of the perfect oval face. 'Running away was more his style.'

If so, this time Ensor hadn't run far enough, poor devil. His wife may have been shaken, but her life didn't appear to have fallen to pieces on receiving the appalling news. She wondered what sort of life they'd led together, that Judith Ensor accepted the manner of his death so unquestioningly. But she'd said all she was going to say. Her lips were firmly pressed together, with the look of a woman who wouldn't be persuaded into saying what she'd determined not to.

'I'm afraid,' said Kite, 'there's the question of identification. We shall need someone to do it—you say your brother lives near. Would he be prepared to do the necessary?'

Her grey eyes turned a curiously assessing look on him but she shook her head and spoke decisively. 'No. I don't want him bothered. I'm quite capable of doing it myself.'

The photographs displayed around the home were enough to leave no doubt that Philip Ensor was indeed the man last seen lying on the mortuary slab at his autopsy. But formal identification was a necessity in any sudden, unexplained death, when anyone had been unlawfully killed, one of the more harrowing experiences which had to be gone through. Not, however, one which most wives willingly undertook.

'It might be an idea to have a word with your brother, all the same. He may know something about your husband's—'

'If Phil didn't confide in me, he certainly wouldn't in Lew! I might as well tell you they didn't exactly get on. But last Saturday, in case you're getting the wrong idea,' she added ironically, 'we—my brother and sister-in-law and myself—were at a family wedding over at Sutton Coldfield, and the celebrations went on until well after midnight. You'd be wasting your time.'

'Let's have his address, all the same,' Kite said.

She shrugged and gave it.

'When are we likely to find him in?'

'Most of the time. He's unemployed.'

Abigail considered briefly. 'Sergeant Kite will drive you over to Lavenstock and bring you back while I see your brother.' If Kite was surprised at this, he said nothing. 'In the meantime, would you mind if we took a look at your husband's belongings? It might give us some ideas where to start, help us to get a better picture.'

She readily gave permission. 'Go ahead, what there is. He wasn't a man for keeping things.'

Which proved to be absolutely true. Philip Ensor might have been a man living in a hotel, for all the personal possessions he'd left behind him. Some clothing, good but unexceptional. A few expensive but unused toiletries, the varying brands suggesting they might have been given to him as presents. An innocuous choice of books and CD discs, revealing nothing but a mediocre taste. The personal papers—in the shared desk were only insurances, tax papers, documents relating to the house. He'd had a mortgage he could well afford, contributed to a pension fund that would leave his wife in comfortable circumstances—though not suspiciously so. His bills were paid. He'd evidently lived a life so blinding in its ordinariness that it was in fact quite extraordinary.

*   *   *

Lew Walker hadn't done anything like as well for himself in life as had his sister.

Not only was he unemployed, he lived in an undistinguished terraced house in a narrow, shabby street leading off the main Birmingham road, about as far a cry from Yorkfield Avenue as you were likely to get. He'd missed out on his share of the family good looks, too, though what he had would undoubtedly have been improved by a shave and a haircut, and less of a scowl. Sullen and uncommunicative, he reeked of cigarette smoke and left the television horse-racing blaring in the spotlessly unimaginative living room, while waiting for Abigail to state her business. In the background his wife hovered, a tired-looking, colourless woman, with bulging, thyroid eyes, dowdy and depressed. Abigail would have felt the same, married to Walker.

'Do you mind?' She had no compunction in going to the set and turning down the sound. The man stared at her, but said nothing. The woman's eyes flickered.

It took Abigail about two minutes to realize Judith Ensor had been right. She was wasting her time here. The shocking news she had to pass on seemed to have no more impact than if the victim had been some unknown politician who'd been assassinated at the other side of the

85

world, rather than their brother-in-law. No expressions of sorrow or surprise escaped their lips. Not even a dear me.

She pressed on, feeling frustrated. The decision to spend time here she could ill afford, while Kite ferried Mrs Ensor to and from Lavenstock, had been prompted by a hunch that Judith Ensor didn't want her brother to talk to the police. She'd evidently boobed, and was now going to have to hang around at the pub where she'd arranged to meet Kite. Neither of the Walkers had anything relevant to contribute to the sum of her knowledge about Philip Ensor, much less the mystery of his death. Mrs Walker opened her mouth to speak only once, and looked at her husband for permission before she did. Abigail had posed all the questions she could think of, and was about to leave, when the woman surprised her by speaking directly to her, and for the first time meeting and holding her eyes.

'You'll have to excuse me, I have to go to work. Down the road at the Shangri-la café on the corner. They don't like us to be late.' She left the room, a moment later the front door banged, and after a few more unproductive words with her husband, Abigail, leaving him to light yet another cigarette, followed suit.

*   *   *

The Shangri-la lived up to its name only in that

it was clean, bright and reasonably comfortable.

'You've something you wanted to tell me, Mrs Walker?' Abigail asked of the woman behind the counter, as steaming water spat into the pot of tea she'd ordered.

She nodded. 'Table over there, in the corner—I'll join you in a minute.'

Abigail poured herself a cup of the strong brew, helped herself to a ginger biscuit from the cellophane-wrapped pack of two she'd bought. Avis Walker dispensed microwaved faggots and mushy peas to an elderly couple at a table by the window before coming across to lower herself on to the chair opposite, carrying a cup of tea for herself.

'Can't spare long, they'll all be coming in wanting lunches and sandwiches any time now.' She nodded in the direction of a builders' yard on the other side of the road. She was wearing a red plastic apron that matched the table coverings and its reflective glow added a little colour and animation to her pale face. Released from the presence of her husband, it seemed she was prepared to talk. 'You want to know about Phil, then? Well, I can't tell you much, but never mind what *he* says, there'd been something wrong between him and my precious sister-in-law, some big row or other recently. I don't know what about.' *He* evidently referred to her husband.

'Not a female, according to Mrs Ensor.'

She considered this, measuring sugar from a dispenser into her tea. 'No, I'll give Phil his due, I don't think he went after women, though who'd blame him? That Jude!'

'I thought you were friends? Didn't they move here to be near you?'

'To be near us? That's what she told you?' The humour of the remark struck her, and the sudden smile made her tired, drawn face nearly pretty. 'That's a laugh! First time I'd seen her for months, that wedding last week. Only went there to show off her new car and her fancy clothes.'

'So why do you think they did come to live here?'

'I've wondered about that. It was very sudden. He was still working at Bletchley, there seemed no reason.' She sipped her tea, then said suddenly, 'I'm sorry what's happened to him, he was a nice chap, you know, Phil. Not somebody you'd ever get close to, mind, you never knew what he was thinking. Deep, you know, and quiet. But very generous. He's lent Lew a fair old whack one way and another, and not got it back, either—and was Lew ever grateful? He was not! That's often the case, isn't it? Folks don't like to feel beholden—you noticed?'

'I know what you mean.' When you had no choice but to accept favours and had to remain under an obligation, gratitude could turn itself inside out. 'What did your husband do, when

88

he was in work?'

Avis Walker shrugged. 'You name it, he's tried it. But nothing's worked out for him. He's got past bothering now.' She finished her tea and pushed her chair back as the elderly couple left and a group of displaced-looking teenagers wandered in. 'Sorry, but that's all I can tell you; I'll have to go now.'

'I'm very grateful to you. Could I wait here until I'm due to meet my sergeant? He shouldn't be more than ten minutes or so, now.'

'Stay as long as you like. You stay where you are and I'll get you another pot of tea when you've finished that—on the house.'

PART TWO

The party for the new neighbours is in progress at Simla, and Francis Kendrick, having downed a glass of wine and made what he considers is quite enough small talk, is about to make his excuses and leave them to it, when he glances outside and sees one of the children, Lucy, or the one they call Allie—he can't remember which is which, only that she's the shy one—standing alone under the big conifer on the lawn.

Maybe it's the height of the tree—they've just been discussing it in the drawing room and someone has estimated it to be nearly a hundred and fifty feet tall, which sounds about right, supposing it to have been planted at the time the house was built, a century and a half ago— maybe it's this height, juxtaposed with that of the small solemn child, three foot six at most, which holds his attention. He likes the way she's listened to the conversation and then gone out to see the tree for herself. She stands dwarfed by its immensity, overawed by its size.

He puts down his empty glass, steps over the low windowsill into the heat of the summer-evening garden and, unaware of Hope's eyes following him, walks across the grass towards the little girl.

She is Allie—properly Alice—he discovers, not Lucy. She wears a cotton frock, bare legs and sandals, and her hair is side-parted and held back with a blue hairslide in the shape of a butterfly. She has a small chip on one of her front teeth. He can't think who she reminds him of. They talk about the size and age of the conifer, and he tells her that it is correctly a Sequoiadendron giganteum, *known variously as the sequoia, the Wellingtonia, the Big Tree or the Mammoth Tree, that it belongs to one of the tallest and oldest family of trees in the world, and that its potential height is over ninety metres.*

He watches her listening to him, big eyed and serious, absorbing the information, which he imparts to her in the same way he would to an adult. He'd be hard put to it to know how to speak to her otherwise, in what might be considered a more appropriate way, but in any case, he's never been one to underestimate what children can comprehend.

Allie thinks about it, scuffing the toe of her shoe in the deep, sun-warmed layer of brown needles beneath the tree, raising dust, and fingers a piece of the thick, fibrous, spongy bark which he tells her the tree regularly sheds. She reaches up to one of the sprigs of unripe green cones on the gracefully swooping branches, some of which touch the ground. She breathes in the resiny smell, it's like Dettol.

Belatedly, he says, 'What are you doing out here, all on your own?'

'I'd finished my lemonade and I wanted to see the tree. My friend Angel and me don't like grown-up parties.'

'Don't you? Then we should be friends, Allie. I don't like them, either,' says Francis, and the smile few are privileged to see lights his face. He

94

knows now who she reminds him of. She is an Arthur Rackham child, thin and spindly, a child in an illustration, with windblown clothes and hair, who dances under witchlike trees with spiky, insubstantial fairies and elves. Or Titty in Swallows and Amazons, *still on occasions his preferred bedtime reading. He smiles again. 'Have you ever heard of a pianola?'*

'No.' She considers gravely. 'Is it some kind of piano?'

'That's right, a mechanical piano. I have one, a similar sort of thing at any rate, called a Polyphon, that plays a tune with the same name as yours. Would you like to hear it?'

'Yes, please.' She turns, says something over her shoulder, and reports back, 'Angel says she'd like to hear it, too.'

After a moment of attentive regard, Francis answers, seriously, 'Come along then, both of you.'

The sun has passed behind the sequoia and the shadows in the garden are lengthening, columns of midges dance around in what is left of the sunlight, making it thick and soupy, as the tall man and the little girl walk back to the house.

CHAPTER SEVEN

'What?' Hope turned from the window to answer something Dermot Voss had said to her. The word was sharp enough to come to Sarah's ears over the murmured conversation. She watched the pair of them as her own conversation with Meg Saunders, the wife of the self-satisfied man who owned a thriving local timber yard, wound down. Mrs Saunders was clearly disappointed to find Sarah was only incidental to the scene and would soon be gone, and had lost interest on hearing that Dermot didn't have a wife whom she could cajole on to the various committees she chaired. Someone else spoke to her and she turned to answer with alacrity, blocking Sarah's view of her brother-in-law.

Dermot was feeling hard done by, his worst fears about this gathering fulfilled, and not only because of the quality of the wine, which was indifferent. The information relayed to him through Sarah, via Doreen Bailey, about the occupants of the gloomy old house (even gloomier and quite as old as Edwina Lodge, he'd discovered when they arrived) had not filled him with enthusiasm, while meeting them had put even more of a damper on his easily dampened spirits ... this middle-aged brother and sister, tall, thin and besandalled, unnervingly alike. Distantly polite, not the sort one warmed to . . .

He repeated his question to Hope. 'I was asking you what kind of books your brother writes?' He found her difficult and abrupt, though rather better than the brother, quite certainly the Cambridge professor whom he'd briefly met, years ago, but who showed no recollection of ever having met Dermot. There was no reason why he should remember, of course. As far as Francis Kendrick was concerned, Dermot had merely been the young man behind the camera in a stiff, awkward interview with one of the outside-broadcast team, and, if he were wise, he'd have put the incident which had occasioned the interview firmly behind him. He'd spoken briefly when they were introduced, then retreated into an abstracted silence before disappearing into the garden.

'His books are mostly concerned with Byzantine art,' Hope Kendrick said in answer to his question at last, dragging her wandering attention back to Dermot and then becoming animated as she cited the number of books her brother had written, the critical acclaim he'd received . . .

Dermot listened with half an ear, but brightened as the other sister, Imogen, re-entered the room, ushering in more guests and seeing them settled in a hostessy kind of way. This was more the type of woman he could

98

appreciate. She had talked amusingly, when he first arrived, about living in Brussels, a city he knew fairly well. He knew from gossip relayed through Doreen Bailey, via Sarah, why she no longer lived there, though she didn't mention this to him. He'd realized immediately that she was still committed to this almost-ex husband of hers, but the situation offered possibilities, all the same . . .

She now signalled across the room to Hope, who excused herself to Dermot and went to greet some newcomers, while he let himself drift in her wake towards Imogen.

*   *   *

Gil Mayo ate another handful of salted peanuts and wondered what the heck he was doing here. Parties of any kind were anathema to him, and as an overworked policeman his spare time wasn't so plentiful that he could afford to waste it in what he considered to be meaningless chit-chat with people he didn't know and would probably never see again. But he'd agreed to come, to take time out from the madhouse the station seemed to have become this week, a situation that had made his successful seminar no more than a beautiful memory. He'd played his part tonight with good grace and circulated obediently around the crowded room, making himself pleasant. He'd now wedged himself into a corner, hoping to remain unnoticed until Alex gave him the sign they could depart—a forlorn hope for one of his size and personality: he was a big man, with a presence as solid as the Rock of Gibraltar—not easy to miss. But, alone for the moment, his policeman's eyes were everywhere, noting, filing, remembering, instinctively sensing the undercurrents, the feeling in the room of something not quite right.

His eyes lit on Dermot Voss and Imogen Loxley, whom Voss was entertaining with audible accounts of how he'd picked out Lavenstock with a pin, come across Mrs Burgoyne and become intrigued with the idea of himself as an entrepreneurial landlord. Intriguing chap, Voss, on several counts. Through his job, widely travelled in many of the most dangerous spots in the world. Quick-witted, with an Irish fluency with words which enabled him to recount his travels so as to make them seem both fascinating and amusing, when often they must have been neither, involving him as they did in the worst situations mankind could create for itself. As if he enjoyed living on the edge, or it hadn't quite got through to him. Mayo would have liked to continue their conversation, if only to find out whether he was right in his assessments. He mustn't, however, monopolize the guest of honour. Most of the women in the room were dying for the chance to talk to him. Voss was the sort who would be attractive to women, there was a sort of daredevil look about him that they seemed to go for . . .

'What are you doing here?' said a voice. 'Wouldn't have thought this was your scene.'

'Nor yours, Henry.' Mayo was relieved to find a kindred spirit at his side—Ison, the local police surgeon, looking as ill at ease as he felt himself to be in this gathering, far cry that it was from the less salubrious places and circumstances where they usually met.

'Viv brought me,' Ison replied, rather as if he were an umbrella picked up as an afterthought in case of rain, and Mayo remembered that Vivien Ison taught geography at the Princess Mary where Hope Kendrick also taught, and that they were near neighbours of the Kendricks into the bargain, their home being just a little further down the hill, in a cul-de-sac off Albert Road. Ison was a short, brisk man, with a bristly moustache and bright eyes, reminiscent of some small, furry, bustling animal who, over the years, had become more than just a colleague with whom Mayo worked. Work, plus a mutual respect and liking, was what had initially formed a bond between them, but it was a shared passion for music which had fostered the friendship.

'Me, too,' Mayo said gloomily. 'I mean, Alex brought me along with her. She's standing in for Lois, who couldn't come tonight.'

'That situation working out all right?' Ison

asked carefully.

'I think so.' Mayo's reply was equally cautious, given more in hope than in certainty. His glance travelled across the room towards Alex, at the moment talking with evident interest to the woman he'd been introduced to as Sarah Wilmot. He caught her reflection in the big, dim old looking glass over the mantelpiece, softened by the evening light, and was momentarily reassured. Too often, lately, he'd felt something overbright about her, like a splintered reflection of her sister, Lois, and it was bothering him.

She'd recently astonished all who knew her by throwing in her hand, leaving her successful and promising career as a police sergeant, and begun working with Lois in her smart interior-decorating business. She'd so far resisted any attempts to involve her in a partnership, for which Lois undoubtedly, if mistakenly, blamed Mayo. Hardly new. Lois French blamed most of Alex's misfortunes on Mayo, including the major one of living with him.

But Lois was wrong about him trying to influence Alex in any way. In fact, he had quite a load of guilt on his shoulders about her decision to quit the Force, though he'd never actively encouraged her in that. Stood objectively aside, and let her make up her own mind. And her own mistakes. *Had* it been a mistake? He was damn sure dabbling in interior decorating wasn't going to prove stimulating or challenging enough for her in the long run.

The sun had passed behind the sequoia and dusk was gathering in the big dark room, the light absorbed by its heavy furniture, drawing its sombre colours into itself. It was a relief when Imogen began to move gracefully around, flicking on lamps that focused a kindlier radiance into the centre of the room, lighting faces, gleaming on glasses, on the women's clothes and their bare arms, leaving the shadows to the corners.

Alex was wearing a full patterned skirt that caught the light in its folds, and a kingfisher-blue silk shirt which emphasized the dark blue of her eyes. Her dark hair was a little longer than she'd worn it when in uniform. She wore his ring, a Victorian sapphire and diamond cluster—but still on her right hand. He swallowed a sigh.

He came to earth again to hear Ison harking back to the last time he'd been called out on police work. As usual, the doc couldn't resist the opportunity to talk shop. He was asking about Abigail's case. 'Any developments on your body by the allotments? I hear the theory that he staggered along and fell down in a drunken stupor is ruled out. Must confess, that was my first impression.'

'Not according to T-L. No alcohol present, for one thing.'

'Then who are we to doubt?' Ison grinned,

103

but Mayo knew his amusement didn't reflect his high regard of his colleague's opinions. Sobering, he added, 'Poor devil. Chance in a million, drowning like that, in such shallow water.'

'Not if you've been hit on the head first.'

Ison was immediately interested, wanting to know the full details of the autopsy. Fortunately, or perhaps intentionally, no one else came near. Everyone in the room must know by now that Mayo was a policeman, and people trod warily when encountering the law, whether they had cause or not.

'Any ideas who he is?' Ison asked.

Mayo told him what they knew about Philip Ensor. 'We've pulled out all the stops and I must confess we're nowhere nearer knowing what he was doing here. Nothing in his line of business in Lavenstock, though Abigail's tried several long shots. And nobody's come forward who'd seen him, despite that photo we issued to the media—not good, but the best we could do in the circumstances. Fortunately we now have a better one.'

Because of the ethics of showing a photograph of a dead face—nonproductive, too, given the state of Ensor's face when he'd been found—it had been a reconstruction involving facial enhancement by an artist. The result hadn't been bad, but the recent photograph of her husband which Judith Ensor had handed over and was shortly to be used revealed all the reconstruction's inadequacies. It was hoped this one might better bring forth recollections on someone's part.

'Early days yet, isn't it?'

'Long enough—nearly a week. We haven't given up yet, though.'

The case wasn't anywhere near being closed. Never would be, though the inquiry was growing sluggish and Philip Ensor was nearly as much of an enigma as he had been at first. Abigail was worrying like a terrier at the idea that Judith Ensor knew more about the circumstances than she was saying, but was getting nowhere with it.

The elder Voss child, Lucy, her job of handing round canapés over, and the attention she'd basked in at first now fading, was starting to whinge a little, fidgeting beside her aunt, bored in this grown-up gathering. He couldn't see Allie, who'd taken herself out into the garden. Francis Kendrick hadn't returned, either. Mayo decided perhaps he, too, might take a stroll around the garden.

He took another cautious sip of the diabolical wine and a glance at his watch, and thought of the pleasant, relaxed evening he and Alex could be having together at home.

The covert glance hadn't been lost on Ison, nor the fact that other people were beginning to leave. 'Tell you what, why don't you and Alex join us for supper?'

'Good idea. Where shall we go? Somewhere

where there's no need to book?'

'Oh, join us at home's what I meant.'

'We'd enjoy that—thanks. But would Viv welcome guests at such short notice?' Mayo had no wish to be the cause of marital dissension.

'Rubbish! I believe it's only cold meat and salad. Anyway, Viv will cope. She'll be delighted.'

Mayo had no doubt about Vivien Ison's ability to cope. She was an energetic, practical woman with short grey hair, who took most things in her stride, including her husband's demanding, and sometimes macabre, job. Ison added, as further incentive, 'I have that new John Eliot Gardiner recording I know you're dying to hear.'

That clinched it. 'Well, if you're sure.'

'Sure I'm sure. Let's make tracks, then.'

The Isons departed to walk the short distance home, leaving Mayo and Alex to follow in their car. They made their round of farewells and were thanking Imogen and her sister at the door when, from somewhere in the back of the house, came a faint and gentle sound, the slow, sweetly measured musical-box notes of 'Alice Where Art Thou?'

'Oh, do listen!' Alex exclaimed, enchanted.

'That's Francis's Victorian Polyphon,' Imogen smiled. 'You put an old penny in it and it plays the tune you choose. Allie's very favoured to be allowed a demonstration.'

For a moment, they stood in the shadowed hall, lit only by gloomy stained-glass windows, the dark staircase with its tall carved newel posts winding upwards into infinity. What was it that held them all still? Those poignant echoes of the old house's past ... musical soirees, drawing-room ballads, young ladies in ringlets and crinolines? Or some moment of precognizance? Mayo shook himself and moved to the door.

But in the weeks that followed, he was to remember time and again that haunting tune, the overpowering smell of roses from the garden, and the look on Hope Kendrick's face.

*　　　*　　　*

'Nice kids,' remarked Vic Baverstock over Monday-morning breakfast at Edwina Lodge. From the window of their downstairs flat, he watched Lucy and Allie trotting between their father's car and the house, importantly helping him to stow photographic paraphernalia into the boot of his car, plus a grip for what looked like an overnight stay away from home, encouraged by Dermot, who knew the value of volunteer labour and wanted to get off as soon as possible.

'They're noisy,' replied Tina, without any reference to truth.

She'd been born with an argumentative and contrary nature, and disagreed with her husband on principle, contradicting him almost every time he opened his mouth to speak. He constantly reminded himself that, being thin and colourless, and of no great significance as far as looks went, this was her way of getting attention. If so, it wasn't a very successful ploy. People still did their best to avoid her. And Vic himself continued to air opinionated views, even on subjects he didn't much care about, simply to keep his end up, so that their conversation resembled an acrimonious game of pat-ball.

'All kids are noisy,' he said, although it had been only the elder child, when he'd met them in the garden the previous day, who'd seemed uninhibited and full of high spirits. The younger one had played with the ends of her hair, seeming too shy to open her mouth. They jigged about on the front doorstep now, waving as their father finally drove off, shouting goodbyes in their shrill childish voices before going indoors.

'Not all children make their presence felt so obviously, by any means, if they're well brought up,' Tina continued her complaint, punctuating it with a sniff.

Vic gave up the unequal struggle and poked without enthusiasm at his bowl of yoghurt and muesli, thinking it resembled sweepings from a stable floor, while his mouth watered for bacon, sausage, eggs, the works. Vegetarian food was all right in its way, but it needed imagination to give it a kick, you had to be committed enough to food to make such a regime palatable, and Tina was basically not interested in eating, regarding it as a necessary evil, nibbling minute quantities while barely giving herself time to sit down and consume them. Now there was a thing, he reflected, the manager of a wholefood shop who wasn't interested in food! No wonder the customers didn't actually roll in—or quickly made some excuse to leave if they found themselves there by mistake. If you'd been born in Lavenstock and grown up with a centuries' old tradition of consuming the products of pork butchers' shops in the form of pigs' trotters and tripe, black pudding, pork pies, faggots and peas, you didn't take kindly to being lectured on the virtues of a healthy diet by someone who was patently no advert for her own products. Being skinny and intense wasn't admired around here. They thought her advice a bit of a cheek. Vic considered it a pretence.

Like this pretence that she found children a nuisance, when she pursued motherhood as determinedly as she pursued every other craze in her life—he couldn't think of it as anything else but a craze: Tina as a parent hardly conjured up visions of dewy-eyed madonnas or fruitful earth mothers. He switched off the subject, which he preferred to ignore—not the idea of having a family, for he was extremely fond of children, but the processes entailed in getting one. All these charts and temperature-taking and other things which he'd rather not think about, too damned clinical, by half. Not to mention sex at the approved time, whether one felt like it or not. Off-putting, to say the least. Especially since Tina didn't inspire him to feel much like it at all these days.

'That wretched paper girl's left her bike inside the gate again!' she declared suddenly, assuming her on-the-warpath expression as she spied Patti Ryman's bicycle in the bushes, and Patti talking to Henry Pitt.

'If she didn't hide it, it'd get nicked. You can't expect her to push it around while she's delivering that load of papers.'

'She shouldn't be delivering papers at all.'

Vic was inclined to agree—the bag for them was very near as big as the girl herself—but he couldn't be bothered to argue. He was going to have indigestion all day as it was from that bloody muesli.

'You don't need to go yet—and you haven't finished your breakfast,' she accused him, as he pushed his chair back from the table. 'It's only quarter to eight.'

'Not really hungry,' he lied, thinking of the hot sausage sandwich he'd have time to pick up if he left now. 'And I want to be in early this morning. There's old Pitt—I can offer him a lift.'

'He likes to walk to work.'

'Well, he's only got to refuse, then,' Vic

retorted, making his escape before he said more than he ought. He had his own reasons for keeping Tina sweet at the moment, apart from the fact that he was sorry for her over the way Mrs Burgoyne had let her down over her promise to let them have first refusal to buy Edwina Lodge.

He was just in time to catch Henry Pitt, from the upstairs flat, a plump, white-haired old man who was looking flustered, mumbling something Vic didn't catch, touching Patti's sleeve then edging away from her, his face growing even more pink as he spotted Vic.

'Well, thanks, Mr Pitt,' Patti said, giving Vic a bright smile as she hurried off to complete the rest of her deliveries. 'Don't forget to be there. It's really important.'

'Assignations?' Vic asked Henry jokingly, his gaze appreciatively following Patti's neat little back view. Even the hideous school uniform couldn't hide that Patti Ryman was growing up, fast. Her legs, when she'd worn those miniskirts during the holidays, were worth more than a second look.

Henry flushed even more deeply as he answered Vic's flippant remark. 'Oh, it's something and nothing.'

He didn't refuse Vic's offer of a lift, although it would mean abandoning his walk to work. He would arrive far too early at the town library, where he stamped books and put them back on the shelves contentedly all day long, where he

111

made his way every day with his doddery-looking walk that must surely be deceptive, since he had no car and rarely took the bus, and sent for a taxi only on odd occasions. Couldn't be as old as he appeared, not yet retired and on the pension, Vic reflected, though he wasn't looking as benevolently smiling today as he normally did.

'How's things, then?' Vic asked when they'd joined the traffic flow and were bowling down the hill.

'Oh, coping you know, coping.' Henry paused. 'Well, to tell the truth, not happy with the way things are going at the library, Vic, not happy at all.' He had a gentle, cultivated voice, he wore knitted waistcoats and, in winter, a fur hat with ear-flaps. He'd lived with his brother, Charles, until Charles died and their house had become too much for Henry to cope with alone. Harmless old boy, a big soft Nellie, really, but basically OK.

'Oh, you mean the cuts and that.'

'Yes, that's just what I do mean.' Henry was silent for a while, then burst forth, growing more and more agitated as he elaborated on his theme. They were being forced to close down another branch library, due to spending limits set by central government ... 'Closing down *libraries,* imagine! We're becoming a nation of Philistines!' he cried. 'Not to mention the shortsightedness of it! How can we grumble about children doing nothing but sit in front of the telly, if we don't encourage them to read?' He went on in this vein for some time. 'It's hardly surprising they're growing up illiterate, can scarcely even write their own names!'

'I suppose not,' answered Vic, who rarely read anything other than *Exchange and Mart* and hadn't given the subject much consideration one way or another, although, working as a clerk in the council treasurer's department, he could hardly be unaware of the swingeing cuts in local government spending. He was rather taken aback at the gentle Henry's vehemence.

'Well, that's how it seems to me,' said Henry with an apologetic smile. 'I'm sorry, I can be a bit of a bore on the subject. It shouldn't matter to me, I'll be retiring shortly, but it does, I'm afraid, it still does.'

'Think nothing of it,' replied Vic, who'd been listening with half an ear anyway, thinking that if he got a move on, he'd still be in time to nip round the corner to the sandwich bar where the lovely Mandy would slip three sausages in his bap, rather than the stipulated two, at no extra charge. It wasn't only the sausages that made his mouth water again. 'What are you going to do with yourself, then, when you retire? Got all your plans made?' he asked Henry heartily.

Henry looked bleak. 'I'm not sure. My brother and I—we used to spend our holidays in Greece, the country fascinated him, and we'd intended to go there more often when I retired—but I don't somehow feel inclined to go alone. To tell you the truth, I can't imagine what I shall find to do without my work,' he added, in a forlorn burst of honesty. 'I've worked in the library for forty-eight years.'

Forty-eight years! Jesus. Vic tried to think up something useful to say, but could only dredge up a cliche he was himself sick of hearing. 'Oh, I don't know. You wait. When I meet blokes that used to be in our office, they tell me they don't know how they found time to go to work. You've got plenty of hobbies, I suppose?' Vic was a great believer in hobbies. His was singing in a male-voice choir. Very therapeutic, letting off steam by belting it out—and useful, too, if you needed an excuse.

'I like cooking. I read a lot.'

'You want to get yourself an allotment, keep you more fit than reading.'

'An allotment? Good heavens, I don't know the first thing about gardening!' Henry laughed gently. 'I am happy to say I have never *seen* a spade.'

Poor bugger, thought Vic, not realizing Henry was quoting, he's going a bit gaga already, even before they shove him out on to the scrapheap. Get worse if he wasn't watched. You could never tell with these old blokes when they got to that age, up to all sorts, they were. He thought with sudden unease of the empty sherry bottles he'd noticed recently in the shared dustbin, of lonely old men sitting on park benches, loitering outside school gates, of the two small girls at Edwina Lodge, and wondered what Henry could have been talking to little Patti Ryman about.

*   *   *

After those who went out to work had left, and the children been packed off to schools and playgroups, Ellington Close took on its usual peaceful daytime languor. Mothers thankfully made themselves a quiet cup of coffee and looked for their horoscopes on the telly, the postman came and went, the three retired couples rose and had breakfast, and Stanley Loates put his mother's soiled bed linen into the washing machine.

Trevor Lawley, from number thirteen, went in search of his cat.

CHAPTER EIGHT

It had been a week of disasters, one of those weeks that occasionally descend like the wrath of God, even on well-conducted police stations such as Lavenstock Divisional Headquarters. Murphy's—or somebody's—Law, saying that if something can go wrong, it will, with Detective Superintendent Gil Mayo under pressure too, and—just another natural law of life—passing on the heat to the Poor Bloody Infantry below. A week best forgotten, but not yet over, culminating in this.

This was something the Super hated more than any other single crime, as his bleak face showed, and the reason he'd been one of the first on the scene. And not alone in that, Abigail Moon thought. Professionals, accustomed, but not yet, thank God, desensitized to the murder of a young person, a child—and this one not much more than a child, fifteen, sixteen at most. Life barely begun for her. Thought at first to be much younger, so small in stature was she, but underneath the dark-green school uniform the small round breasts, the smooth curves of her developing young body confirmed she was older. Yet the face of innocence looked up at them from the fallen carpet of leaves. Unblemished, but dead. Oh, certainly dead.

Patti Ryman, the paper girl.

Poor, poor child, poor creature, muttered Doc Ison, tight-lipped, he who had brought her into the world, and never thought to see her out of it. He knelt, shaken out of his usual professional detachment, beside Timpson-Ludgate as the pathologist delicately probed and examined: bluff and hearty, renowned for his mordant humour, he too was silenced by the terrible waste of a young life.

'What could she ever have done to deserve that?' Ison asked.

Probably nothing, thought Mayo grimly, overhearing the muttered question. Nobody knew better than he that the times we live in mean that murder doesn't necessarily require provocation any more—or only one so slight as to be incomprehensible to any sane person, to anyone but the killer.

On the other hand . . .

There were many things on the other hand. Youth, however innocent it seemed, was rarely completely so these days. They knew more at eight years old than Mayo had known at twenty-eight—which wasn't to say he hadn't always wanted to know. He'd been born with an avid curiosity about the human race and what makes it tick, what causes it to go off the rails. It was what made him a good copper and occasionally a bad risk as a friend and companion. It was why he raged inwardly, in tune with Ison, against what could have brought little Patti Ryman to this violent end.

The playground drugs scene? A quarrel with a boyfriend, after experimenting with sex, becoming pregnant? Teenage prostitution, leading to murder? Unthinkable only a few years ago, any of them, but now all too possible.

But there was that other thing, the possibility of this being one out of a series of murders, which until now had been principally Hurstfield Division's problem, but now was in everyone's mind here: two other young girls over there had been raped and brutally battered to death within the last few months, another was missing. Younger than Patti, but two of them in school uniform, like her, and all of them with fair hair, like Patti's.

And yet . . .

Murder this undoubtedly was, though possibly not a sex crime. It seemed unlikely that she'd been raped or sexually assaulted, for although she'd been discovered lying on her back with her skirt rucked up around her thighs, she'd been fully clothed and there was no indication so far of any sexual interference. Timpson-Ludgate had refused to be categoric about it until he'd had the chance to do a more detailed examination, but it wouldn't be what he expected to find. And, now that he'd gently turned her over, it could be seen that her mane of crimped fair hair was clotted with blood.

'There you are. Her skull's been smashed. With,' he added, looking more closely, 'what looks like a single blow to the back of her head. Savage, though, some weight behind it. And if you ask me what with, I can only say,' he went on, parting the hair carefully, 'it was probably something narrowish, flat, heavy, what say you, Henry? We'll get a better picture later, but take a look.'

Thus called upon, Ison squatted further down beside Timpson-Ludgate so that he, too, could examine the wound. Mayo didn't feel a minute inspection was called for on his part. He looked briefly, then at the rest of the body, the way her skirt had been dragged up, and at her black leather school shoes. He frowned.

There'd been no problem with identification. Everyone around her knew Patti. Knew her and liked her, a cheerful girl, delivering papers for pocket money before she went on to school. No problem with establishing the time of death, either: the doctors were saying she couldn't have been dead much more than an hour, which tied in with the time she normally arrived here on her round.

'PM nine a.m, tomorrow morning,' Timpson-Ludgate announced, peeling off his gloves. 'Best I can do.'

It was quicker than Mayo had expected.

As the doctors took their leave, the SOCOs moved in. Mayo took the opportunity—while the cameras flashed and captured the scene on video and Dexter applied his forensic skills to collecting the usual samples—to walk around and fix the scene in his mind: a roughly rectangular wooded area which sloped down behind the gardens of Edwina Lodge, Ellington Close, and the house called Simla, running down to the car park of an engineering factory on the lower road, from which it was separated by high chain-link fencing surmounted by barbed wire. The rest of the wood, except where the residents had put up their own more decorative woven fencing panels, was fenced off with wire strung between concrete posts, fronted with scrawny quickthorn hedging. A narrow dirt path between the first house in the Close and the garden of Edwina Lodge—six-foot boarded fencing on the one side and a high brick wall on the other—led into this shared piece of private woodland, to which all the residents had legal access and where the older children played. Scruffy woodland of little more than an acre, the children probably thought it paradise. Ropes hung from trees, 'camps' had been dug, a stream, little more than a trickle, had been dammed with stones and diverted.

But now, apart from the shirt-sleeved police swarming all over the wood, and the sounds of their voices, the Close itself was silent as he guessed it rarely was—older children now in school, younger ones kept protectively indoors. Murder close to home had a sobering effect.

He completed his circuit of the wood and came back full circle. 'Somebody's going to miss this,' Dexter was saying. 'These don't come cheap. Hundred and fifty nicker at least, I'll bet, probably more.'

'Hundred and fifty, for a biro?' Kite echoed. 'Strewth!'

'It's a fountain pen. Last you a lifetime, this would.'

'If you don't lose it,' Kite said, looking at the slim, mottled brown-and-gold plunger-action pen with the gold fittings, engraved with a stylized gold flower, which Dexter was carefully putting into a polythene evidence bag. 'Or drop it at the scene of a crime.'

'There'll be prints, hopefully,' Dexter said, moving off.

'Who was it found her, Martin?'

'Chap at number thirteen,' answered the lanky sergeant, running his hand through his curly, fair hair. 'Name of Lawley, looking for his cat. He was going to take it to the vet today, for an operation on its ear, but he can't find it. Maybe the moggy's got wind of what's to happen to it and it's taken off, you know what cats are. Anyway, Lawley came in here calling for it and found the girl, recognized her immediately.' His usually cheerful face was grim. 'Lucky it was him, and not any of the children.'

Every other policeman there, those who were parents and those who weren't, was undoubtedly thinking the same thing. 'Anyone taken his full statement?'

'On my way now.'

'Don't forget to ask him if he's lost a pen,' Abigail reminded him.

As she spoke, someone called out to Kite from the other side of the wood. The sergeant raised a hand in reply, but the dead girl was being placed in a body shell, and he remained quietly with the others while she was removed to the waiting ambulance, thence to be transported to refrigeration in the mortuary.

Her parents would have to be told.

'There's only one, her mother. Divorced,' Abigail said, 'and she was an only child.' She looked up from her clipboard, pushing her hair back. 'Life's rotten, sometimes.'

She didn't usually let things get to her, but this was different. This he could understand. In the rare moments when he was feeling low, when he'd been a parent coping on his own, his wife dead and his daughter Julie still a teenager, this was the sort of thing Mayo had always dreaded. But Julie had never remotely encountered any violence, she was alive and well and living abroad at the moment, he'd never personally had to confront such an appalling tragedy as was facing this unknown woman, Patti's mother, whose life would never be the same again.

And it was Abigail who was going to have to tell her.

Informing a parent that their child's life had just been snuffed out was the worst task any of them ever had to perform, but it was something they'd all had to do, and would no doubt have to do again. He thought about suggesting someone else do it, but he knew Abigail wouldn't appreciate it. She never asked for concessions.

He watched her for a moment, and was reassured. Cool, apparently unruffled, wearing a summer skirt and a light cotton shirt this hot morning, her bronze hair drawn back into a thick plait. She'd cope.

'There's also an aunt,' she was saying, brisk with herself once more. 'She lives here in the Close, a Mrs Bailey, the mother's sister, and she wants to be the one to tell her . . . it seems they're very close. I'll give her time to break the news, get the worst over, before I go and see Mrs Ryman. By the way, she's asking to speak to you personally, before she goes to see her sister. She won't speak to anyone but the "top man". Claims she knows who did it.'

'She does?' He gave her a sharp glance. 'With good reasons? Or just suspicious?'

'I don't know. She wouldn't say anything more.'

'I'd better see her, then.'

Was this, after all, going to be one of those open-and-shut cases, where it was immediately apparent who the perpetrator was? Murder occurring out of the blue, for no reason, by some anonymous stranger, was a far rarer phenomenon than some of the more lurid press would have their readers believe. Trouble had more often been openly brewing before suddenly erupting, with disastrous repercussions. Friends, relatives, neighbours could, and often did, point the police in the right direction, leaving them few problems, save those of calming down the participants enough to make a coherent statement. If it was so in this instance, nobody would be better pleased than Mayo, but he doubted it. With nothing more than his gut feeling to go on, he somehow doubted it very much.

'We've talked to the neighbours, all sixteen houses in the Close, but no joy,' Abigail went on, tapping her clipboard, 'from those we've asked so far, that is—nobody saw or heard a thing. A lot of them had already left for work before she was found, mind, we'll have to see them later . . . and two families are on holiday. The rest are mainly mothers with young children, one or two retired couples. I'm just about to start on the two big houses, then we'll do the rest of Albert Road down as far as Patel's, the newsagent she worked for. It's going to be manpower-intensive again,' she added wryly.

Mayo's mind was already working on it, on the transfer of personnel from the Ensor case, which was now going to have to be put on to the back burner. With the department still working through the backlog of summer holidays, several people on annual leave, everything else would now have to go by the board. This investigation would take priority, he would personally see to it that it did. They'd give it all they'd got, work round the clock. Exhausted men and women, stretched resources, escalating overtime figures and budget allocations were the least of it.

'It might help if you left those two houses to me. I've met the owners—briefly, but at least it gives me a bit of an edge. I can make a start with them.' It was doubtful that they could have seen anything behind their shrubberies and high walls. But he knew instinctively that his personal involvement was needed here, that the occupants—the Kendricks at Simla, certainly—should be handled with care. They knew everybody that mattered, they still had poke. He couldn't afford any cock-ups where they were concerned. But there were other, less obvious reasons why he should concern himself with them, reasons he couldn't explain even to himself, but were amounting almost to a conviction ... shades of the party he'd attended, of something he'd missed, or subconsciously sensed out of kilter. Catches of that old tune, 'Alice Where Art Thou?', which had haunted him maddeningly ever since, began another replay in his mind.

'Right,' he went on, suddenly realizing that he'd been elsewhere while Abigail had been putting him in the picture, a bad habit of his that he knew irritated the hell out of other people, who thought he wasn't paying attention, especially since he rarely missed anything. The ability to think and operate on two levels was a facility he'd developed out of necessity. 'That seems to be it, then, so far?' he said, recapping correctly on what she'd been saying.

Patti, it appeared, had left her bicycle where she invariably parked it, just inside the gates of Edwina Lodge. After leaving the papers there and at Simla, she'd gone on to deliver in the

Close. The canvas bag, with most of the newspapers and magazines still in it, had been found at the entrance to the path leading into the wood. Traces of blood, still wet and sticky, indicated that she'd been attacked when she was halfway along it, and presumably by someone who must have come up behind her. But she'd actually been found here, a hundred yards further into the wood.

Why had she been going into the wood at all?

He stood back, hands in pockets, to get a better view. The Ellington Close houses were all set at angles to the wood, so that only the frosted-glass bathroom windows upstairs overlooked it. Number one had a bedroom window that obliquely looked over the path, but could be discounted, since the occupants were away. Only the upstairs windows at Edwina Lodge overlooked any part of the wood. Nothing could be seen of the path from Simla, the angle of vision was wrong.

Whoever had made the attack had still taken a very big risk of being seen. True, it was breakfast time, a busy hour of the day with everyone intent on their own concerns: preparing to leave for work, getting children ready for school, no time to be interested in what was happening outside. All the same, people must have been about all the time, walking past the end of the pathway, leaving in their cars.

They were making a fingertip search of the wood now, outside the taped area around the body and the delineated access path to where it had lain, looking for the murder weapon. Brambles and nettles grew in profusion at its edges, unidentified fungi grew in the undergrowth and on rotten tree stumps, nasty to the touch. There were still damp, muddy areas, even after weeks of dry weather, and evidence that dogs were irresponsibly let out to exercise here. Garden rubbish—and other things which had no business to be dumped there—had been thrown over the fences of those gardens backing on to the wood. 'The best of British,' he muttered under his breath as he left, on his way to see Mrs Bailey. It was a long time since that sort of thing had fallen to his lot, thank God.

'Sir!' It was young WDC Platt, hurrying to intercept him. Her pretty face was pale, her curls damp with the heat.

'What is it, Jenny?'

'We've found the missing cat, sir. It's dead.'

She was looking upset, the way people did over animals, and shocked, evidently thinking, what a place to dump a dead cat, where children played! A hitherto safe area, where they wouldn't now be allowed to play for some time, even when the police were finished with the locus, Mayo guessed. Parents and children alike would, understandably, be wary of this little wood for some time to come.

'Perhaps you should come and see, sir,' Jenny suggested. He saw there was something more by her face.

Abigail accompanied him as he walked over to where Kite and a group of uniformed men were gathered around a deep tangle of undergrowth, and as she peered down at what was there, he heard her indrawn breath, and understood why when he also looked.

Not just any old cat. A big, sleek tortoiseshell, a handsome animal, plump and healthy-looking, despite its reputed ear trouble. It wasn't going to need the vet now. It appeared to have been stabbed, not once, but many times. It had had its throat cut. He gently touched the animal. The fur was still warm, the body not yet locked in rigor. He turned away, sickened.

'Poor beast. See we get blood samples.'

'Sir?'

'We'll need to establish which is the cat's blood out there, and which came from the girl.'

Jenny looked even more upset, but she pulled herself together quickly. She was turning out to be one of his best officers, proving to be hard-working and methodical, though she sometimes had to have things spelled out for her. She would probably do all right for herself in the Force, in a steady, unspectacular way.

'We'll have to have another think now about where Patti was killed, won't we?' Abigail,

128

naturally sharper and more intuitive, was saying. 'If the traces of blood further back along the path weren't hers, she might have been attacked right by where she was found.'

'Could account for why nobody saw or heard anything of the attack, too. And for the absence of any drag marks on the heels of her shoes or along the path into the wood,' Mayo said, 'or the unlikely possibility that her killer picked her up and carried her further into here. I suppose he could have dragged her by her feet, but if he did, there'd have been marks on her, on her clothing. And anyone who did this,' he said, jerking his head towards the body of the cat, 'he'll have blood on him, maybe scratches, unless he wore gloves. I'd guess by the size of it, this puss was a bit of a tiger.'

There was another shout. One of the uniformed constables had found what was almost certainly the weapon.

It was a flat, heavy length of iron, flaking with rust, about eighteen inches long by two inches wide, the sort used to brace the concrete posts between which the wires at the bottom of the gardens in the Close were stretched. Its narrow edge suggested the profile of the weapon used to inflict the wound on the back of Patti's head. Typically, the builders who'd put the fencing up in the first place had simply dumped the surplus material among the nettles and docks in the wood, rather than go to the trouble of carting it away. The killer had made no attempt to hide the piece of iron, perhaps thinking it would be lost among the dozens of similar pieces left lying around, that the blood would be indistinguishable from the rust marks on it, perhaps not thinking at all, only wanting to be rid of it. Only it wasn't, like the rest, half obscured in the encroaching bindweed and nettles, but had landed on a broken piece of the concrete fencing post, staining it with wet blood. Even then, it had needed someone as sharp-eyed as the youngest constable there to notice the stain.

'Nice one, Kevin,' commented Kite to the young PC, who flushed and tried to look nonchalant.

Dexter, summoned to look at it, pulled down his mouth. 'Don't expect we'll get any prints from that rough surface, even if he didn't wear gloves, but we'll collect some blood and so on from it, all right. And there'll be some of this muck and rust in the wound.' He indicated the flaking surface of the rust-scabbed and soil-encrusted iron bar as he bagged it in a polythene evidence bag and labelled it.

'Do your best, Dave.'

Mayo was at last able to leave them to it and went, with Abigail, to seek out Mrs Bailey at number sixteen, while Kite went three doors down to take a statement from the man who'd found Patti's body.

CHAPTER NINE

The tortoiseshell cat's name was Nero, and the Lawleys had obviously been devoted to it. The news of how it had been killed devastated Trevor Lawley. 'God, that's sick!'

'Yeah. Makes you wonder, doesn't it?' Kite agreed.

'I mean, you hear about folk doing these sort of things to animals but you never think ... hell, how am I going to tell the wife? Much less the kids!'

His Black Country accent came out strongly. He was a smallish man, thin and nervy, dressed in a dark-blue-and-red checked workshirt and jeans, and in his distress over his cat he seemed almost to have forgotten why he was being interviewed.

'Just my rotten luck, ain't it?' he moaned, when Kite managed to bring him back to finding Patti Ryman's body. 'I tell you straight, I rue the day we ever come here. It was only a council flat we had but we'd have been better stopping there. One thing after another it's been since the day we moved in. First the wife loses her job, then I'm made redundant, we haven't a snowball in hell's chance of paying the mortgage and no hope of selling the bloody house, neither. We don't need this! If anything'll put the kibosh on selling it, this will!'

With all these troubles, it was perhaps understandable that Lawley was morbidly self-obsessed with his ill fortune, and Kite schooled himself not to remind him too tersely that life wouldn't be fun for Patti Ryman any more, either, or her mother. 'Mr Lawley, just tell me what happened this morning,' he said shortly, making a mental note to ask whether the Lawleys had quarrelled with anyone who might have taken their revenge through the cat, though Lawley was quite likely to be as paranoiac about that as everything else, to see himself surrounded by enemies. They were doing another quick round of the Close, anyway, after discovery of the cat, and in a close-knit community such as this, with everyone aware of everyone else's business, any quarrels between neighbours would soon come to light.

Kite's tone, if not the words, had got through to Lawley, making him pause in the airing of his grievances, gnawing his lip. 'Sorry. Just got to the stage where I can't take much more, know what I mean? It's a shame about the little wench.'

'How well did you know her?'

It wasn't a question to keep him calm. 'What do you mean, how well did I know her? Here, you're not thinking I had anything to do with it? Bloody hell, I only knew her through her

132

bringing the papers!'

Trevor Lawley had been the one to find her, he might also have been the last one to see her alive. Why Patti Ryman had died was as yet a mystery, and there was no reason to believe Lawley had anything to do with it but there was every reason why he should, like anyone else, be subjected to questioning, and Kite told him so. He doubted whether Lawley even heard him.

'Look, she was a nice enough kid as far as I could tell, and I'm sorry this had to happen to her. Why, she used to stop and have a word with Nero of a morning,' he said, as if the cat had been a human being and their niceness to him was the criterion by which Lawley judged every other human being. 'He'd taken to sitting on top of the fence post by the path, and she'd stop for a minute or two and he'd let her stroke him under his chin, where he liked it—he wouldn't have let anybody do that, I can tell you! He was sixteen,' he said, back with his preoccupations. 'That's a good age for a cat, but he could've lived for years. He shouldn't have died like that! Just let me get hold of the bastard what did it! What sort of sicko could do that to a poor, defenceless animal?'

Kite had had enough of this. He said sharply, 'Patti Ryman was sixteen, too. Shall we keep to the point, Mr Lawley?'

Like a finicky housewife, the other man bent to straighten the fringe on the hearth rug,

133

perhaps aware he'd gone over the top in his lament for his cat, more likely just out of a habit of obedience. The house was soulless and unimaginative, so immaculately clean and tidy, without a book or a magazine or a child's toy in sight, that it was hard to imagine any family life existing in it, much less any pet being allowed to form part of the household. Perhaps it only looked like this because it had to stand in permanent readiness for inspection by any possible client who might suddenly appear on the horizon. More likely Mrs Lawley was one of those obsessive housewives who have a personal vendetta against anything likely to harbour dust and germs.

Either way, Kite began to feel sorry for him. He thought of his own untidy, sometimes chaotic household, centred around two noisy, pre-teenage boys, and his cheerful, always on the go, slightly zany wife, Sheila, and was suddenly, thankfully, happy.

'So, to recap. You went looking for your cat and entered the wood at half past eight, when you saw the body of a young girl you recognized as Patti Ryman?'

'Well, I didn't know her last name. I only knew her as Patti.'

'Did you touch her?'

''Course I didn't touch her! I rushed home and dialled 999, for God's sake, for the ambulance.' He stopped. 'I think I knew she had to be dead, though, the way she was lying there—her clothes, know what I mean . . . Was she raped?'

When Kite didn't answer, he added, with unexpected sharpness, 'If you're looking for perverts, mate, you want to look at that bloke at number seven, not me. Can't keep his eyes off of the kids!'

At the door, Kite remembered he hadn't asked about the pen.

'A what?' Lawley said, when he'd described it. 'A bloody pen, that price?' He jerked his thumb towards the For Sale sign. 'You have to be joking!'

At least, thought Kite as he left, he'd succeeded in bringing some amusement into Lawley's day.

*   *   *

The bay window at number seven gave Stanley Loates an oblique view of the police activity in the Close. Despite the uncomfortable racing of his heart, he watched their comings and goings compulsively, his jaws masticating one lump of treacle toffee after another from the paper bag in his pocket, telling himself repeatedly that he'd nothing to fear. He'd already been questioned twice—once about the girl, and then that young woman detective constable with the curly hair had come back about the cat. He'd told her that he'd seen nothing of Patti the paper girl that morning. She'd seen how surprised he was about the cat, and he was sure she'd believed him on both counts. She'd been very polite, thanked him and told him not to bother getting up out of his chair to see her to the door, sir, as though he was an old man.

Stanley wasn't old—nearly fifty, but that was young these days—a fattish, flabby man whose shirt and ill-fitting, baggy-bottomed trousers never met neatly, an unprepossessing man with sweaty palms and thinning, fairish hair. He lived with his mother, who was old and senile and ought by rights to be in a home, where she could be looked after properly, anyone said so. But to all such advice Stanley turned a deaf ear. She was his mother, he'd never let her be put away, he told them. He was a good son.

Maybe a few gullible souls were fooled by this, but not anyone who knew the two of them.

The truth was that the council-owned homes were full, with long waiting lists, and though Hilda Loates had enough funds in the bank to pay the costs of a private one, Stanley had no intention of wasting what was left of his inheritance. She'd sold his father's run-down business (thus depriving Stanley of the only job he'd ever had) and the old house in Grover Street, for what little they would fetch, having taken it into her head to buy this house as an investment, telling him with a cackle he could always sell it at a fat profit when she was gone. That was five years ago. She hadn't gone yet and you couldn't give these houses away now.

All this, however, was only partly why he didn't trouble himself about finding another job, but stayed at home and cared for her. The truth was, Stanley didn't dare to suggest such a thing as a home to his mother, for he was still terrified of her, as he had been all his life. His brain told him it was quite impossible that she, a weak old woman, could take him, a grown man, by the shoulders and shove him into the dark cupboard under the stairs as she used to when he was a child, but his mind didn't believe it. She was capable of anything. She'd be able to rise from the dead, he was sure. She'd always had a vicious tongue, and though what she said nowadays, after her stroke, was mostly rubbish, she was aware of everything that went on, and she could talk intelligibly if she wanted to. The reason she didn't, very often, was that she knew her gobbledegook speech made life more difficult for him. So he gritted his teeth and carried on. He was prepared to do whatever he had to do for her. Whatever. He knew she couldn't last that much longer and after that—bingo! Life would begin, at last, for Stanley Derrington Loates.

She'd driven his father to an early grave. Alfred Loates, who built up a successful shoe-retailing business in the days when personal service to customers meant something, had been a small, spry, cheerful man, but even his unfailing optimism had eventually been defeated by her. He'd lost heart and his business had gone down the pan. But she wasn't going to defeat Stanley.

And he wouldn't be scared by the police, either.

He decided to have a doughnut and a cup of drinking chocolate to soothe his nerves before he went out and finished tying up his beans.

*　　*　　*

'Mrs Bailey's house is the first on the right, number sixteen, the one with the wishing well in the garden,' Abigail said.

And the frilly nets, and the ding-dong door chimes, and the blaze of petunias and French marigolds lining the path, Mayo found as they walked up to the front door.

'This is Detective Superintendent Mayo, Mrs Bailey,' Abigail said as the door opened on the first ring. 'He's the senior officer in charge of the case.'

'Thank you for coming.'

Her eyes were red and swollen, her voice congested with weeping, but she was in command of herself. 'I was just off to work when I heard,' she began, indicating the pink tracksuit trousers and T-shirt that were presumably her working garb, evidently comfortable, if all too revealing of ample curves. 'It's my morning for Simla, but they'll have to do without me today. My sister's going to need me more than they do.'

The tiny hall was uncomfortably crowded with Mayo's large form, and Abigail, plus Mrs Bailey. 'What am I thinking of, keeping you standing here! It won't take any longer if we go and sit down somewhere,' she said suddenly, opening the door into a spotless front room that smelled of lavender furniture polish.

Waving them to a large, puffy, be-flowered settee with extra cushions embroidered in pansies, she sat down opposite. 'We've never had children of our own, me and Bob, and she was like my own daughter, our Patti.' Tears welled again and it was moments before she could speak, after employing an already sodden wad of tissues she pulled from her pocket. 'I'm sorry, but it's just—I blame myself, I blame myself. I told her, see, that there was nothing to worry about. If all he does is look, I told her—'

'Mrs Bailey, who are we talking about?'

She stared at Abigail. 'That Stanley Loates, of course, at number seven! Dirty old devil! Getting his kicks watching her bend down over the letter-boxes to push the papers in. She asked me what should she do and I said leave it, I'll give him the side of my tongue when I get the chance. And now look what he's done. I should've told you lot right away, when she first complained.'

'I doubt we could've done anything, except warn him off,' Abigail said sympathetically. 'We can't stop anyone looking out of his own

139

window.'

'Well, he wouldn't have gone on to rape and murder her if he knew you had your eye on him, would he?'

Mayo said, 'I'm afraid it's not quite so simple. For one thing, we don't know yet if she was raped, and it seems unlikely.'

But sexual motivation in some form or another couldn't be discounted, not when the victim was an attractive fifteen-year-old schoolgirl so small she might easily have been mistaken for a child, especially in her school uniform. Perhaps the name of Stanley Loates would appear when the computer came up with the names of all known child molesters, though it wasn't one known to Mayo. At any rate, along with all the others he'd be requestioned, minutely and at length, in a painstaking reworking, resifting and correlating of the data already collected in attempts to throw light on the deaths of the two little girls in Hurstfield.

'It seems more likely Patti died from a very violent blow to the head, Mrs Bailey,' Abigail said.

'What, him, violent? Hitting her? Stanley Loates?' Mrs Bailey's astonishment was enough to stem her tears. 'He'd be hard put to it to hit the top off a soft-boiled egg! Still, it just shows! You never know with that sort, do you?'

*   *   *

140

Ways in which the two deaths, the girl's and the cat's, could be—must be—connected, were running through Abigail's mind, all of them nasty. Yet however bizarre the possibility, it had to be assumed that the two killings, so closely related in time and place, were related in other ways, too.

She'd joined two of the other officers—Kite and Jenny Platt—for a quick sandwich in the snack bar a few doors away from Patel's paper shop. It was pretty basic, but when you were on a job like this, niceties didn't take priority. And since they were the only customers, inevitably, ideas began to be batted around.

'She heard what she assumed was someone torturing the cat, went to investigate—and he hit her on the head—?' Kite suggested.

Abigail shrugged, gulping down coffee from a thick white beaker and finishing a hot sausage roll that filled a corner but didn't satisfy. 'I can't think of any other reason why she'd have gone in there. She couldn't have had much time to spare, with school starting at half past eight. But she was fond of this cat, you say, Martin?'

'According to Lawley. If she did hear the noise, she couldn't have known it was Nero, of course, but it seems he used to wait for her every morning . . . well, that's what Lawley said. And apparently Nero was everybody's favourite.' He paused. 'Though not for some sadistic bastard, he wasn't.'

141

'No ill-feeling between the Lawleys and anybody else in the Close—nobody likely to kill their cat to get at them?'

'It would seem not, and I'd have problems believing anyone killed it simply to lure Patti into the wood.'

'But she *was* there, Martin, they died at about the same time; she may have seen who was harming the cat.'

'And the bastard killed her for that?'

It was an unlikely scenario, Abigail had to admit. 'And in any case, if he was behind her, as he must've been for her to have got that wound on her head, he would surely assume she hadn't seen him anyway.'

'Unless she saw him and turned to run away. Scared he was going to turn on her, maybe?'

It was, at that moment, fruitless speculation. Of more immediate moment was the question of the allegations against Stanley Loates, as she pointed out. How much credence could be given to them, apart from the fact that they came from two independent sources? How much of it was simply malicious gossip and suspicion? Loates was known as a loner, an oddball, a man who kept himself to himself and apparently didn't mix with his neighbours, who didn't fit into the same pattern as those other families in the Close ... and people were always suspicious, ready to point the finger at what they didn't understand.

'Well,' Jenny Platt put in, unexpectedly, 'all I

can say is that if I had a life like his, I'd stare out of the windows a lot, too. You should see that mother of his! Can't be much else for him to do except look after her and that'd be enough to get anybody down.'

Except for the coffee machine burping behind the counter, there was a silence after this outburst. Jenny's young face was flushed, earnestly trying to put another point of view.

'Is she bedridden?' Abigail asked.

'No, she just sits in a chair by the fire—full on, even today—and makes life miserable for him. It's difficult to understand what she says but she can convey a lot with her eyes. He never goes out unless one of her old cronies comes to sit with her, would you believe, but there's no love lost between them. Mind you, he's pretty loathsome himself, but just because he's always looking out of the window doesn't mean he had anything to do with Patti . . .'

'Don't forget the kids he watches, Jenny.'

'Yeah.' Jenny looked down at the grey coffee in her beaker.

'I know we can't jump to conclusions, but you don't suggest we ignore the possibility?'

''Course not. That wasn't what I meant. I'm only trying to be fair.'

Abigail was quite aware that, despite her defence of Stanley Loates—or at least, of his rights—the last thing Jenny wanted was to go back to number seven and talk to him again. She'd no need to say how much he made her flesh creep, that she hated the foetid smell of the house, the overpoweringly heated sitting room where that ancient old woman sat silently in the chair by the fire, but Stanley Loates had to be questioned, and the sooner the better. And Jenny's—or anybody's—feelings, however, weren't paramount in this, something Jenny knew, and accepted.

It was unfortunate for DC Farrar, tall, blond and good-looking, with his propensity for saying the wrong thing at the wrong time, that he should have entered the café in time to overhear the last exchanges, and to have summed up the situation with his quick intuition.

'Just lie back and think of England, Jen,' he advised, smirking as he came back from the counter with his coffee and a pie.

Abigail gave him one of her looks. 'There won't be any need for that, Keith,' she said, making her mind up. 'Sergeant Kite will be interviewing Stanley Loates, and you'll be going with him. I want Jenny with me when I go down to see Patti's mother.'

'Right, ma'am,' said Kite, catching her eye and turning a look on Farrar that wiped the smile from his face.

CHAPTER TEN

Mayo drove himself back up to Albert Road,

after a snatched lunch and a couple of hours at his desk, during which he returned numerous phone calls and spent a brisk half hour with his part-time secretary, Delia, disposing of all but the most pressing of his commitments for the next couple of days and dealing with the reports that had landed on his desk. He noted in passing that Abigail had left him word that another prestigious car had gone missing, this time a top-of-the-range Rover, and that the file on Philip Ensor had grown no thicker.

He drove out of Milford Road and was caught, as usual, by the badly phased traffic lights at the corner of Victoria Road, swearing as he waited for them to change. Like every other frustrated motorist in Lavenstock, he didn't understand why the devil Traffic couldn't get it sorted, why you only went forward two or three cars before the lights went again to red, why there had to be these long periods when no traffic lane at all moved, as if frozen at the whim of some higher authority.

But it was this hiatus which afforded him the glimpse of Alex in the Italian restaurant on the corner. She was sitting at a table a little way from the window and facing him, though she was too immersed in conversation with the man sitting opposite her to look up and see him. Her companion had his back to the window and Mayo had no chance, before the lights changed again, to assess who it might be. He frowned a little. A client? She hadn't said she was lunching with anyone—but then, of course, there was no reason why she should have.

She'd been smiling, leaning forward in a friendly, even intimate, way. There'd been wine on the table.

*   *   *

His first call was to Simla, the house he'd previously visited in vastly different circumstances—the welcome party for Dermot Voss and his family—but he was unlucky in that only Imogen Loxley was at home. She'd told him when he'd telephoned to arrange his call that her sister Hope, as he'd expected, would still be at the Princess Mary School where she taught and wouldn't be home until around half past five. He intended to see her when he made a visit to Patti's school the following day, but he was disappointed now to find that her brother Francis was in London, lunching with his publisher, combining the day with doing some research at one of the museums—Imogen couldn't recall which—and had arranged an overnight stay in the hotel he always used on such occasions.

He was informed of all this in a prettily furnished room which overlooked the garden, a large room giving an overall impression of lightness—an astonishingly attractive room to find in that dark house, whose heavy, fusty, last-century ambience he'd found so depressing on his last visit. Here, there was a thick blue carpet, with a Chinese hearth rug in creamy pastels and deep, chintz-covered armchairs. Taupe-grey velvet curtains stirred in the breeze from the open window. Flowers were massed in bowls, and the walls painted in a shade that glowed like lighted alabaster, iced with a delicate white cornice and frieze. Imogen Loxley looked equally elegant, and expensive, decorated with the sort of gold jewellery he thought should be described as 'understated', wearing a slip of a dress, cream coloured, short and sleeveless, nothing to it—though one thing he'd learned was that the cost of women's clothes couldn't be judged by how much there was of them.

Come to think of it, Alex was spending a lot on clothes lately. He'd accidentally come across one of her bills and had to be resuscitated by a large malt. Not like Alex, to be extravagant . . .

Imogen had offered him tea but he'd declined, and they sat opposite each other on twin sofas set at right angles to a pretty marble fireplace that was crowded with silver photo frames, where she gave him the information he needed. Hope Kendrick, it seemed, had left that morning to drive to school at about twenty to eight, earlier than she normally set out, having allowed time to run her brother to the station to catch his train; he would take a taxi

147

when he returned home the following day.

'And you, Mrs Loxley?'

It had been Christian names when they'd been introduced at the party, but somehow the circumstances didn't seem to warrant their use now. She'd addressed him formally when he arrived and he'd responded likewise, feeling it was better to keep this on an official footing.

'Oh, I like to start my day in a leisurely fashion. I made my breakfast and brought it in here while I watched the breakfast news until after the headlines came on at eight. I didn't realize anything was amiss until I noticed all the cars arriving.'

'But you didn't see them from here.' Simla was a house with a long frontage, narrow from back to front, with most of the principal rooms facing the garden at the rear. From this window could be seen that giant tree they'd all been talking about at the party, and the rose beds which stretched across the garden in front of the windows. Though extensive, sloping down to the wood at the bottom, with overgrown banks of laurel and rhododendron separating it from the back gardens of Ellington Close, it wasn't a garden to write home about, apart from the roses, which were magnificent, their heady and pervasive scent mingling with that of the roses in the room. 'You can't see the road from this room.'

'No, I was in my bedroom at the front by then. I sat by the window, looking out for the

148

postman, but he was late, he didn't get here until after nine.'

It was a long time to sit watching for the postman. But as she spoke, he caught the hint of pain in her voice, perhaps over an expected letter that hadn't come, the almost inaudible indrawn breath, a small, abrupt dismissive movement to herself. The hairs actually stood up on her slim, bare brown arms, as if a goose had walked over her grave. He was reminded that Alex had told him she was separated—from Tom Loxley, wasn't it? That Euro MP who'd made his mark over European Agricultural Policy... Hadn't he had something pungent to say recently on the subject of British cheeses (as one smart-aleck journalist had it) and the European diktat as to how they should be manufactured?

'She'd delivered our paper as usual, you know, poor child.'

'You saw her bring it?'

'No, she must've left it before I went back to my bedroom. She used to deliver first to next door—Edwina Lodge—and leave her bicycle there before she came on here.'

'You'll have a good view of the entrance to the Close from your bedroom, then?'

Ellington Close was approached by a narrow road between the two older houses, walled either side, after which it broadened out into a rough crescent shape.

'Yes, there's a side window, as well as one at

149

the front, but I saw no one, other than the people who lived round about, setting off for work in their cars. I'd no idea what was happening until Doreen Bailey rang to say she wouldn't be in today and told me why. I'm so sorry I can't help you. Believe me, I would if I could—I've a daughter about the same age, away at school.'

Following the direction of her involuntary glance at the collection of photos on the mantel, he saw a girl with a thin, clever face, smiling up at the man next to her, who had his arm around her shoulder. 'Is this her?' he asked, studying it with interest. 'I can see the resemblance.'

'Yes, that's Melissa. Mel, we call her.' Her smile was that of any proud mother, but it also seemed to him slightly strained. Understandable, if her marriage was breaking up, and there was a daughter to consider ... She said nothing about the man in the photograph, whom Mayo had recognized from TV appearances as Tom Loxley.

There seemed nothing more to pursue here at the moment, until Francis Kendrick returned. He left with a general impression that despite her outwardly cool poise, she had been distinctly on edge throughout the interview, and had been relieved when it was over.

* * *

150

Sarah Wilmot hadn't been in when he telephoned but it was possible she'd returned meanwhile. It was unlikely, he thought as he crossed the road, that she'd be of much help, in view of the short time the Voss family had been in residence, and he'd have to see her brother-in-law later, but both had to be routinely questioned, and it would fit in with his busy schedule if he could see her now.

Edwina Lodge was one of those red-brick Gothic edifices whose ornate and irregular design seemed to have no relevance to its function. Having received no answer to his first ring, he circumnavigated the house but found no one at the back either. He guessed that it had been converted vertically, with the three flats in one half, but he gave up trying to work out what the interior layout might be. The back of the house overlooked the wood; it would be difficult to see very far into it through any of its lower windows because of the garden's slope, though it didn't seem impossible for anyone to have made an escape from the wood via the garden and then the front entrance. The same, of course, would apply to the garden at Simla.

Both front gardens had very little depth, probably due to the widening of Albert Road at some time, and were filled by dusty spotted laurels. Here, a heavy, ornate arch attached to the side of the house marked the entrance to a broad driveway leading to something that looked like a fairly derelict coach house at the end. The drive was paved with blue bricks and a high wall ran alongside, behind which ran the road into Ellington Close. This was the wall, presumably, against which Patti had been wont to prop her cycle.

He was standing back and trying to decipher the entwined initials below the date, 1859, on the stone cartouche in the centre of the arch when someone came up behind him.

'Were you wanting anything?' asked a suspicious female voice.

He turned to see a thin, sharp-featured young woman, laden with carrier bags, with hair that appeared to have been cut with a knife and fork, wearing a grey T-shirt stretched across her nonexistent bosom, and baggy flowered shorts.

On hearing who he was, Tina Baverstock, for so she announced herself, with a gleam in her eye and the eagerness of the inveterate gossip, promptly invited him in for a cup of tea. Such people being as gifts from the gods to policemen hard pressed for information, Mayo accepted. He was lucky she was here, she informed him, Monday being the day when her wholefood shop closed. 'A lot of people don't like it—they expect everybody to keep open all hours nowadays, but I have my customers who know when I'm open and when I'm not. Anybody wants anything, they'll take the trouble to come at the right time.'

152

Or go somewhere else, he thought, amused, as he followed her in.

The entrance to her ground-floor flat was via a side door, where a back staircase, originally built to keep the sight of servants from offending the eyes of visitors, ascended to the upper storeys. The inside of the house confirmed his assumption that the house would be a rabbit warren. Its division into flats seemed to have happened more by an unforeseen accident than through any planning on the part of an architect. The Baverstock living room, at any rate, was an uneasy compromise, wrought from what must once have been a gracious reception room, now ruined by having had a partition thrown across it to make the kitchen, cutting the deep cornice in half and regrettably bisecting a large window.

Tina Baverstock emerged from this kitchen area with tea, predictably a herbal infusion. Well, he'd drunk worse in the interests of getting at the truth. In any case, he suspected she might take offence if he didn't drain it to the dregs. She began talking at once while she was pouring the tea, greedy for excitement, the way some people always were, even in the face of tragedy; perhaps, he thought, striving for charity, through the need for drama in their lives ... there couldn't, after all, be much of that, working in a healthfood shop.

'She shouldn't have been delivering papers,

153

that Patti, it isn't safe, they shouldn't allow girls to do it—' was the first thing she found to say of the murdered girl.

'She used to leave her cycle here, I understand,' he interrupted without too much compunction, abandoning charitable thoughts, but all that did was to start her off on another tack.

'Yes, but not with *my* approval. It fell over once and scratched our new car. She was cheeky when I reprimanded her about leaving it there—but what could I do when the landlord supported her?'

It was clear that her opinion of Dermot Voss was not high, either. Rankling amongst other things was his refusal to promise them a new bathroom installation, and his disturbing them by leaving home at ungodly hours in the morning. 'Half past seven this morning—and by the look of what he was stowing in the boot, he won't be home tonight, either. Not much of a father to those children.' She sniffed, unattractively.

'Presumably that's part of his job.'

She must surely know Voss's circumstances, he thought, but she seemed to have taken against the poor devil, without a good word to say for him.

'But he was back within half an hour, in a right old state about something or other,' she said with satisfaction. 'Then another car came and picked him up about an hour later. I

154

should think his own had broken down, it doesn't seem to be very well maintained. My husband says the engine sounds as rough as— well, rough.'

She'd evidently expected things to take a turn for the better when the house ownership had changed hands and was disappointed that they hadn't, and she'd turned her spite on to Dermot Voss. Her neighbours fared no better when she moved on to them: Henry Pitt, who worked in the library and who let horrid cooking odours float down the stairs, with never a thought of opening a window. And James Fitzallan, who rented the attic as a sort of *studio*—

'He's an artist?'

Her look suggested there were artists and artists. He suspected she'd never actually seen his work or been into this studio and that it ate into her soul. The gossip continued, spilled out, venomous, unlovely.

'I saw her talking to him, you know, this morning.'

'To Mr Fitzallan?'

'No, no, Henry Pitt.'

'What time was this?'

'Quarter to eight. They seemed to be having what I can only say was a very *animated* conversation! Not the first time I'd seen them talking, either. Of course, I'm not one to gossip, but he scuttles away quicksticks every time any other woman approaches him and it's funny he happened to be on his way out so often, just at the time she was here to deliver the papers, when the library doesn't open until half past nine! Well, I mean, a young girl and an old man like that—*unhealthy,* I call it.'

'Are you saying, Mrs Baverstock,' Mayo asked coldly, 'that Mr Pitt could have had something to do with Patti Ryman being murdered?' He was aware by now of disliking her extremely.

She flushed bright red at his tone and bridled. 'How could he have? He got straight into Vic's car—my husband's—and went into town with him. Naturally, I didn't mean to imply—'

Why, he'd wondered while she was complaining, if she equally disliked her neighbours and living here so much, didn't she move, surely she and her husband earned enough between them for something better? Her last words as he left were enlightening on this point. 'Of course, things would've been different if that woman had kept to her promises—Mrs Burgoyne. She always promised she'd give us first refusal to buy this place when she left, that's the only reason we've stayed here, but she conveniently forgot that when she had a better offer.'

'Thank you for your time,' he said, and with relief went to where he'd left his car, further up Albert Road.

For a moment, there, he'd contemplated

asking her if he might look through her bedroom window, which must overlook the back garden, but had immediately decided that the unlikely chance of there being a possibility of seeing into the wood from there wasn't worth it. He wished he hadn't been such a coward, but he'd a strong feeling there was every possibility of her being the type of woman who'd immediately think the suggestion an invitation to rape.

CHAPTER ELEVEN

It was the young, uniformed constable, Kevin Marsden, he who had distinguished himself by finding the murder weapon and was now keeping an eye on the entrance to the wood, who first noticed the commotion.

He set off at a run towards the end of the Close, from where shouts and scuffles travelled on the still, early-afternoon air, putting out a call on his radio as he did so. Kite and Farrar were, as it happened, just rounding the corner on their way back to the crime scene and within seconds, close behind Marsden, they all arrived at the spot where two people were struggling on the pathway outside number seven, Ellington Close.

Mrs Loates had finally flipped. She had somehow tottered out of the house before

Stanley could stop her, and in the struggle to get her back inside, had fallen to the ground, where she now lay, mumbling and muttering and offering passive resistance. Her flowered quilted dressing gown had fallen apart to reveal a dingy flannel nightdress that had ridden up over her mottled, varicosed legs. The legs terminated in zipped felt bootee slippers. Her hair, stiff and iron grey, hung in two rat's-tail plaits down her back.

Stanley was trying to yank her to her feet, desperately begging her to come back inside the house. 'Come indoors, do, you'll do yourself a mischief!' When that failed, he tried another tack. 'Everybody's looking at you, Mother, you're making a spectacle of yourself.'

Groups of neighbours stood around, embarrassed, unwilling or unable to intervene. A mother with a baby in her arms clutched her toddler's hand. An elderly couple stood together by their gate, stunned by this further chaos and disorder which had descended on their hitherto quiet and respectable Close. Trevor Lawley came out and hovered on the sidelines for a moment or two, then went back indoors.

Stanley's normally doughy face was red. Hilda Loates had once been a big, strong woman and his belly quivered with the effort of trying to lift her. She looked at him balefully and let her weight sag slackly against him. The three policemen arrived.

Thankfully, Stanley left them to it. He relinquished his hold on his mother and stood back, breathing heavily as they manoeuvred her bodily into the house and put her in her chair.

The spectators muttered together in shocked tones and presently went back into their own houses.

Inside the house, Stanley said, 'Should we give her some brandy?'

'Don't let him near me,' the old woman said suddenly, muffled but quite clear. 'He's after me—he wants to kill me!'

'Now then, Mrs Loates,' Kite said, and to Marsden, 'Get an ambulance,' not liking the bad colour of the old woman's face.

'Right,' Marsden said, thankful to have something to do that didn't involve watching the old woman. Domestics of any kind he hated, one involving a batty old woman without her teeth in he could do without any day.

The others stood around, keeping a wary eye on her. She seemed to have shot her bolt with her accusation at Stanley, however, and sat slumped into the chair where she'd been placed, her mouth opening and shutting like a fish. Kite sent Farrar to find a blanket and he came back with an old-fashioned pink sateen eiderdown which they wrapped around her. Her eyes wandered and her colour came and went alarmingly. She sat speechlessly now, huddled into the eiderdown, chumbling her lips, seemingly unaware of the crowded room.

'What brought this on?' Kite asked her son.

'God knows.'

All at once the old woman began talking again. Kite was getting used to her and had no trouble in understanding her when she said, 'He did it, him, our Stanley! He did it, I saw him.'

'Take no notice of her,' Stanley said scornfully. 'She's daft as a brush. She doesn't know what she's saying.'

It was possible to feel sorry for him. His eyes swivelled round in his head like a hare's, the sweat stood thickly on his pale skin.

A malicious spark glinted in his mother's old, black eyes. 'Threw it over the fence, he did.'

Stanley gave a groan.

'Threw what, Mrs Loates?' Kite asked, and guessed: 'The cat?'

'Ar. Been peeing all over his lettuces, that's why. Used to fancy a nice salad, I did, but not now.'

Marsden gave a snort and was quelled by a look from Kite. But once started, there was no stopping Hilda Loates, though she wasn't making sense any more. Her face was plum-coloured. Farrar had made tea for everybody but she knocked the mug out of Stanley's hand when he attempted to get her to drink. 'Where's that ambulance, for God's sake?' Kite muttered.

'It's here.'

'Now, what's all this, Mrs Loates?' the paramedic was beginning, when she made a sort of bubbling sound. She went rigid and the dark colour drained from her face. In a flash, she was wrapped in a blanket, lifted on to a stretcher and borne away in the ambulance.

'You can come with her,' they said to Stanley but he refused, though he promised to assemble what she'd need and take it to her later, and when the ambulance had disappeared, sat down heavily on the sofa. He looked drained and exhausted, and sagged against the back cushions with evident relief. His eyes, however, were surprisingly bright and alive. At one point he put a hand over his mouth and Farrar thought, *The bugger's laughing!*

'I've said, I know nothing about all this,' he grumbled in answer to Kite, who chose to lead in with a question about the cat when it came to question time, but he knew he was cornered, with little alternative now but to tell the truth. He showed no remorse for what he'd done. The animal, it appeared, had been annoying him for years. It seemed to regard anywhere it chose to roam as its own territory and nothing Stanley could do deterred it. 'Scratching in the seed-beds and piddling all over the veg!' His indignation mounted. 'If I had a dog, I'd be had up if I let it roam all over other folks' gardens, but cats—they can let 'em go where they

161

bloody well like and nobody can do anything about it!'

'Doesn't mean to say you can go around killing 'em,' Kite stated, staring out into the small garden, dominated by tidy rows of vegetables and a small greenhouse, with espaliered plums against the side fence and a couple of ballerina apple trees dead centre.

'I tried everything else—cat-pepper, string, you name it, made not a blind bit of difference.' A painted tin cat with glass eyes, meant to intimidate genuine members of the species, leaned impotently against the fence, bearing witness to Stanley's wasted efforts. 'It used to sharpen its damned claws on my apple trees!'

'All the same.'

'Didn't mean to kill it, though,' he said suddenly. 'I was cutting string to tie the beans up, see, and there it was, bold as brass, behind me. It shot off when I shooed it away but it caught its claw in the netting. I lunged out at it and nicked it with the knife. After that—well, it was yowling fit to bust—I had to put it out of its misery.'

Kite, sickened, recalled the number of slashes in the cat's body and didn't believe a word. 'And then you threw it over the fence.'

'As far as I could.'

There was no reason to doubt this, at least. A good heave and the cat, thrown over the hedge from here, could conceivably have landed where it had been found.

'I'd like to talk to you about Patti Ryman, Mr Loates,' he said.

Stanley's eyes swivelled. His eyes lost some of their brightness. 'I've already said, I don't know anything about her. I didn't even know what she was called till today. She was only the paper girl.'

Beads of sweat stood on his pallid forehead. Unappealing at the best of times, now, stressed by what had happened with his mother and under pressure about Patti, he was probably showing up at his worst. Kite by now had an inkling of what Jenny Platt had been getting at but he wasn't going to let up out of a misplaced sympathy, simply because Stanley was inadequate, pathetic, because he'd been screwed up by his mother. The man was a toad.

'You like children, Mr Loates?'

Stanley blinked. 'Like them? I suppose so, they're all right.'

'You give them sweets, watch them when they're out playing.'

'What of it? I wouldn't do them any harm. I like them, yes, and what's wrong with that? Don't you like kids?'

Nothing wrong with liking them. Maybe something wrong with a society that had to suspect everyone who was kind to children of having an ulterior motive. But.

'Patti—' Kite said.

'I liked her as well,' Stanley interrupted defiantly. 'She was a bonny little thing, she used

163

to wave to me at one time, I don't know why she stopped. I wouldn't have harmed a hair of her head.'

There was a certain ring of truth about this, but Kite had heard protests of this nature too many times to have much faith in them. He gazed out of the window, at the garden into which Stanley had put most of his time, energies and talents. The chain-link fencing at the bottom was completely obscured by the quickthorn planted in front of it, which he kept well clipped and which had consequently by now thickened into a well-nigh impenetrable barrier. There was no way that this man, flabby and out of condition, could have got over that and into the wood, and back, not without some assistance, such as a ladder which he might have pulled over after him—had he been more athletic—still less reason for him wanting to do so.

And if he'd gone into the wood by the conventional route, Stanley Loates, slow, lumbering, ungainly, would have been hard to miss, making the return journey between the front of his house and the path.

'What'll happen to me?' he asked. 'About the cat?'

'A report will be made to the Crown Prosecution Service. What happens then is up to them, and Mr Lawley, whether he wishes to bring charges or not. And if he doesn't,' Kite added, piling it on, 'you'll be lucky if the

NSPCC doesn't.'

Whichever way things went, he couldn't see life being very happy for Stanley Loates in Ellington Close.

*   *   *

Abigail Moon leaned forward, peering through the windscreen for a possible parking space amongst all the vehicles parked nose to tail either side of the streets, while Jenny Platt drove slowly.

'How the heck do the people who live round here manage?'

'Anybody's guess.'

They were at the bottom of Albert Road, near to the house where Patti Ryman had lived. A run-down area of terraced houses, small factories, corner shops, a deserted Methodist chapel and a huge, hangar-like building painted in shouting primary colours that was a DIY store proclaiming itself open 8 a.m. to 8 p.m., with an enormous, near-empty car park. Jenny was muttering about leaving theirs in the car park and be hanged to it when a battered Cortina was driven conveniently away from the kerbside.

The area on the whole was not, in any sense of the word, attractive, and Mailer Street, when they walked round the corner and came to it, stood out like a beacon in comparison, being on the edge of what had been selected by the council as an experimental improvement area, extending from here to the Leasowes. The street itself was short, comprising decent little terraced houses built of dark brick, sloping down to the fish-and-chip shop on the corner of the main road. Now restored to its original appearance when it was first built at the turn of the century, it had a rather self-conscious charm. Encouraged by what the council had done, the residents had made their own contribution by way of window boxes and tubs. The steps of every house were swept clean, the windows polished, as if vying with each other for points on the respectability scale. Bollards, painted a handsome dark blue and gold, had been set into the cobbles, top and bottom, to prevent vehicle access, presumably in the interests of safety as well as nostalgia: the road at the bottom provided a never-ceasing flow of traffic, much of it heavy, on its way to the motorway, less than a mile off.

By the door of Linda Ryman's house, petunias and helichrysum spilled luxuriantly from a trough, and the brass knocker was highly polished.

Doreen Bailey was still with her sister. The two of them were in the living room at the front of the house—there was probably only a kitchen behind—drinking the last of what, in Abigail's experience of these sort of situations, was likely to have been an endless succession of cups of tea. Unlike her older sister, Linda

Ryman showed no signs of tears, but her eyes were huge and overbright in a face drained of all colour. She gazed unseeingly into the dead coals of a living-flame gas fire, her feet neatly together on the hearth rug, her hands clasped tightly on her lap.

'Go easy on her when you see her,' Mrs Bailey had warned. 'She's had some hard knocks.'

Yet however difficult life had been for her, it hadn't left its physical stamp. At the moment, her face was set into a mask of grief, yet it remained unlined, pretty, incredibly youthful-looking. The age gap between the two women was so large she might have been Doreen Bailey's daughter rather than her sister. They bore a faint, family resemblance to each other, but otherwise they were quite unlike. Where Doreen was a large and comfortably upholstered mother figure, Linda was a small, slim, blue-eyed blonde, as her daughter had been.

But Abigail guessed, despite the air of helplessness, that she was a fighter, one who hadn't let life get her down. She'd done wonders with the house on a limited budget. The sitting room was attractive in a do-it-yourself stripped pine, dried flowers, Laura Ashley way. Built-in shelves in the corner were painted matt green and displayed a collection of pretty white china ornaments. Some old chairs were neatly slip-covered in a blue and green patterned fabric. A school photograph on the mantelpiece showed a younger Patti, her fair hair long and silky, unpermed.

'Come on, m'duck, drink your tea,' Doreen said gently, lifting the cup and saucer from the coffee table and putting it into her hands. Linda drank as obediently as a child, evidently still in that state of shock where Abigail doubted any possibility of getting anything useful from her.

'What will happen now?' she asked dully. 'What about the funeral?'

Abigail explained that there would be an inquest, probably on Thursday, which would be adjourned for further police inquiries to be made, after which the coroner would release Patti's body, and the funeral could take place. 'The inquest will be resumed as soon as we've found out who killed Patti, and why,' she added gently. There was no need to mention to her the necessity for identifying the body, since this appalling task Mrs Bailey had already offered to relieve her of. And, mercifully, her mind seemed to have blanked off the horrors of a postmortem.

After telling her what she needed to know, Abigail stood up and Jenny followed suit. 'We'll leave you now, Mrs Ryman. I have to ask you some questions, but they'll wait until you feel able to answer them.'

'Now's as good as any time,' Linda said unexpectedly. 'I'm not going to feel any better

168

tomorrow. And it helps to talk.'

Abigail hesitated. 'If you're sure . . .' She glanced at Mrs Bailey inquiringly.

'She'll be all right, won't you, m'duck?'

Linda nodded.

'Well then—' They reseated themselves. Jenny took out her notebook.

There were the usual routine questions, designed to establish the normal course of Patti's days and to find out whether anything unusual had happened during them which could give a lead on her murder. But her life appeared to have followed its usual innocent pattern of school, homework, sports practice, with all her spare time spent with her friend, Gemma Townsend. They were bosom friends and did everything together.

'Nothing in the least unusual happened? Nothing she seemed worried about?'

'She was a bit preoccupied last week—her new school project was bothering her a bit, I think. She was doing well at school, she always worked hard—but it was the start of a new term, different teachers. If there was anything else, she'd have told me. We've always been like that with one another. I've never kept anything from her and she wouldn't keep anything from me.'

Parents often said that, and the truth was hard to bear. 'What about boyfriends?'

That roused Linda enough to earn Abigail a sudden, sharp look. 'Are you asking was she pregnant? Well, I can tell you she wasn't, not yesterday, anyway. And she didn't have any one particular boyfriend, I made her swear she'd tell me if there was anybody, I didn't want her making the same mistake as me, did I? I was only sixteen when she was born, you know, and that's a rotten start for anybody.'

'You're divorced now, I believe?'

Doreen Bailey intervened tartly; 'He pushed off when Patti was eighteen months old.'

Linda shrugged. 'Things were never right between us from the start. He was only a couple of years older than me and he wasn't ready for marriage any more than I was.'

'It must've been hard for you, left on your own.'

'I wasn't sorry. We've managed. I'd always kept my job on at Nancy's—the hairdresser up the road, worked there ever since I left school—and I've had a good family behind me.' She attempted a smile at Doreen, and Doreen put her arm round her shoulders and squeezed.

'Come on, Lindy, bear up, you've done wonderful, so far.'

'Does her father keep in touch with Patti?'

'He's dead,' Doreen Bailey informed them, pursing her lips. 'Killed just after he left them, in a motorbike accident, and good riddance.'

'Doreen.'

'All right, I'll say no more.'

'I should never've let her take that paper round!' Patti's mother said suddenly. 'I tried

170

not to be overprotective—you need freedom when you're young, but it was a mistake—I wouldn't have let her keep it on when the dark mornings came but I thought, this time of year ... and it's a nice neighbourhood. She begged me, see, wanted to feel she was pulling her weight. Girls that age want clothes and things like their friends, and she knew I couldn't afford them.'

'It's unlikely the paper round had anything to do with it,' Abigail said gently, and as the difficult, unshed tears began at last to threaten, she thought it might be tactful to leave the sisters alone for a while. 'Is it all right if we take a look at her room, Mrs Ryman?'

'Linda, please. It's just at the top of the stairs.'

No more than a boxroom, really, with the dressing table doing duty as a desk, a T-shirt draped over the mirror to avoid distraction. Bookshelves showing a fairly wide reading for her age, with copies of *King Lear* and *A View from the Bridge,* plus A level text notes, on the bedside table. The top dressing-table drawer held a brush, comb and electric hair-curler, the others nothing but underclothes, T-shirts, tops and sweaters. In the single wardrobe were a couple of summer school-uniform cotton dresses, some school shirts, two very short skirts, jeans and a leather jacket. Sandals and a pair of the ugly, clumpy shoes girls favoured at the moment stood on the floor. The walls were

171

covered with the usual pop-idol posters, pictures of animals and two RSPCA posters. There was also an RSPCA collecting box. It was the room of any teenage girl, with nothing in it to give any sort of clue as to why she'd been murdered.

When they returned to the living room, Linda's tears had dried. 'We've been talking over what you said about there being anything different, well, it's probably nothing—'

'Anything at all, it doesn't matter how unimportant it seems.'

'It's just that she came home in a taxi last Saturday from Gemma's.'

'Taxi?'

'I made it a rule she had to be in by ten unless it was something special, and she always kept to it, she knew how I worried.'

'But it wasn't usual for her to take a taxi?'

'Heavens, no! Gemma's mother always brought her back if it was late, but she's a doctor, and she was called out during the evening. She knew she was likely to be away for some time, so she told the girls to ring for a taxi when Patti was ready to go home, and gave her a ten-pound note to pay for it. She rang up a minute or two after ten—Dr Townsend, I mean—to see if she'd got home all right. She's a single parent, too, so she knows the problems. Patti came in the door just as I was putting the phone down and wanted to know who'd been ringing and—well, it ended up with a bit of an

172

argument.'

'Why was that?'

'It didn't amount to much, but she went on a bit about being checked up on, and having to be sent home in a taxi, and taking money from Gemma's mother like that—why couldn't she come home on the bus, she was old enough, you know the sort of thing.'

'It's not what happens on the bus, it's when you get off—I hope you told her that,' her sister said.

"Course I did, but girls of that age, you can't tell them anything. Though I think it might just have got home to her. She went a bit quiet after that, and then said she was sorry for giving me all that hassle. It wasn't long before she went up to bed.'

CHAPTER TWELVE

By the time Mayo had finished talking to Tina Baverstock, he felt in need of something long and cool to wash away the taste of her nasty herbal tea. And not only the tea. The Drum and Monkey was just around the corner. What was ten minutes to a thirsty man?

It was a pleasant pub with a forecourt and tables, and a shady corner, fortunately empty. He carried his half of ginger-beer shandy to the table under a sycamore, threw his jacket on to the bench beside him, took a long, cool swallow and sat back, reviewing his thoughts.

Going straight from one house to the other had given him no opportunity so far to assess the interview with Imogen Loxley, but uppermost in his mind was the notion that if she'd been truthful about sitting at her window like the Lady of Shalott, looking out for the postman—and there was no reason at this stage to think she'd any conceivable reason to lie, or conceal the truth—it seemed clear that Patti's murder had occurred after she'd delivered the paper to Simla and before Imogen arrived upstairs at, say, five past eight, no more than a fifteen-minute time span. Unless the assailant had either been lurking in the wood before she was attacked, or entered it via one of the gardens which adjoined it—and presumably escaped the same way. But how could he have known Patti would go into the wood?

He didn't in any case see how anyone planning a murder would have contemplated one such as this, with all the attendant risks. There could have been no guarantee that the perpetrator would have got away without being seen or heard. When questioned about their movements, few people could be exact about what they'd been doing at a precise time during the day, but breakfast-time was different. The human race is on the whole more habit-orientated than it cares to admit. Morning routines are established by office, school and factory starting times, and in his experience, people usually knew exactly where they were, or should have been, when the day was beginning—and which people they normally encountered. A stranger hanging around was almost certain to have been noticed. On the other hand, a moment only would have sufficed to slip along that path and disappear from sight, and the same would apply when he emerged from the wood, not much later.

But it was fruitless at this stage in a murder inquiry to start looking for any sort of pattern. Until more facts were collected, names of witnesses had been obtained, others eliminated from the inquiry, until a suspect emerged and the motive became clear. Speculating before that, there was always the danger of jumping to wrong conclusions . . .

A kamikaze wasp, intent on suicide, zoomed in on his beer mug. He moved his glass further into the shade, covering it with his hand. The wasp decided to concentrate on his ear. He flipped irritably at it and watched it land on the table, legs in the air. Gotcha! Where were we? Wrong conclusions . . . ah, yes.

It's a well-known fact that nobody can ever concentrate wholly on one subject for any length of time. According to the shrinks, at any rate. The more you try, the more the mind wanders . . .

All right, then. Who had he been, the man with Alex? Jealousy was an immature emotion, not to be considered in well-adjusted senior police officers. Anyway, it wasn't part of his make-up. He was curious, that was all. Far be it from him to be suspicious of every man Alex had dealings with. She'd worked for years in a man's world, and not without exciting admiration, and it had never been a problem for him. And it was months—well, a long time, anyway, since he'd thought of Liam, the Irishman. The bad-news man, the playboy of the western world, the hound who'd spoiled so many of the best years of Alex's life, kept her dangling with promises he'd no intention of ever fulfilling, playing up his so-called need of her, until at last, seven years on and no further forward, she'd come to her senses, seen things as they really were: the wife in the background, still the semi-invalid she'd always been, and Liam, no nearer asking for a divorce than he'd ever intended.

It was several years now since she'd gathered her courage, moved away and given him the push.

He'd gone, gone forever, hadn't he? Hadn't he?

Of course he had. But Alex had never blamed him entirely, always made excuses, always saw the other side of the equation. Could it explain that brittle, nervous excitement about her recently that he couldn't understand and didn't want to ask about, not even tentatively or obliquely? And she'd been smiling and lifting her glass to the man opposite her in the restaurant . . .

What the hell.

He took a long, reflective pull of his shandy.

And became aware of increasing activity outside the church on the opposite side of the road, of the number of cars parking there. He watched more arrive, driven mostly by women, but with one or two men among their number. As they walked up the path to the church door, and he decided from their casual clothes and their demeanour that it was unlikely to be either a wedding or a funeral they were attending, a red Renault drew up. Sarah Wilmot got out, locked the door and also made for the church.

Mayo finished his drink, strolled across the road and followed the rest of them up the yew-bordered path through the old churchyard, shaded by ancient oaks, renowned in spring for its great sheets of daffodils, its tombstones now laid flat and the graves grassed over for easy maintenance, their occupants far too long dead to care.

Sarah was sitting motionless in one of the back pews, while the people he'd seen entering moved purposefully about the church. A regular hive of activity, it was. Someone was practising on the organ. 'Jesu, joy of man's desiring'. Trite, but gentle and oddly appropriate, and played well. There was to be an organ recital next month—he'd spotted a notice stuck up in the porch as he came through. He made a mental note that it might be worth attending.

Sliding into the pew beside Sarah, he was struck by her unexpected sombreness. She looked as wholesome and healthy as when he'd met her at the party, her face, as well as her smooth bare limbs, tanned pale gold, and her short, toffee-coloured hair streaked with the sun. She smelled of bluebells and fern. She glanced up when she saw him and smiled, and immediately the impression of some dark shadow hanging over her was gone.

'Did you want to see me? I thought someone from the police would be coming round, but to tell the truth I'd forgotten you were a policeman. I suppose you have to ask me questions.'

He hesitated. 'I don't want to disturb you if—'

'That's all right, I just came in for a few minutes' quiet. It isn't often churches are open on weekdays, these days. Go ahead—unless you'd rather we went across to the house?'

He shook his head. 'This'll do. I haven't much to ask you ... you don't know the neighbourhood yet, won't know which comings and goings are normal, which are out of the ordinary, who's a stranger and who isn't. For the moment, we're just checking on when people left home this morning.'

Routine comment. True, of course, but also,

even at this stage, a matter of being alert to catch nuances, things let slip, of patiently picking up discrepancies or seemingly irrelevant pieces which might eventually fit together.

'Oh, that's easy,' Sarah said. 'Dermot left at half past sevenish, or maybe a bit later. I suppose by the time he'd walked back home it must have been after eight. I wasn't there, I'd left with the children for school at five past eight.'

'Walked back?'

'Didn't you know? He had his car pinched this morning.'

'I wouldn't necessarily be told about it. Not my department.'

'Oh. No, of course, it wouldn't be. He parked it outside Patel's while he went in to get some cigarettes. There was quite a queue and when he came out it was gone. He had to come back home to report the theft and make arrangements for another car and so forth. He's not due home tonight and of course, his overnight bag was taken as well—plus his personal camera. His company's lent him another car but it's really messed up the day for everyone. He was livid.'

Tina Baverstock, though she'd been wrong in her assumptions about the car breaking down, would testify to this fury. She'd heard the door bang. Mayo mentally slotted these times in with the others. Picaddilly Circus in the rush hour wasn't in it, all of them milling around at the same time, and still no one seeing hide nor hair of the murderer.

The church was High, with lace on the altar cloths, candles and a sanctuary lamp burning, a faint smell of incense mingling with the flowers. A young priest in a black cassock moved quietly among the groups. A faint murmur of conversation made a background susurration.

'What are all these people doing?' he asked, curiosity finally overcoming him as a woman with a large tote bag and a camera slung over her shoulder passed them and took up a determined stance in front of a marble monument on the wall, produced a notebook and started making notes. 'Who are they?'

'Oh, church recorders,' she answered, smiling at his mystified expression. Here, she explained, to make a detailed inventory, to record minutely every part of the church and its furnishings, whether it be silver, woodwork, memorials, books, or anything else . . . 'In case of damage, or loss—or theft, which I don't suppose I need to remind you about. My mother's in a similar group, that's how I know about it.'

St Gregory's was a fourteenth-century church which had been enlarged and overrestored by the Victorians. Pevsner hadn't found much to remark on in Lavenstock, other than the public-school buildings, the Tudor almshouses and various ancient inns and dwellings in the mediaeval streets leading from the Cornmarket down to the river. St Gregory's, if Mayo remembered correctly, had received scant mention, apart from the fine organ and some stained-glass windows by Kempe. What a pity. As with the town, there were more subtle attractions than the patently obvious.

'Did you see Patti at all this morning?'

Her face clouded. 'Not this morning, no. I didn't see anyone; I left Dermot to it, got the children into the car and drove off.'

The music changed. More Bach. 'Lovely,' she said.

'Do you like music?'

'Oh yes—but that's not why I'm here.' She gave him a quick, sideways glance. 'I—I actually slipped in to say a quick prayer for her, for Patti, and her mother, but—I'm not sure part of it wasn't for myself. My own sister, dying so recently . . . it brings it back. How little we *know* anyone, really.'

Now why had she added that last remark? What did she mean by it? Her head was bent and the wing of butterscotch hair partly obscured her face. She looked up with an unreadable expression and gave a little embarrassed half-laugh.

'When are you expecting to return home?' he asked.

'I don't know, but I can't stay here much longer. I've a job—and a flat I must get back to—but there's millions of things to do here, yet—' She looked at her watch. 'Today, I've to find a *chimney-sweep,* would you believe, before Dermot can have gas fires fitted ... buy new curtains ... pick the children up.' She laughed. 'I'll be glad to get back to work! No reason why I shouldn't, now. I've actually found a housekeeper. Mrs Bailey's agreed to come in when I've gone, to see to the cleaning and cooking and look after the children when Dermot's not there. She's very good with them and they adore her. She's delighted with the idea, it means she can give up her job at the supermarket. But now this has happened she may not want to start for a while ... Patti meant an awful lot to her.'

'Mrs Bailey doesn't seem to be the type to let it knock her off her peg for long.'

'I expect you're right. Imogen Loxley did offer to see to the children pro tem, she and her brother and sister seem to have taken a shine to them, Francis is trying to teach them to play Mah Jong but—I don't know ...'

Francis, he thought, jolted. Francis Kendrick? That dry, intellectual stick. Well, well. Then he remembered the Victorian music box and the tall man holding the hand of the little girl as they crossed the lawn.

'Tell me about the other people at Edwina Lodge. I've already met Mrs Baverstock.'

She met his glance and grimaced. 'Her husband, Vic, he's OK. He's nice to the children, makes them laugh. I've scarcely spoken to Mr Pitt. He seems a sweet old soul but I suspect he's shy of women. He ducks his head and scoots whenever we meet.'

'What about the mysterious man who has the attic floor—Mr Fitzallan?'

'Fitz? Oh, there's nothing mysterious about him,' she said casually. 'He's a spare-time artist and he rents the attics as a studio, that's all. He runs a successful design consultancy in real life.'

'Fitzallan Associates?'

'Yes, I think that's the name—d'you know it?'

'I've heard of it.'

A faint smile played round her lips. 'He's painting a portrait of Allie. Oh Lord, that reminds me!' She looked again at her watch. 'If there's nothing more—I have to go and find a pet shop before the children come home. Disaster struck this morning. Goodness knows how it happened, but after they'd gone to school I found their hamster lying dead in its cage. I'll have to get another, otherwise they'll be heartbroken. Will they know the difference, d'you think?'

'Wouldn't bank on it,' Mayo answered, remembering a similar experience in Julie's childhood. However, he told her where the nearest pet shop was, gave her a few minutes and then followed her out into the bright sunlight, pausing to make a note of the organ recital. The organist was not to be the woman he'd just heard playing, but Francis Kendrick. A man of many parts, Kendrick. And high time he made contact with him.

As he walked back between the yews he thought of the other name that had been mentioned—James Fitzallan. He remembered the case, and nearly all the details. The wife who'd died in suspicious circumstances. And that other woman, and her child.

*   *   *

Abigail Moon came into his office as soon as he got back to the station, with a report on the Stanley Loates incident. 'He's a creep,' she said forthrightly. 'Anyone who could do that to a dumb animal could do anything.'

'And that, of course, makes it certain he killed Patti, as well as the cat.'

'Oh Lord, of course not! But—I don't know—he could have, I suppose—not intending to kill, but a mindless reaction because she saw what he'd done—? All right, I know—I'm letting my prejudices show.' She ran a hand through her hair. 'More to the point, there's someone come in with some information. He's in with Martin Kite at the moment—his name's Pitt, Henry Pitt.'

*   *   *

'I feel I ought to tell you,' Henry Pitt had begun, nervously looking around the interview room as though expecting to see jack-booted inquisitors behind him and thumbscrews on the wall, rather than a tattered copy of PACE and Martin Kite sitting opposite. He coughed, blinked like a nervous rabbit, smoothed back his hair. His hands, Kite noticed, were smooth and white, the backs covered with freckles and pale gold hairs.

'Yes, Mr Pitt? What is it you have to tell us? I take it it's about Patti Ryman?'

'Patti, oh dear, yes. Someone at the library heard about it on the local radio.' For a moment Henry looked as though he were about to burst into tears. His soft lower lip trembled, tears did actually come to his eyes, but he took out a large handkerchief, blew loudly into it and then said, 'I'm sorry, it was such a shock . . .'

He'd taken time off from his work at the library, come in of his own accord and asked to see the detective superintendent in charge of the case, at what cost to himself Kite could only guess. In Mayo's absence, he'd been offered Sergeant Kite as a substitute, plus a sympathetic presence in the shape of WPC Platt, and a cup of tea, which he hadn't touched. None of it seemed to have had any effect. 'It's all so difficult—'

'Well, let's begin with the last time you saw Patti,' Kite said, patiently.

'Yes. Yes, of course. It was this morning, when she was delivering my paper. We often used to have a little chat. I was very fond of her.' His lips began to tremble again but as he met Kite's gaze, kindly but sharp, his hesitant manner suddenly left him. He may have given the initial impression of being a doddery old fool, but he was an intelligent man, must be well aware of how this conversation might be interpreted, and Kite had no doubt it had taken some courage to square up to what he had to say.

'Take your time, Mr Pitt.'

'Thank you.' He breathed deeply, and then began to speak slowly, anxious to get things in the right order. 'I first met her when I was taking a collecting box round the Close for the RSPCA. She was at her aunt's house—Mrs Bailey, you know—and she started chatting. I could see she was as passionate about cruelty to animals as I am, and she wanted to know if she could become a collector as well, but of course she wasn't old enough. I gave her a collecting box for her own use, and she used to put a small amount in every week, and something out of her birthday and Christmas money, that sort of thing. Well, that's how it began—I came to look forward to seeing her smiling face every morning. Occasionally we had a few minutes' conversation, but usually it was just to pass the time of day and so on, nothing more, you understand.'

'Yes, I understand.' Kite had heard similar protestations hundreds of times. This time, there was more than a ring of truth in what the old buffer had been saying so far. Kite, who wasn't easily fooled by anyone, thought him almost painfully honest and well-intentioned. 'And this morning?'

Pitt licked his lips. 'This morning was different . . . she said she had a problem. That was how she put it, a problem, and could she talk it over with me. I asked her why me—was it something to do with her schoolwork? You see, sometimes I'd help her to find books she needed for her school projects and so on, but she said no, it wasn't that, it was only that she couldn't think of anyone else who'd understand. That made me think it was something the RSPCA should know about, and I told her she should report it, but apparently what was bothering her was something quite different. "I think it's what you'd call a moral dilemma, Mr Pitt," she said. "Like when you think you know something bad about a person, but you're not quite sure."'

'Was it anything that had a bearing on what's happened to her?'

'I don't know. She said she'd no time to talk about it then. I suggested she came to the library after school and I'd take my tea-break in the library cafeteria with her, and we'd discuss it then. But of course . . . when I heard the news . . . dear God, what are we coming to?'

'All this happened before she went to deliver her papers in the Close?' Kite asked, shuffling papers to give Henry time to get over his distress.

'Oh yes, she always came to Edwina Lodge first—and then Simla—before she went on there.'

'If it wasn't anything to do with the RSPCA that was bothering her, why do you think she came to you, in particular?'

'I really can't think,' Henry said humbly.

CHAPTER THIRTEEN

Police cars were still parked at the entrance to the Close when Sarah arrived back at Edwina Lodge after picking the girls up from school, but luckily the children either didn't notice them or saw nothing untoward in them being there. It wasn't going to be possible to keep them in ignorance of the terrible events which had happened in the wood for long, however. News of that sort couldn't be kept secret. They'd met and talked to Patti, been promised a go on her grown-up bicycle. But how did you tell young children something like that without frightening them half to death? Especially now, just when they were beginning to come to terms with the loss of their mother.

Later that evening, when they were in bed, Sarah sat back, nursing a whisky, richly deserved, she felt, after a day of enforced domesticity—how did mothers stand it, day in, day out?—coupled with the terrible news about Patti Ryman, and ending with a protracted scene with Lucy over the hamster.

'This isn't Goldie!' Lucy had declared, immediately she opened the cage to give the animal its food. 'It's somebody else! What's happened to her?'

'What makes you think it's not her?' Sarah had prevaricated, furiously cutting Marmite sandwiches, pouring juice, knowing she was being cowardly.

'I just do! It's not Goldie! What have you done with her?'

Sarah knelt down by the cage and tried to tell both children as gently as she could what had happened, wondering if she could use the hamster's demise to introduce the subject of Patti, but to her horror both children had burst into noisy sobs and whatever she said couldn't pacify them, especially Lucy, who could create a scene better than anyone when the occasion demanded it.

It was at this point, when she was kneeling on the floor with her arms around both children (at least around Lucy—Allie was pulling away, as usual, stiffening whenever she was touched) that blessed intervention came in the person of Imogen, there to deliver a parcel for the children, from Hope. The tears gradually subsided. When opened, the parcel was found to contain a pair of dolls, one for each child. Hope, it appeared, had been embarrassed about giving the presents herself, as well might she be, considering the one intended for Allie, Sarah thought, considerably taken aback by it.

'I know, I know!' Imogen said, holding up a hand, forestalling comment. 'I did try to dissuade her, but you know what Hope's like. They've no sentimental value for her—she was never one for dolls.'

It was obvious to Sarah that she *didn't* know what Hope was like. She was stunned by her generosity, but at the same time, appalled. Mainly at the total unsuitability of Allie's present, which was not a plaything but an expensive antique in near-mint condition, a genuine, simpering Victorian doll with a rosebud mouth, wearing plum-coloured, lace-trimmed silk, and kid boots. But the sight of Allie's enraptured face, besotted with love at first sight, like a mother with her first-born baby, effectively scotched any possibility that somehow, tactfully, the doll could be returned.

The one designated for Lucy wasn't nearly such a thoroughbred, but that didn't matter. Lucy hardly ever played with dolls. She thanked Imogen politely for the jointed wooden Dutch doll, dressed in national costume, and was playing with it for the moment, introducing the now apparently accepted hamster to it, with the hamster receiving most of the attention. It wouldn't be long before she put the doll on one side in favour of her new computer game.

Allie was sitting on the floor with her doll cradled tightly in her arms, covering it with wet, messy kisses, boding ill for the pristine, the pink and white face. 'Now come along, Angel,' she announced, prim as a Victorian nursemaid, 'I'll read you a story I've written and draw you a picture, but then you'll have to go straight to bed.'

Sarah exchanged looks with Imogen. *Angel?* Maybe Hope, even if unwittingly, had done more than she realized.

*   *   *

Now, Angel having been tucked up in bed beside Allie, and Lucy's doll, as yet nameless, lying on the floor in the corner of the bedroom with its limbs at all angles, Sarah abandoned the whisky, which she didn't really care for and, disappointingly, always looked better than it tasted, and escaped from Dermot, if you could he said to escape from someone who barely seemed to know you were there. He was ostensibly immersed in a fat file concerned with the legal intricacies of being a landlord, but he

191

didn't look as though his heart was in it. Something of greater moment was absorbing his thoughts.

Out in the garden, the new swing hung loose on its ropes from the old pear-tree branch. Sarah perched on it, absently propelling it back and forth, one toe barely touching the ground. In the dusk, the Welsh poppies which had seeded themselves between the cracks of the old blue bricks of the path glowed like small harvest moons, orange and gold. The deep honey scent of dame's violet hung on the air. On the other side of the great beech hedge was the wood, silent now, where the sound of men's voices had rung for most of the day.

Although Sarah hadn't known Patti, had barely spoken to her, the poor girl's murder seemed to add another dimension to the shock of her own discovery of the previous day.

She'd been putting off thinking about *that* for too long—ever since yesterday, in fact, when she'd knelt on the floor of her bedroom with the old tin trunk beside her, but no amount of procrastination was going to make it go away.

The trunk had held the last of Lisa's personal possessions to be disposed of. The rest—the pretty shoes and slender suits she'd been so looking forward to wearing again after the baby was born—Dermot had donated to charity shops immediately after the funeral. It wasn't until yesterday that he'd asked Sarah if she'd mind going through the trunk. He simply couldn't face it himself, he said, and she'd steeled herself to do the task straight away, in order to get it over with, though suspecting it might awaken memories grown neither less painful nor less vivid.

Lisa, surprisingly for one so much of the moment, had kept more memorabilia from her childhood and adolescence than Sarah had. Perhaps she'd just never got around to throwing them out. Sarah began to sift through the oddly assorted layers—toothily smiling Donny Osmond posters, the ivory-backed prayer book her godmother had given her when she was confirmed, a pair of ballet shoes, a riding crop and hat, old school photographs—one of them with Sarah, taken when they were gap-toothed six- and seven-year-olds. She shook out an acid-yellow minidress Lisa had begged and schemed and cried for—just why, wasn't now clear, and put it on the 'discard' pile, before turning to Lisa's jewellery box.

'I've kept her engagement ring myself,' Dermot had said, 'and if there's anything you think the girls might like when they're older, put them on one side. Anything else, you're welcome to have for yourself, or to get rid of, just as you think best. There's one or two things of value, but you know she mostly preferred costume jewellery, though none of *that* was cheap, as I remember!' he added, with a wry lift of the eyebrow.

Sarah didn't imagine there would be much to her own taste. Lisa had, surprisingly, loved the sort of dramatic costume jewellery that made an impact, as if feeling her personality lacked some definition. Whereas, small and sparkling, full of life, she hadn't needed jewellery at all.

Sarah set aside a couple of gold chains for herself, then a heavily laden silver charm bracelet that she was sure would delight Lucy, and for Allie the single strand of cultured pearls, identical to the one Sarah herself possessed, chosen as eighteenth birthday gifts by their father. She gathered up the rest and put them back carefully in the velvet-lined trays to return them to the box. The girls might like them when they were older. It was a large box, covered in ivory leather and lined with red velvet, whose loose, padded bottom had collected a little fluff and dust. Lifting it to give it a brush, she saw a manila envelope underneath. Inside was a photograph. Taken somewhere foreign-looking, hot. Italy? Greece? A blinding light, deep shadows, a café table under a tree. A man with a thin face, smiling into the sun.

On the back was written: *Darling Lisa, as requested. Until I can be there again in person. Ever and always, my dearest, yours.* It was unsigned, but dated New Year's Day of the previous year.

The face smiling from the photograph wasn't Dermot's.

*   *   *

Sarah found it hard to accept that Lisa, open and honest as the day, could have risked everything—her marriage, her children's happiness—by carrying on a secretive, underhand affair. That it was an affair, Sarah had no doubt. There'd been no dubiety about the message. Unmistakable. Darling Lisa. A few lines on the back of a photograph, and Lisa's memory was diminished, tarnished. Lisa, the last person to have done such a thing. Well, she hadn't been canonized, no one had ever said she was better or worse than the next woman. But—Lisa!

Perhaps she'd really been in love with him, this 'yours'. Sarah paused. Would *I* do *that* for Simon? Better not think about that.

Ever and always, yours. Darling Lisa. Who was he, and did it matter now, anyway? Yet Sarah had a sudden sense that it did, a feeling of impending disaster. The hairs on her skin stood on end. Nonsense.

She slid off the swing and walked to the grainy, splintery wooden seat set under the wall which supported a great swathe of honeysuckle, facing the view over Lavenstock. In the dusk, lights twinkled palely below; in the distance, the hills, blue in the daylight were

195

now dark against a sky the colour of a 'Peace' rose. Night insects danced, moths fluttered dustily in the grass.

Behind the puzzle of why Lisa, of all people, had had this secret, was a plunge of unexplained fear.

A footfall on the path. Fitzallan, looming tall beside her. A hand on her shoulder, his deep voice: 'Something wrong? You're shivering like a leaf.'

'Oh! Oh, Fitz, it's you.' She came back from a long way, feeling that she had to make an immense effort. 'It's nothing, a ghost walking over my grave.'

'I'm sorry. I'm intruding.' But he didn't go away. Instead, he pulled his Aran sweater from his shoulders and draped it around hers, and sat on the seat beside her, where a warmth that had nothing to do with the sweater presently enveloped her. She'd hoped he would come and join her. Since showing her his paintings in the attic, it was becoming almost a nightly ritual to sit here on the seat before he went home to his house, fifteen miles away. They never talked much. He had a great capacity for silence, this man. Quite often, she'd wondered about that house of his, his lonely life since his wife had died.

'Want to tell me what's wrong?' he asked.

That face, the one in the photograph. Undistinguished, a stranger's face, yet half recognized. No one she'd ever met, she was sure

196

of that, there was no voice that went with the face. A man glimpsed in the street, across a shop counter? A restaurant? Some politician or other in the paper? Not recently, or she'd have remembered—surely . . .?

Fitz would know what to do if she told him. He was that sort of man—partly due, she felt, to having gone through his own personal hell while his wife had been alive, about which she now knew a little—but mostly because that's how he'd been born. Knowing what to do, and unswerving, once he set his mind to it.

'I *can't*,' she said, hoping this didn't sound as feeble as she felt it did, but she was unused to bottling things up. 'I would, believe me, but I just can't.'

'Well, if you start to feel differently—I'm here.'

He smiled at her, his brilliant eyes lighting up. He wouldn't press her, she knew, but yes, if anything could have made her feel better at this moment, it was to know that Fitz was there.

'The police came to see me today,' he said suddenly.

'They're talking to everyone.'

She waited but he didn't say anything more.

She had a feeling that he was trying to bring himself to tell her something, but she knew him well enough by now to know that he'd only do it in his own time.

* * *

Down at the police station in Lavenstock, those who could were going home. It had been a long, long day.

Abigail Moon drove home to her cottage under the hill, thought about a glass of wine, thought about having to open a bottle when she only wanted a glass and decided against it. Thought about ringing Ben, then looked at the clock and decided against that, too. Made herself a tuna fish sandwich, went to bed, thoroughly restless, knowing she wouldn't sleep, and went out like a light immediately her head touched the pillow.

*   *   *

Detective Constable Keith Farrar slipped his key into the lock of his front door, let himself in quietly, wiped his feet on the mat and without putting on the light—so as not to disturb Sandra—tiptoed into the spotless, state-of-the-art kitchen, where a corner of the table was set out for one. A meal of unimaginable dreariness awaited him in the fridge. Cutting into the cold lamb and beetroot, he saw the letter on the table, propped against the glass dome that covered a plate of bread spread with healthily polyunsaturated margarine. His heart sank. Another hospital consultation for Sandra. Almost certainly another disappointment. He felt deeply sorry for her, but even sorrier for himself, wistfully imagining a life with a wife who had a baby to occupy her, rather than needing to fill in her time by keeping the house as sterile as an intensive care unit, and nagging him about promotion.

*   *   *

Martin Kite arrived at his warm, untidy home, as different from the house where he'd interviewed Trevor Lawley that morning as chalk from cheese, just as his wife was going to bed. She saw how tired he was but he surprised her by putting his arms fiercely around her and holding her head against his shoulder, and even more by not uttering a single complaint about Daniel and Davy not yet being in bed and having the television on loud enough to keep half of Lavenstock awake.

*   *   *

Gil Mayo was in that state of wakefulness which even a steady walk home through the dark, sleeping streets of his manor had failed to lull. He was happy on two counts when he walked through the door of his upstairs flat: to find Alex not yet in bed and that he'd missed her sister Lois by about ten minutes.

'Shut up, Bert!' he said by way of greeting to the parrot, who was resenting the close attention being paid to Alex and was responding in his inimitable way. When he could make himself heard, Mayo asked carefully after Lois and Alex responded just as carefully. Relations between himself and the spiky Lois, he sometimes felt, were rather like that of his cat and his parrot. Correction. His *landlady's* villainous-looking grey cat, and his daughter Julie's parrot, wished on him when she'd decided to leave for foreign parts. Pesky old Moses, who also answered to the name of Go Away, sometimes now managed to insinuate himself into the flat because Alex couldn't bring herself to boot him out, and with the bars of the parrot cage between them, the two nonhumans regarded each other warily, like Tweetie-pie and Sylvester, like himself and Lois.

He poured himself a dram of The Macallan while Alex went to prepare him something to eat, sank on to his favourite sofa and put his feet up on the new upholstery, letting a warm feeling of home envelop him. Clean, tidy, stylishly decorated, smelling faintly of polish. He'd once questioned the wisdom of living with someone who was so congenitally tidy-minded as Alex, even fearing it might break up a beautiful relationship, but in fact he'd come to see certain advantages. He now made no objections to having his books alphabetically arranged, or his CDs neatly shelved, and even responded positively to having his socks paired and tucked together, rather than having to search for a mate.

He sipped his Scotch and began to rehearse variations of the same question: 'So who was that you were having lunch with?'—'Who was that man I saw you with in the Italian restaurant?'—'Why didn't you tell me you were meeting a man for lunch?' Worse and worse.

A loud clattering was issuing from the kitchen, the volume of which was unfortunately not guaranteed to be commensurate with the quality of what was produced. Farrar's wife, Sandra, wasn't the only one who wasn't interested in cooking, though Alex was learning, having begun to get a grasp of the situation when she'd cottoned on to the number of times Mayo mentioned his mother's treacle sponge, or one of Julie's more exotic dishes. Plain, unimaginative food, mostly salad, was the order of the day when it was her turn to cook. Perhaps Julie would come home one day and teach her properly.

'I forgot—letter from Australia on the mantelpiece,' she said, popping her head round the kitchen door, tuning into that telepathy between them which was still a source of wonder to him.

Slitting the envelope open, he skimmed it quickly for what he always hoped to read—but his daughter wasn't coming home, not yet, nor likely to be, he saw as he came to the last paragraph. Since giving up her place at catering college, eschewing meat and opting for a life in faraway places, she'd found an exciting life in Australia and was now planning to start up a restaurant with a friend.

He went to tell Alex what the letter had said. 'Vegetarian restaurant in Sydney—wonder what the Ozzies'll make of that?' he grinned, hovering hungrily in the kitchen door. 'Good smell.'

She waved a fork at him. 'Go away. You know I can't do anything properly when anyone's standing over me. I'm not your Julie and this needs concentration. I'm doing you a steak, with a pepper sauce I got from a recipe in the paper. Don't mind if I don't join you? I'm not hungry.'

Whisky glass in hand, he leaned against the doorjamb, seeing himself reflected in the dark window, relaxed in his shirt sleeves, the whiteness of the fabric making his dark face look all the darker, the slatey eyes under the thick brows watching her steadily, his dark hair crisped with grey. He said the last thing he meant or ought to have said, albeit with a smile: 'You won't, not after eating with Lois and stuffing yourself with pasta at lunch-time.'

She barely missed a beat. Smiling in return, she said, 'How did you guess I had lunch at Gino's?'

'I saw you when I was stopped at the traffic lights.'

There was a short silence, accompanied by a horrid smell of burning. 'The sauce! Hell's teeth!'

Alex grabbed the pan and rushed it to the sink, where she turned the tap on and spent some time getting rid of the ruined sauce before turning round and leaning with her back against the sink unit. 'So much for that. Plain grilled steak, I'm afraid.'

'You'd better turn it over, then, otherwise that's going to be charcoal as well.' He liked his steak rare.

He realized, when he was finally sitting down to what he considered to be a near-cremated steak, that his ill-judged remarks were going to be passed off, as though nothing had been said, but when she'd brought cheese for him, a small slice of hazelnut chocolate cake to satisfy her own sweet tooth and late-night, decaffeinated coffee for both, she sat down opposite and said seriously, 'Something quite exciting's appeared on the horizon, Gil. I do want to talk to you about it sometime, I'd appreciate your advice, but it's not the right time now, not while you've got your plate full with this case.'

Had she really been going to tell him, or had he forced it into the open with his snide remarks, for which he was truly sorry? And had the rug pulled from under his feet? Wasn't that just like a woman—whet your appetite and then refuse to satisfy—

'Sure you won't have a piece of this cake? It's from Dowley's.'

'No, thanks, and I thought you weren't

hungry.'

'It's longer than I thought since supper-time. And that pasta I was stuffing myself with at lunch was an omelette.'

'Don't forget the wine.'

'You saw a lot in a few seconds at the traffic lights. What can I do to convince you that—'

'Try me and see,' he said, pulling her to her feet.

PART THREE

Hope Kendrick is sitting in her empty classroom, waiting to be summoned to talk to the police in the headmistress's study. The weight of Patti Ryman's death feels heavy on her shoulders. It brings back painfully, in a roundabout way, memories she's striven for years to forget.

She'd dreamt of him last night, as she regularly does, as she has for more than twenty-five years, though his face is becoming less clear with every year that passes. Sometimes, she can't remember his face at all, and that really frightens her.

Well, he'd been tall, had to be, of course. Taller than she is, but even so, not the same height as Francis. A big, blond man with light, Scandinavian blue eyes, broad shouldered and athletic-looking. Not the usual picture of an academic, but Sven had never been what was expected. A brilliant mathematician, he was first her tutor at Cambridge, then her lover. Her face twists. She's aware that everyone considers her a dried-up old prune, who has never known love, much less sex . . . even Francis, perhaps especially Francis, never suspected, though neither of them, Sven or herself, had ever deliberately sought to keep it a secret.

She'd introduced him to Francis with caution. Her brother received him with his usual suspicious reserve, but as it became apparent that Sven was going to be part of the continuing scenery, when it was obvious that he was intellectually at least Francis's equal, his wariness gradually gave way to respect, liking, and finally, acceptance. She had, ironically, been delighted.

After that, it was Francis with them everywhere they went: she, Francis and Sven, their friend. Cycling out for tea at one of the villages, picnicking in the river meadows, the Cambridge college, gardens, punting on the Cam, tennis, music at King's . . . a summer of roses and wine. And love, unsuspected by head-in-the-clouds Francis, as she'd never hoped or expected to find it. Sven, making her come alive, filling her with passion. Sven, watching her, smiling when their eyes met, Sven watching her watching Francis . . .

And then, the summer was over and the days were lengthening. Something was wrong. Sven growing very cool towards Francis. Then Francis catching flu, really bad flu, so that she had to cancel the week with Sven in Prague, where he'd been invited to lecture. After which Sven had bowed out, saying, 'I can't compete, and I won't play second fiddle.'

She'd managed to reply, though she was choking, scarcely able to breathe. 'He couldn't help catching flu.'

'No, but there was no need for you to stay behind with him. He wasn't that bad.'

This time she couldn't answer.

'I don't know why I'm surprised. It's only what I should have expected. He always comes first, doesn't he? Doesn't he?' His gaze had held hers. 'He always has and always will.'

Scalded, she'd refused to think about the

subtext there. It was over without argument, without the opportunity to speak in her own defence, though she would have offered none. And she'd been too proud to tell him she was pregnant. No one had ever known that, not even Francis. Well, by then, Francis had had troubles enough of his own.

She sits now in the quiet room, seeing what she has become, a gaunt, desiccated, angular spinster, nearing fifty. Motionless, the sun focusing on her clasped, ringless hands like a burning glass, allowing herself for once to think of the child—the children—wonderful bright children, like Patti Ryman and the little Voss girls—that she might have had, not resolutely shutting them out of her life and thoughts as she normally does.

The head comes in to say the police are ready to see her. A woman fifteen years younger than Hope, smartly dressed, made-up, a woman whose style the girls secretly admire, in contrast to Hope, whom they pity. She has children of her own, a husband who is a captain of industry. She runs her school, her home and her family with equal efficiency. She is successful, dazzling. What a terrible thing this is, Miss Kendrick, we mustn't let it get out of hand, though. Keep the girls busy, life must go on.

Hope gets to her feet, her shoulders sagging. She feels drained, but she must talk sensibly to the police. She follows the head to her study. Life must go on.

CHAPTER FOURTEEN

Patti had been a model pupil, according to her headmistress, conscientious and hard-working, homework always handed in on time, consistently high marks in class and in exams, popular with staff and pupils.

Her form tutor, Miss Kendrick, neither as young nor enthusiastic (and nowhere near as ambitious of her school's position in the league tables) as the head, gave a modified version of this when she was left alone with the two police officers in the latter's room. 'Patti hadn't been with me for long—I'd had her as form pupil only from the beginning of this year, but I taught her maths for the last two. She was conscientious, though she did not, in my opinion, have a first-class brain ... I wouldn't have encouraged her to have too high expectations, it would have been unrealistic. She *might* have gone far—but only by overstretching herself.'

There was implied criticism of the headmistress here, and when Hope Kendrick spoke of high expectations, she was probably meaning Oxford or Cambridge, but Mayo looked at her with more interest, seeing in her an authority he hadn't expected, and finding himself in agreement with what she'd said. He'd never seen the point of pushing children beyond their limits, either, a counterproductive act if ever there was one.

'Well, we're not here to assess her academic prowess,' he said. 'We just want to get a general impression of what she was like, to find out if anything might have been worrying her, if anything happened lately that could possibly have led to her death.'

'Teachers, I assure you, are the last to be told if anything's worrying children! I can only say that she didn't appear to be worried. I always found her a cooperative girl, lively in class, not half asleep as some of them are from staying up too late watching television—not even from getting up early to deliver those papers. I saw her collecting them from Patel's yesterday as we passed.' She softened the implicit disapproval by adding in a low voice, 'Poor child,' yet flushed as she did so, almost as if embarrassed to show compassion.

'What time would that be?'

Quickly recovering herself, she gave the time as twenty to eight, or thereabouts, which agreed with the time her sister Imogen had given. She was absent-mindedly fiddling with the cap of a biro she'd picked up from the orderly array set out in a tray on the large clutter-free desk, and staring at Mayo in a slightly puzzled way; when she saw he'd noticed, she looked away, confused. 'I left earlier than usual, though I had a couple of free periods first thing. I was driving my brother to

Birmingham New Street to catch the eight fifteen to London.'

My brother. Three syllables, with a wealth of undertone. He remembered the way Hope's eyes had followed Francis, on the evening of the party, as he stepped over the windowsill from the crowded, chatter-filled room into the silence of the rose-scented garden. That damned tune began re-echoing through his head again, 'Alice Where Art Thou?', the measured notes tinkling like drops of water, sweet, melancholy, maddening.

'I'm afraid I haven't been much help,' she apologized, still fiddling with the pen. The plastic clip finally snapped off 'I was . . . fond of Patti—she was a sensible girl, if a little immature for her age in some ways—though in my opinion that's no bad thing. They're grown up before they've left the cradle, these days.'

He'd heard she was a bit of a martinet, and could well believe it, suspecting that she was respected, if not liked. She was more at home here, mistress of her own environment, than she had been in the party scene, when she'd been tense and uneasy, out of place. But she wasn't comfortable, being questioned. Something odd and unaccountable about both her and her brother remained lodged as a question in his mind.

'As to what Patti did, or what she was like out of school,' she said finally, 'I don't know, you'll have to see her friends for that.'

* * *

A bubbly personality, Patti, ready to have a go at anything, according to her friends when spoken to, some of them in tears, all of them subdued, overawed by having the make-believe horror of the telly made real, brought so abruptly into their own young lives.

Anything? Well, anything for a laugh, nothing heavy.

Not, according to her special friend, when Abigail and Mayo drove off to talk to her at her home, anything *forbidden*. Patti liked fun, but knew where to draw the line, said Gemma Townsend severely, a tall and self-possessed girl, neat and conservative with long, smoothly combed, silky dark hair. A direct contrast to Patti, little and fair, liking fun clothes and fun hairstyles. Patti certainly wasn't into drugs. Boyfriends? Gemma shrugged. Nobody special, though a lot of boys fancied her. She and Patti had decided they weren't going to get themselves seriously involved. They wanted to get good A levels, and the two didn't mix. Neither was all that interested in boys, anyway.

'I see,' Abigail said, noncommitally, wondering if the two girls had gravitated towards each other subconsciously, each seeing the other as a foil. Where Patti had apparently seemed young for her years, Gemma appeared much older than hers, very controlled, though

214

her dark eyes still revealed a bewildered and youthful misery when she spoke Patti's name.

'More coffee, anyone?' asked Gemma's grandmother, graciously.

'Thank you, no, Mrs Sinclair.'

The grandmother, a slightly flustered, faded woman with faraway eyes who lived with her daughter and granddaughter, seemed to be regarding this visit of the police as some sort of social occasion, the rules of which they were transgressing by asking questions not quite in the best of taste. Gemma was actually being seen at home because she was allegedly suffering from a heavy cold, though there were precious few signs of it, apart from the fact that she was extremely pale. A diplomatic cold, perhaps, because she couldn't face school and all the fuss and melodrama and emotional hoo-ha among the other girls over what had happened to Patti. Abigail felt some sympathy with that.

'Think about the last few days, Gemma. Did Patti mention anything that had upset her, anything unusual?'

Gemma looked down at her feet, neatly shod in well-polished tan leather, smoothed her carefully pressed skirt over her nyloned knees. Her clothes looked as though they'd been bought by her mother at Marks and Spencer. On her slender middle finger, oddly, gleamed a cheap little brass ring, decorated with a skull and crossbones. 'She was going to ask to be given a different paper round. She didn't like the one she had.'

'She'd had it for some time, hadn't she?'

'Yes, but it was a pain having to lug that great heavy bag halfway up the hill from the paper shop. And she said some creepy old man in one of the houses was watching her all the time. It was a rush to get to school on time, as well.'

'OK,' Abigail said. 'Let's talk about last Saturday night, Gemma, Saturday the second.'

A wariness in Gemma's eyes. 'What about it?'

'Patti was here, with you, wasn't she?'

'Oh dear, poor little Patti! She so enjoyed the lemon pudding I made for supper!' Mrs Sinclair interjected, dabbing at her eyes, as if the news had just struck home.

There was an awkward pause, during which nobody seemed to know what to say. Mrs Sinclair smiled vaguely and picked up her knitting. Abigail began again.

'Yes, well, you—er—had supper, then she left in a taxi,' she stated again. 'What time would that be?'

Gemma glanced sideways at her grandmother. 'About quarter to ten, I think. I'm not sure.'

'Mrs Sinclair?'

'Oh, don't ask me!' the grandmother answered vaguely. 'I went to bed early with a migraine.'

216

Mayo wondered who was supposed to be keeping an eye on whom, when Gemma's mother wasn't here. 'Which firm did you ring, Gemma?' he asked.

She was smoothing her skirt again. 'I don't remember, not really. I think we got it from the Yellow Pages.'

'If we looked at the Yellow Pages now, would it jog your memory?'

'It might.'

But the book couldn't be found. 'I expect my mother has it in the surgery, and she always locks the door before she goes out.'

It was a group practice, two other doctors besides Amanda Townsend, housed in the one half of a pair of large Edwardian semis, with the Townsends living in the other half. The receptionist had gone home, and neither of the other two doctors were in.

'We always used Woodruff's when my husband was alive,' Mrs Sinclair remarked inconsequentially as they left. 'A very reliable firm. We never had any trouble with *them*.'

*　　*　　*

'Very cool, our Gemma,' remarked Abigail, as they left the doctor's house.

'Telling lies, what's more. Can you see her not remembering the name of the taxi firm? Well, we'll find out, it'll take us a bit longer, that's all; there aren't that many taxi firms in

Lavenstock. Though my guess is, for some reason Patti *didn't* go home in a taxi. But I can't see any way of making Gemma tell us why.'

'There'll be a boyfriend in it, somewhere,' Abigail said, not believing Gemma, either. 'If Grandma hadn't been there, she might've told us.'

'If Grandma hadn't been there we couldn't have interviewed her, at her age, could we? Not without breaking all the rules in the book.'

*   *   *

A man known to Mayo, Chief Inspector Uttley of the Hurstfield Division, a colleague of long-standing, was in charge of the investigation there into the murders of the two little girls, and the disappearance of the third, all of which had fallen within his jurisdiction.

They'd made arrangements to see him and went in Mayo's car, which he allowed Abigail to drive. Mindful of the honour, she reciprocated by not talking, leaving him to enjoy the music he preferred when driving but which, truth to tell, sometimes got on her nerves. Hers not to reason why. Twenty miles, and a good deal of Shostakovich's Ninth later, they arrived at Hurstfield Police Station, where Uttley was waiting for them with coffee and sandwiches.

'A right bugger, all this,' he greeted them, shaking his head, waving a hand like a ham in the direction of the several fat files in readiness

218

on his desk. Fred Uttley was an old sparring partner of Mayo's, a big, solid man whose belly strained the waistband of his trousers, a tough copper of the old school. But, handing the bulging folders over, knowing what they contained, his usually genial face took on a greyness. 'Help yourself to what you want from them, but I warn you, it won't be much.'

They leafed through the material while they drank the coffee, but what they read choked the bread in their mouths, and in the end the sandwiches were left uneaten and curling up at the edges.

It was seven months, in January, since the first child, Nicola Marchant, aged eleven, had been found, raped and brutally battered, lying in the snow. She'd been out tobogganing one Saturday afternoon with her friends, on a hill not a hundred yards from her home, and had left them at three-thirty, as instructed, before the winter afternoon began to get dark. She had never reached home. Her body, with her long blonde hair cut off at the roots, had later been found tossed into the ditch by the roadside, her sledge thrown on top of her. Snow had fallen intermittently all that day, until well into the evening, obliterating any tracks or traces the killer might have left.

Rachel Williams, thirteen the day before she disappeared in April, was on her way home from school when she was killed. She'd waved goodbye to her friends on the school bus, turned down the country road on which she lived and was never seen alive again. She hadn't been found for six weeks, when council workers using a mechanical hedge-flail had come across her, dumped like discarded rubbish in the ditch below, six miles from her home, and, like Nicola, her fair hair had been hacked off. She too had been raped and repeatedly bludgeoned with a heavy instrument.

'A hammer,' Uttley said. 'Same bloody hammer in both cases, or identical ones. The bastard probably saved it to use again.'

The MO had been similar in all respects. DNA tests confirmed it was the same man responsible in both cases. There had as yet been no trace of the third missing child, Tracey Betteridge. A few weeks ago, she'd gone to visit her grandmother who lived just around the corner from her own suburban road, and hadn't been seen since. Her disappearance might, or might not, be connected to the other two.

A lifetime of police work had rendered Uttley not insensitive, but not easily upset, either, yet these events had shaken him to the core. He had grandchildren of his own and obscurely and needlessly blamed himself for not yet having got to grips with the situation. 'I shan't sleep at nights, and that's a fact, until we've put the scumbag that's responsible where he can't do any more harm. Preferably pinned to the floor by his balls.'

But his turned-down mouth suggested his hopes weren't high, snatched at random as the children appeared to have been, with nothing at all to give a clue as to their abductor, not a shred of evidence, anywhere. Appeals, reconstructions on *Crimewatch*, miles of foot slogging, knocking on doors, hundreds of hours of tireless questioning, thousands of witnesses, yards of computer print-outs, nothing had come of it.

If Patti's death had indeed been linked to these other murders, it was a depressing prognosis for the apprehension of her killer.

Uttley was bitter. 'The only way we're going to catch him is if little Tracey turns up and he's made some mistake.' His eyes boded no good for whoever was found to be responsible. 'Or if it turns out he's made one with your Patti.'

*　　　*　　　*

'But they've nothing to do with Patti, have they?' Abigail remarked in an unusually dispirited voice on the way home. During the last couple of hours, she seemed to have lost some of her resilience. 'If we're looking for a pattern, we're not going to find it there.'

Mayo, chin sunk into his collar, thinking over the last depressing session, didn't think so either. Serial killers were creatures of habit, apt to keep to more or less the same modus operandi, and Patti's murder was unlike the ones they'd been reading about, in almost every respect. The full autopsy report on her body had confirmed Timpson-Ludgate's original opinion that she hadn't been raped, for one thing, and for another, it had been a single blow which had killed her—wielded with enough savagery and strength to shatter her skull, to be sure, but she hadn't been senselessly and repeatedly battered, as the other two girls had been. It wasn't a hammer belonging to the assailant which had been used, either, but the first weapon that had come conveniently to hand. Nor had she been abducted and taken somewhere else to be killed. All the victims had in common, in fact, was their fair hair—hardly conclusive proof of any connection. And Patti's hair hadn't been cut off.

He sat back with his eyes closed, the radio switched off, his thoughts grim. Like Uttley, he promised himself no rest until they'd found the killer. The burden was heavy, but it was his responsibility. The third day after the murder, and the bastard still free. Yet he knew that the search could go on for months, years even. If you didn't find them fast, often you didn't find them at all.

As the tree-crowned Kennet Edge flashed by on their left, and they entered the outskirts of Lavenstock, children were coming home from school, humping the oversize bags they all seemed to find necessary to carry their school kit around in. There'd been nothing in Patti's school bag to excite attention—her school books, plus gym kit, towel, a hairbrush, deodorant and a small leather purse containing less than a pound. The newsagent she'd worked for, Surinder Patel, had been worried that she hadn't returned to leave the empty delivery bag and to pick up her school bag and hat, which she always left with him before cycling off to school for half past eight. He blamed himself for not raising the alarm earlier, but his corner shop, as well as being a newsagent's, was also a sub-post office and general grocery store, and that was his busiest time of day, when people were coming in for papers and cigarettes, and bread and groceries were being delivered. Long before he'd had the chance to do something about it, Patti was dead.

Just why had Gemma been pulling the wool over their eyes? Farrar had been detailed to canvass all the local taxi firms, and, knowing Farrar, it would be done thoroughly, but Mayo was damn sure none of them would have received any call on Saturday evening for a taxi to take a young schoolgirl home. Narrowing his eyes, he visualized the town map which occupied most of one wall in his office.

'Turn off and drive round the ring road,' he said suddenly to Abigail as the Kubla Khan glass domes of the new shopping centre at the top of the town came into view.

She obeyed without so much as raising an

eyebrow. They followed the road as it skirted the main thoroughfares and swung round into Colley Street. At the stop by the Punch Bowl they had to wait until a number 12 bus pulled out, which lumbered in front of them all the way to Milford Road, where Mayo instructed Abigail to abandon the ring road and drive into the police-station car park.

Back in his office, he traced the same bus route on the map with the arm of his spectacles. It went along the ring road, then made a detour into the town centre. Past the Saracen's Head and across to join Albert Road and thus into Colley Street. Past the police station, and eventually round to the end of Mailer Street, where Patti lived.

'But—have a look at this—from the bus stop in Colley Street—'

'The quickest way to Mailer Street is the path across the back of the allotments.' It hadn't taken Abigail long to pick up his reasoning. Her eyes took on a gleam of realization. 'And you think—?'

'It's a possible hypothesis,' Mayo said slowly.

'More than that, surely? It was the same Saturday night Ensor was killed there, wasn't it? So it's not out of the way to think that she might have seen something!' The idea had re-energized her. 'I think I should go and see Gemma again. And this time get the truth out of her. I'll go carefully,' she promised, pre-empting any warning he might see fit to give.

224

'After what happened to Patti, no wonder she didn't want to talk, poor kid.'

*   *   *

Abigail would have preferred to speak to Gemma on her own, but since Gemma was in the eyes of the law still a juvenile, it was necessary to go by the book and have an appropriate person present. In this case, Gemma's mother, not the grandmother. The evasions didn't trip quite so easily from Gemma's tongue in her presence.

Amanda Townsend was several inches shorter than her daughter, a pretty, dark, energetic-looking woman in her mid-forties, but one whose every gesture indicated that she wasn't one to stand any nonsense. She sat next to Gemma on the sofa, looking expectantly at Abigail, wearing a beige cotton skirt and a plain white shirt, no make-up. Too busy, perhaps too self-fulfilled in her career to feel the need to bother about her appearance. Maybe it was the grandmother who'd chosen Gemma's clothes.

'I just want to go over what you said again, Gemma,' Abigail began. 'About the taxi on Saturday night. We haven't been able to trace a taxi firm that came here to pick anyone up.

Gemma, this time dressed in jeans, albeit carefully pressed ones, and worn with a neat print blouse, gave a choked sort of gasp and then burst into tears.

Her mother let an arm rest across her daughter's shoulders for a few seconds, gave a squeeze, then announced briskly, 'That's enough of that, Gemma. Dry your eyes and tell Inspector Moon what she wants to know. She's not going to bite.'

It seemed as though that might be the least of what Gemma feared. In a rush, scrubbing at her eyes at the same time with a tissue, she gulped, 'She didn't take a taxi home.'

'Well!' Her mother eyed her speculatively. 'How is it you were able to give me the correct change, three pounds fifty?'

'We just guessed that's what it might have come to, about six fifty. Patti put that, apart from her bus fare, into the RSPCA box, so it wasn't really dishonest. It wasn't her fault about the taxi, anyway—it was me! She only did it because I asked her to, Mum!'

'Did she, indeed?' The tone was not encouraging, but Gemma knew now there was no going back.

There was, as Abigail had known there would be all along, a boyfriend in the picture. Not Patti's, however, but Gemma's. 'What boyfriend's this?' Dr Townsend interrupted sharply.

'His name's Nige.' Gemma's chin went up, a small act of defiance, but she skated on hurriedly with the rest of the story, twisting the little brass ring with the skull and crossbones

226

on it around on her finger. Gemma had known, she said, that if she went down to the amusement arcade by the market he'd be there, it was where he spent his evenings—

'Hm,' was her mother's only comment.

Hearing the tone of it, and as familiar as Gemma's mother evidently was with the arcade and the sort who hung around there, Abigail saw immediately why this Nige hadn't been introduced into the Townsend family. She wondered briefly where Gemma's father was. Divorced, as Patti's had been? One could see that drawing the two girls together. Orphans of the marital storm, perhaps.

They'd all had a coffee together, Gemma was saying, when Patti had caught the bus and—Abigail listened impassively—Nige had brought Gemma home on the back of his motorbike. Her grandmother was still in bed and hadn't known a thing. Not even that Gemma had been out.

In view of all this, looking at Amanda Townsend's determinedly noncommittal face, Abigail had it in her heart to feel sorry for Gemma. Threats of wasting police time, which had been in her mind when she arrived, she pushed away as unnecessary.

'I'm sorry, Mum,' Gemma apologized tearfully, swallowing hard, and turning to Abigail. 'I suppose I should've told you before, but I—There's something else.'

'More?' repeated her mother ominously.

'Patti got off the bus at Colley Street and took a short cut across the allotments. She could've stayed on and ridden round to the end of Mailer Street but it would've taken ages and she was already a bit late.'

Bingo! Even the fact that the idea had been Mayo's, and not hers, couldn't lessen Abigail's small surge of triumph. 'And?'

'She was halfway along the path at the back of the allotments when she saw two people struggling. One of them seemed to knock the other flat to the ground. She wondered if she ought to have gone to fetch help or something, but it would have made her even later, and, well—you don't interfere in anything like that if you've any sense, do you?'

'That's right, Gemma, you don't.'

Abigail visualized the allotment site, the small green huts amid the neat rows of vegetables, here and there a vivid patch of flowers for cutting, beans climbing up their supports. The colour would have been leached out by the moonlight, but the same moonlight and residual light from the sodium streetlamps in Colley Street would have cast enough light for Patti to see clearly as she took the path towards the Leasowes, giving her a good view of the central road, the place where Ensor had been found, and possibly even a good view of their faces.

'But then,' Gemma said, licking her lips, 'there was that piece on Radio Lavenstock about that man who'd been found dead there. And she began to be worried that she ought to tell someone.'

'She didn't know who they were? Didn't describe them, or anything?'

'No—but I think she might've known, really, after she'd thought about it. She kept saying she didn't know what to do. I think she was just too scared to say.'

CHAPTER FIFTEEN

Speculation ran like a buzz of adrenaline through the incident room where the team waited for the Superintendent. The ending of another frustrating day. Largely unproductive routine: legwork, telephoning, questioning, with sources beginning to run dry, a feeling that the inquiry was reaching stalemate. And now, with tidings of this new development filtering through, it was kiss goodbye to any thoughts of taking it easy. They revved up with cigarettes and coffee, in the circumstances not a man or a woman there begrudging the extra effort that would be needed.

Kite alone was bouncing around as if it were first thing in the morning. Keeping up with his high energy levels was other people's problem. He began opening more windows before Mayo had the chance to do it himself. It hardly made a dent in the atmosphere, since Inspector George Atkins had his pipe well away. He came back to the front desk and reread the information Gemma had given them, propping himself against a desk, arms folded, crossed legs stretched across the gangway. 'Silly kids. If they'd simply come straight out with it—'

'It's obvious why they didn't.' Abigail pressed the last drawing pin into the visual-aid board and laid down the black marker pen. 'Patti thought at first that it was nothing more than a fight she'd seen. According to Gemma, it was only after she heard on the news on Sunday night that a man had been found dead down there on Sunday morning that she began to worry. She dithered about coming forward because she knew both she and Gemma would be in dead shtuck over her not taking a taxi home, not to mention compounding it by short-cutting through the allotments, that time of night.'

'What devious lives adolescents lead!'

'And the ones you'd least expect to. Gemma Townsend, of all people, and this Nige.'

'Nigel Worsfield, a name not unknown to us down here.'

'OK, I know, bunking off school, petty shoplifting when he was younger—but fair's fair, he's had a job down at Everett's garage since he left school and not been in trouble since. Hardly someone her mother's likely to approve of, though.'

'Excuse me, Sarge.' A WPC, looking pointedly busy, with a file under her arm and balancing two styrofoam cups of coffee, was endeavouring to get past.

Kite amiably angled his long legs to one side. 'Any mates Patti might have been pairing off with?' he asked.

'Apparently not. Patti had been covering up for Gemma—you know, saying she was with her when Gemma was really with Nige and so on, but she doesn't seem to have had any particular boyfriend of her own. Don't think we shall get anywhere pursuing that line—the odds are that she saw Philip Ensor being murdered—and that makes it an entirely different ball game.'

Mayo evidently thought so as well. When he showed his face in the incident room, the buzz of talk died down in the expectation of what was to come, the cigarettes of the circumspect were put out as officers grouped themselves in front of him to hear what he had to say.

'Firstly, thanks for staying on. You should all have made yourselves familiar with the new developments by now, but just to make sure everything's crystal clear . . .'

He drew their attention to the diagrams Abigail had drawn on the board: the names of Philip Ensor and Patti Ryman, side by side, with details of the assaults on each circled and radiating from them. Lines from each circle were now joined together at the bottom.

'None of you need me to spell out what this means. We now have a possible motive for Patti's murder—I say possible, we must keep an open mind, but at least it gives us something to work on, in both cases. It's beginning to look something like this: she takes a short cut home, via the path that runs along the back of the allotments, and sees this struggle going on between the two men. They're milling around on the road which runs through the centre of the allotments, but they're not so far away that she couldn't have recognized their faces—or the face of one of them, at least. There was a full moon that night and in any case, she must have passed fairly close. One of the men dies. Leaving aside the question of whether it was accidental or not, the other man panics, fearing this girl will tell what she saw.'

And that, Mayo was convinced, was why she'd died. He made a positive effort to sound unemotional about it, to control his own anger that Patti's life should have been forfeit—not to satisfy the urges of a random child killer, something quite outside the boundaries of comprehensible human behaviour—but worse, in a way, simply because the poor unfortunate child had stumbled upon an act of mindless violence against another person. And had been deemed expendable because of it.

'Understood so far?'

The queries which followed were mostly routine, until Farrar asked keenly, 'If it was the

232

same perpetrator in both cases, why did he wait so long to kill her—more than a week later?'

'Good question. Patti at first told Gemma Townsend she didn't know who the two men were, but it seems she might have had second thoughts about that. Presumably the killer didn't realize who she was, either. Not then. I believe it must have come to him later that she was the girl who'd passed them when they were fighting. And had reason to think she'd realized this, too.'

'Wouldn't that rule out anybody who lives on her paper round? They'd have recognized her on the spot, wouldn't they?'

'That may be so, Keith, but I still want every resident in the vicinity retargeting. I recognize how tedious this going over old ground is becoming, and I'm sorry. But we need to find out if there were any links at all, however tenuous they might seem, between any of them and Philip Ensor, and—it goes without saying—especially where they were on the Saturday night that Ensor died. And I particularly want to know what the hell he was doing in Lavenstock that night, OK? Try the hotels again, bed and breakfasts, see if someone's memory can be jogged. It's just possible he was staying under an assumed name.'

Though if he'd been staying overnight, why had his car been left out of sight behind Rodney Shepherd's premises, rather than in a hotel car park? Mayo frowned, studying his methodical notes for a moment. Ensor was where it all began, he was convinced, everything else was the after game. Find out what he'd been doing here and . . .

   .ᐧ'As to why he chose the time and place he did to kill Patti, when he could so easily have been seen . . .' Mayo paused. 'It was a risk I don't think he did choose—in that particular sense.' This, he reminded them, was no psychopath they were looking for, but someone out to protect himself from the consequences of the original killing. Whatever the outcome, the intention had simply been to shut Patti up. It looked as if Ensor's murder fell into the same category, an impulse, or possibly accidental killing after a fight. 'We seem to have come up with a profile of a spur-of-the-moment killer, someone who lands out unthinkingly when he's upset, but sharp enough to seize the opportunity when it offers—remember, in neither case did he go equipped, simply picked up what was lying around for a weapon.'

   'What about the cat, sir?' It was Farrar, once again.

   'I think we have to look on the cat as only incidental—important only in so far as it was the cause of Patti going into the wood. We know that Loates killed poor old Nero, but he's not, for my money, a credible suspect in Patti's murder—and it's even less likely that he could fight and overcome a man like Ensor, so much

234

younger and fitter—just supposing he had cause. Unless whoever killed her was conveniently lurking inside the wood at the same time, which doesn't make much sense, we might line it up something like this: Patti hears the cries of the cat—not on his usual perch—and goes to investigate. The murderer—probably watching out for her—seizes his opportunity and follows her into the wood. He speaks to her, still not entirely sure whether she's recognized him as one of the men she saw fighting, but what they say to each other convinces him that she does. She turns away, perhaps having told him that she must tell the police—and he picks up the iron bar and kills her.'

There was a silence.

'You want to say something else, Keith?'

'Could've been someone who had legitimate business around the Close, like the postman or the milkman, somebody not likely to be regarded as a stranger.'

Mayo followed a rule that at these briefings no one was to feel they couldn't put forward a theory or a suggestion—but why was it always Farrar? It was a perfectly legitimate observation he'd put forward, but Farrar got up his nose, in the way he got up most people's noses. Maybe because he was always so damn right, but—There was always a but where Farrar was concerned. Mayo had had a hint from Kite that the DC was having domestic troubles. Not exactly unusual in the police service, as Mayo knew to his cost. Before Lynne had died, things had not gone smoothly in his own household, so he was even more inclined to make excuses for Keith Farrar, who was in any case a damned good police officer, and would have gone further, had it not been for his attitudes.

'Oh, come on, Keith! Milkmen and postmen have already been accounted for, as you should know,' Abigail reminded him sharply. 'Too busy doing *The Times* crossword, were we?'

Somebody sniggered and Farrar looked at the inspector sourly, smarting at the quip about the crossword, which everyone who hadn't been at the South Pole lately must know he could do in under half an hour, but aware that he'd uncharacteristically slipped up. The first woman Chief Constable in Britain had recently been appointed. Moon was obviously hopeful of being on her way to becoming the second. And he was still a bloody DC, he couldn't think why. Life was a bugger, sometimes.

'Worth repeating, ma'am,' he couldn't resist adding, but Abigail swallowed her irritation and didn't reply.

Mayo kept his eye on Farrar for several seconds. An exchange of good-humoured insults was as common currency in the CID room as anywhere else, but Abigail had been unwontedly sharp, and it showed how on edge they all were. He wondered if the public ever realized how much murder, in particular this sort of murder, affected the men and women inquiring into it.

He was ready to wind the meeting up. He himself had two people still to see—Dermot Voss, who was proving elusive, and Francis Kendrick. He thought it might be a good idea to take Abigail with him when he went to see the latter.

'Right, that's about it. We work all out on this. Any extra hours, let Inspector Atkins know. OK, George?'

Atkins nodded, already relighting his pipe in the expectation of Mayo's departure, drawing his lists towards him.

*   *   *

Back in his office, he found a print-out on his desk concerning the motor thefts Abigail was investigating, plus the details he'd asked for about Dermot Voss's stolen car. He studied it for a while, swinging his glasses back and forth while he thought about it. The beginning of any murder investigation was always a time of frenzied activity—gathering statements, collating alibis. Mayo was quite happy to leave all that sort of thing to be worked out by the computers, after all the relevant names and times had been fed in—as far as he was concerned computers had definitely made a policeman's lot a happier one. They hadn't yet entirely replaced the human element, thank God, but meanwhile, a computer print-out beat pencilled lists on the backs of envelopes, any day. Now that both cases had opened up—or rather, come together—he looked at his list of possibles with a new eye. Excluding those residents in and around Ellington Close, eliminated for one reason and another, he was left with:

'X'. The unknown factor, the mystery man who might exist but who hadn't yet appeared on the scene, whom nobody had ever seen.

Stanley Loates. Mayo couldn't for the life of him see Loates wielding a heavy iron bar on the girl, still less as being involved in a fight with Ensor—apart from the fact that Patti knew him well enough, and would have recognized his flabby form immediately. The same thing applied to Henry Pitt, who'd said he'd stayed at home all night listening to a concert of Viennese music on the radio and had in any case left home on the morning of the crime with Vic Baverstock, while Patti was still alive. Vic also appeared to have a watertight alibi for the Ensor murder, having been out practising with his male-voice choir.

Trevor Lawley had sworn Patti was already dead when he found her. It would be worth checking on him to see if there were any links between him and Ensor. It was believable— just—that he could have hit Patti hard enough to kill her, if he thought she'd done that to his precious cat, at least according to Kite, but Mayo was fed up with theories about that damned cat. Better to work on something with more substance, like his own conviction that Patti's murder had a direct connection with what she'd seen when she was walking home that night.

Which left Francis Kendrick, whom he still had to interview today, time permitting, and Dermot Voss, both of whom should prove interesting. He thought about that for some time, then, after several minutes, he added Hope Kendrick to his list, whom he could believe capable of doing anything to protect her brother. A little mischievously he listed Tina Baverstock, whom he could believe capable of doing anything.

After a moment, thoughtfully, he added Imogen Loxley.

*   *   *

They were talking about mildew, black spot and other esoteric subjects. They'd been going on in this vein for some time. It seemed that Kendrick had a sure-fire way of getting rid of aphids. Abigail passed on her father's hint for using soft soap as a spray. Mayo looked at his watch. He signalled with his eyes to Abigail that the preliminaries were over, and prepared for confrontation.

He'd assumed from the first that the

interview with Kendrick would *be* a confrontation: Professor Kendrick, Cambridge intellectual, versus Gil Mayo, ignorant copper, which was why he'd taken Abigail along with him. Ignorant copper he might seem to someone like Kendrick, but he was also a professional one, and apt to get shirty when people forgot. Abigail being there would have a restraining influence on him. He was willing to be proved wrong, but this was the impression Kendrick had given him when they first met. Kendrick had hardly given him the time of day at the party.

They'd found him dead-heading his roses in the cool of the evening. The shadow of the sequoia fell long over the lawn, there was a spectacular sunset over the distant hills. Mayo had decided to play the part expected of him and to keep initially in the background, letting Abigail do the talking. She was the expert here, after all. She'd struck the right note from the beginning, murmuring something about the roses being a credit to him, which had the effect of loosening Kendrick up a bit and bringing a smile to his face.

'Oh, I didn't plant them. They were here when we came. I don't know the first thing about gardening in general, but the roses were so magnificent, it seemed a pity not to learn how to look after them properly.'

He would, Mayo thought. He'd approach the subject with as much rigour as if it were another academic exercise, master it once and for all and that would be it. Mayo, to whom all gardening was a mystery, could admire that. Perhaps if he himself didn't live in the upstairs flat of a house whose elderly owners lived on the ground floor and kept the garden looking neat and pleasant, if unremarkable, he might be encouraged to broaden his knowledge. Rather like Abigail Moon had done with the garden of her cottage, only it had grabbed her in the way Mayo doubted it would ever grab him. The furthest he got in that line was mowing the lawn, whenever he had the time, for the Vickers. Give him a clock that needed setting to rights, any day . . . not like weeds and grass, which never stopped growing, even after you'd attended to them.

Abigail, catching his glance, smoothly brought the discussion to a close and said immediately, 'You know that we're here to investigate the death of Patti Ryman, Mr Kendrick. Did you know her?'

'The paper girl? No, I never set eyes on her, to my knowledge. My study's here at the back of the house and I'm normally working there when the papers are delivered.'

'I'm told you go jogging in the early morning?'

'I walk,' he corrected shortly. 'And sometimes in the evening, too, for that matter. I try to do six or seven miles, most days.'

Mayo, also a dedicated walker, to whom half

a dozen miles was little more than a limbering up, didn't comment, but Abigail asked, 'Any particular routes?'

'Sometimes as far as Scotley Beeches, or Kennet Edge, quite often just to the other side of Lavenstock and back.'

'Did you go out on Monday morning?'

'No, as a matter of fact, I didn't. I had papers to sort out before my trip to London and was rather pushed for time.'

Mayo spoke up for the first time. 'You drove up to Birmingham New Street to catch the London train, rather than go from Coventry. Why was this?'

The big, raw-boned hand tightened on the secateurs. Kendrick leaned forward to snip off a dead head, precisely before the next bud, dropping it into the wheelbarrow before he answered. 'It may have escaped your notice, Superintendent, but Lavenstock is more or less equidistant from both points.'

'But the train starts at least twenty minutes earlier from New Street. What made you decide to go from there, since you hadn't much time to spare?'

Kendrick treated him to the sort of glance reserved for backward students. 'Oh come, that time in the morning? With all the traffic on our famous one-way system? Any time you might have in hand you're likely to lose it—whereas you can use the bypass the other way. Whichever station you choose there's nothing to it in terms of time. You save nothing but your temper. But in any case,' he added blandly, 'I had a manuscript to deliver to my typist on the way there.'

Manuscript my backside, thought Mayo, becoming more bloody-minded northern the more patronizing Kendrick became. And the traffic wasn't that bad. Unless Kendrick had, in fact, gone from Coventry and used the spare time otherwise. It could be checked. 'The address of your typist, please?'

Kendrick gave it with an amused smile.

'And how did you pay for your ticket? Cash, credit card?'

'In cash.' Kendrick's look managed to convey the impression that credit cards were only for the lower orders, or the feckless who lived beyond their means, and how he paid for his ticket was no business of anyone else, anyway.

'All right.' Mayo changed tack. 'Back to these walks of yours. You didn't go for one last Saturday evening—Saturday week, that is, did you?'

'Are you telling me, or asking me? I don't remember so far back.'

'That was the evening you had your party here.'

'So it was. You were one of our guests, I believe.' Mayo tried not to imagine that the word 'guest' was stressed. 'No, as a matter of fact, I didn't get my walk in that evening.' He

243

smiled suddenly and Abigail, at least, saw that there might, in different circumstances, be a more appealing side to him. 'I play the organ at St Gregory's on alternate Sundays and I usually practise for an hour or so on Saturday evening. I saw no reason why the party should make any difference. I went across after everyone had gone home.'

'That would be—what? Eightish? I myself left just before that ... while you were demonstrating your Victorian music box to young Allie.'

'It's called a Polyphon,' Francis said, after a pause. 'The children and their father and aunt went home shortly after eight.'

'So you'd be home after your organ practice at what time?'

Another fractional hesitation. 'I suppose it may have been around nine thirty. I don't believe I noticed the time.'

'One of your sisters would no doubt confirm this.'

'No doubt they could. Unfortunately, Hope is at a PTA meeting, and Imogen is also out. But I should regard it as an unpardonable liberty if they were asked to. What reason do you have for checking up on me? That night or any other?'

'Oh, we're only eliminating you from certain inquiries, on another murder, sir.' Mayo gave the time-honoured assurance with only the merest glint of irony in his eye. Did the man visibly relax? 'We just wanted to be sure you'd nothing to tell us. Seems you haven't, so we'll leave you to your roses. Unless,' he added, 'the name of Philip Ensor means anything to you?'

'Ensor? No. I don't know anyone of that name. Who is he?'

'You may have read about him in the papers. He was the man who was found murdered last Saturday night, sir, on the Colley Street allotments.'

But Francis Kendrick shook his head.

*   *   *

Mayo felt by no means as cheerful, nor even as insensitively brusque, as he'd sounded on leaving Francis Kendrick. On the contrary, he was, quite suddenly and inexplicably, overwhelmed by the feelings of sadness and loneliness he'd sensed in the man. It wasn't something he'd expected to feel. But that last glimpse of his face, lost and tormented, stayed with him.

Ten days since Ensor's killing, and the days were growing cooler, a different quality could be discerned in the light. Evening was coming on appreciably quicker. The sun was going down over Kennet Edge, in a sky streaked with turquoise and rose-gold. The scent of Kendrick's roses seemed to cling to them as they bowled down the hill once more towards Milford Road.

'Well, do you think he *has* nothing more to tell us?' Abigail asked, turning his own words back to him.

'Remains to be seen.' Mayo did his best to shake off the feelings that Kendrick had stirred up. 'Somebody might remember him buying a ticket at Coventry—stands out in a crowd, that height, doesn't he? But I think he's probably telling the truth.'

'What about the Saturday night, and Ensor?'

'Fisticuffs doesn't seem exactly his thing. Words are more his weapon.' He relapsed into an abstracted silence, until they reached the station.

Once there, they found all the accumulated work of the day awaiting them.

'With all there is to do yet, it looks like being a late session again tonight, Abigail—sorry.'

'No problem. Nobody makes plans when we've something like this on if they've any sense.'

He rang Alex, warning her not to expect him home until late. 'Tell you what, I'll give you a ring when I'm ready, and if you haven't already eaten, you can come down and meet me and we'll grab something quick in the town, save the bother of fixing something when I get in.'

'Good idea. Ask Abigail to join us. How about a quick Chinese? We can be in and out in twenty minutes.'

Well, he'd suggested it.

By the time they'd worked their way through the bean-curd soup and the king prawns and the fried won ton, Mayo couldn't face even a bowl of lychees, never mind the hot banana fritters in syrup which the two women were ordering with every anticipation of enjoyment. Chinese food always had the same effect on him: by this stage in the meal he was replete, full to saturation point, but knowing with certainty that an hour later he'd be feeling hollow, craving a thick ham sandwich with plenty of mustard. What was more, there was the vexed question of what to drink with that sort of food: perish the thought of a decent wine—and the diuretic effects of jasmine tea, late at night, was a problem he could do without. He settled, as usual, for a lager. He always grumbled about coming to the overpriced Jade Lotus, supposedly renowned for its Peking cuisine, but in the end gave in because he knew Alex liked it. The decor was restful, it was discreetly lit and the chairs were comfortable, at any rate.

Plus, it was a chance to step aside for an hour from the sort of case that took over every waking thought—and sometimes sleep, as well. One which he'd had no intention of talking about over this meal, though, not even to Alex, who could usually be relied on to lend a sympathetic and understanding ear, often making valuable suggestions of her own, having been in on the sharp end and knowing what it was like. But tonight, he was a little disgruntled, his intention when suggesting supper out having been to direct the conversation into other, quite different channels. He'd be discreet about it, but steer them back to the point where she'd sidestepped the other day. He needed to lay a few ghosts. And then she'd included Abigail. But Abigail, now having demolished the last of the sizzling bananas, was making noises about an early start in the morning, preparing to leave. Maybe there was still time to approach the subject uppermost in his mind.

It was not to be.

Someone stopped near their table. He looked up to see Dermot Voss, smiling, stretching out a hand, making surprised noises about fancy seeing them here and why didn't they come across and join them for coffee or whatever. Pointing to a table just around the corner, with a mirror opposite his seat, through which he'd presumably seen them, though they hadn't seen him. Damn. Damn it to hell. He liked the volatile Voss and his amusing conversation, but he was in no mood to be entertained. However . . . Swallowing hard, he decided it might after all be opportune.

Alex, in her calm way, was beginning to make excuses, but Mayo smoothly intervened, Abigail said no more about going home, and in

248

no time they were all sitting round the same table, he and Alex, Abigail, Dermot and Imogen Loxley.

Imogen Loxley. Well, now, there was a turn-up for the book. Mayo watched them and wondered what Sarah thought about being left at home with Dermot's offspring while Dermot was out wining and dining an attractive woman—if she knew about it, that was. It occurred to him that young woman wasn't exactly getting a wonderful deal out of all this.

The other four were drinking jasmine tea and Mayo was understanding why they'd chosen it in preference to the coffee he'd ordered. On the same principle, presumably, that you didn't order fish and chips outside the British Isles if you were wise. The coffee was undrinkable.

He put the cup down and caught Imogen's stare before she looked quickly away. If she was supposed to be enjoying herself, she wasn't giving that impression. She joined in the conversation, in a social way, but she wasn't really there. She fidgeted with her spoon. Her white silk blouse was scarcely paler than she was. Dermot, on the other hand, was rattling away like an express train. He was explaining his new job, and how it had necessitated him leaving Milton Keynes, how he'd had the amazing luck to find a profitable investment like Edwina Lodge ... enthusing rather too much, Mayo suspected, over something which had seemed like a good idea at the time but was already turning out to be rather a boring commitment.

'Not a very auspicious start to life here in Lavenstock,' he was saying. 'Food poisoning on the first night, my car nicked—what next? Nothing like this ever happened in MK!'

'Yes, I remember you said before that you'd had food poisoning.'

'Did I? Well, it's not something I'm likely to forget. From some shellfish I ate for dinner, I suspect. Had to rush out of the restaurant.'

'The food's usually pretty dependable at the Saracen's. Did you complain to the management?'

'No. There was no point. Once I'd got rid of whatever it was, I felt all right.'

'Well, as far as your car goes, the problem may have solved itself,' Abigail told him.

'You've found it?'

'We caught someone stealing a car today, and he's asked for others to be taken into consideration, yours among them. You should have it back shortly.'

Dermot's face was a study. 'Well, what do you know.'

Imogen said drily, 'Even Milton Keynes couldn't beat that.'

Later, Mayo was to wonder why the connection hadn't occurred to him earlier, but it was only in the dawn reaches of a sleepless night, the hour between wolf and dog, when everything seems suddenly clear and simple, that a sudden flash of the obvious came to him, illuminated his mind for a single moment and then drifted foggily away as sleep came at last.

A busy day crowded in on him, and it wasn't until later events had brought things to a head that the idea came back to him.

CHAPTER SIXTEEN

In another part of the town, while Mayo was consuming his Chinese won ton, Vic Baverstock was struggling with his conscience, aided by a pint of bitter in the Black Bull.

The Black Bull wasn't his first choice—in Vic's opinion, a low-class dump if ever there was one—but if he'd gone to the Saracen's, Mandy would've been there, at her part-time job behind the bar, and he wasn't exactly flavour of the month with Mandy just now.

He stared gloomily into his beer, trying to shut out the sounds of the jukebox. He wasn't the sort who lied to the police on principle and it bothered him that he'd had to, out of necessity. It had been his rotten bad luck for that bloke to have got himself killed when Vic had been parked on the bit of spare ground in the allotments. Just when he was getting well away with Mandy. Not that he'd known then that the bloke had snuffed it, he hadn't stayed long enough to see. When he'd realized that a serious struggle was going on, he'd got the hell out of it before the police arrived, though he knew Mandy would blame him for choosing a spot like, that in the first place, so near the town centre, and he'd been right, she had. To say that she was pissed off was an understatement.

He knew he ought to go to the police and admit he'd lied when he said he'd been out practising with the choir that Saturday night. They'd find out, of course, if they bothered to check, but so far they hadn't seemed to think it necessary. He wasn't in their line of suspects, he'd convinced them that he hadn't known the dead bloke from Adam, and he'd a bomb-proof alibi for the time Patti had been killed. But the other one—the one who'd done it—well, Vic knew who he was, all right. He'd seen him clearly, though Mandy hadn't, being in no position to be able to, at the time.

But, Mandy apart, Vic had his reasons for keeping stumm about knowing. Tina, chiefly. All the same, he hadn't reckoned with that terrible thing that had happened to poor little Patti having had anything to do with what he'd seen.

Upset, he looked down at the evening paper again, folded small on the table, so that the last paragraph about her murder was uppermost. He'd sweated blood—though he wasn't the only one to be questioned—wondering what interest the police had in *his* whereabouts that Saturday night, why they'd wanted to know if he'd known this bloke Ensor. Now, the paper said they were working on a theory that Patti being killed like that might have some connection with the dead man found in the Colley Street allotments ten days ago . . . Vic took a long swallow of his beer. Gawd.

The thought of an anonymous letter or telephone call crossed his mind, but not seriously. That wasn't his style. Then he remembered DC Deeley, Pete Deeley, used to live across the road when they were kids. Good sort, Pete, a word in his ear and maybe he'd be able to make sure that Vic's name was kept out of it—that was what they said, didn't they? Any information will be treated in the strictest confidence. What they meant was, if you'd been out having it off with the neighbour's wife, they wouldn't let on.

Near enough.

He needed to sleep on it, though.

*   *   *

By eight o'clock the next morning, there was a coffee pot with two china cups and saucers on Mayo's desk, not thick white canteen pottery or nasty plastic cups from the machine. The coffee was real, too. A rich aroma of freshly ground Arabica rose between them as Abigail poured two cups and pushed one across the desk

253

towards Mayo, ready for when he'd finished telephoning. The shot of caffeine felt good, jolted her system into full wakefulness. All the same, she swore she'd lay off it for the rest of the day. She'd drunk too many cups yesterday and her mind had been jumping around all night like a Scud missile.

She was tapping her teeth with a pencil, looking thoughtful, when he finally put the receiver down. 'Right, where were we? Dermot Voss and his car, wasn't it?'

'Yes, but I've been thinking about those Belgian francs in Ensor's pocket.'

'He travelled to Belgium in the course of his business. There only a few weeks ago, wasn't he?'

'That's right, and Imogen Loxley was living in Brussels until very recently.' She stopped, looking down at her notes. 'She's married to Tom Loxley, the Euro MP . . . The marriage is on the rocks, by all accounts.'

'Like a lot more,' he commented drily, but his glance was interested. 'Any ideas why, in this particular case?'

She shook her head. 'Not for certain. But Loxley's been acquitting himself very well in Brussels, making quite a name for himself over the Common Market Agricultural Policy, working hard. Perhaps too hard, leaving her too much to her own devices.'

'Par for the course, in that sort of job. Women like Imogen Loxley, they cope, better than their husbands sometimes. What did you think of her and Voss, dining together last night?'

'Interesting. I gathered we came as something of a reprieve, rather than an interruption. The tension was thick enough to cut with a knife when we joined them.'

He nodded. 'My impression, too. And Alex's. So, what are you thinking?'

She frowned. 'I don't know what Voss can have to do with this, if anything. It's a long shot, but it's possible, I suppose, that Imogen could have met Philip Ensor in Brussels and had an affair with him, which broke up her marriage. Supposing she blamed Ensor for it and finished with him, came back to Lavenstock, but Ensor was still pestering her. She arranged to meet him, Patti saw them struggling—remember, she appears to have been unsure at first about the attacker, and this could have been because she wasn't sure if it was a man or a woman, say if she was a tall woman like Imogen Loxley and was wearing trousers. She'd ample opportunity to watch for Patti and follow her into the wood ... T-L didn't rule out the possibility that a woman could have wielded the murder weapon, if she'd had the bottle for it. And there's the pen, too. A woman's sort of pen—'

'Has it been traced yet?'

'To the manufacturers, yes. But they can't give us the specific retail outlet—Deeley's sifting through all the people they supplied that type of pen to. The makers say the engraving was done after it was bought.'

'Mm.' He brought his gaze back from the Town Hall clock, checked it by his own watch. Two minutes slow. 'She's a bit of a dark horse altogether, Imogen Loxley,' he murmured absently, draining his coffee.

'But you're not sure you can see her as a double murderess.' She sighed. 'Well, neither can I, not really.'

'We should see her again,' he temporized. 'But let's get down to this business of Dermot Voss, first. He says he left his car outside Patel's while he went in for his cigarettes, about seven forty, came out five minutes later and it was gone. That young toerag—what's his name? Oh yes, Mitchison—says he didn't nick it until ten to eight—if he's telling the truth for once in his life.'

'He's no reason not to. He nicked it on the way to work, because his own wouldn't start and he was late, would you believe?'

'I believe it. So what was Voss doing between say, twenty to eight and ten past, when he came back home? Plenty of time for him to have followed Patti into the Close and killed her.' He frowned. 'Voss hadn't moved into Edwina Lodge when Patti saw the fight at the allotments, so she wouldn't have known who he was, then. But she could have recognized him when she did meet him—and very likely put two and two together.'

256

He poured himself more coffee and needlessly stirred the black, sugarless liquid. Abigail declined one for herself and waited for him to carry on. He'd had the faraway look of a man with something at the back of his mind ever since they'd begun to talk.

Mayo felt as though he was suddenly on to something.

That mention of meeting Voss in the Chinese restaurant had reminded him of how Voss had been enthusing about the advantages of the modern house, specially designed for energy-saving, that he'd left behind in Milton Keynes, and in the way these things do, his own pre-dawn flash of insight had come back to him. His subconscious, though possibly not entirely unrelated to the stimulation of a couple of stiff, late-night drams, had been working for him while he slept, gone on working and was now coming up with some interesting conclusions of its own.

Milton Keynes. A place Mayo knew nothing about, a new town, a railway-station sign flashing past the window on the journey to and from London: Milton Keynes, Bletchley . . . He said slowly, thinking as he spoke, 'There had to be a reason for Ensor being in Lavenstock that night, for meeting the man who killed him. Milton Keynes isn't a million miles away from Bletchley, where Ensor worked. If he and Voss had known each other before . . .'

That encompassed a whole load of

suppositions, and he knew it. But hell, wasn't that where it started from, a 'what if' that led on to the truth? Thousands of people lived in each place. The odds on them knowing each other were so long as to be hardly worth considering, without any other connection. Yet he had an irrational certainty that he'd somehow—God help him, he didn't know how—stumbled on to something . . .

He reached out for Ensor's file. 'We know he worked in Bletchley, but where did he live before he moved to Solihull? Let me have another look on what we've got on him, while you find out his previous address.'

Abigail picked up the phone and made the request for an outside line, while Mayo began to read. A glowing report on Ensor had been received from his employers. His business life had evidently been as exemplary as his private one. CL Freightlines had been more devastated to hear of his death than any of his relatives had, including his wife. He'd started in the firm as a trainee salesman at the Bletchley headquarters and had moved up the managerial ladder until he was chief salesperson, or whatever, next stop sales director. Moving house to Solihull had surprised his employers but, although it was less convenient from his point of view, it hadn't made any difference as far as his work was concerned. Solihull was within commuting distance—if you didn't object to getting up that much earlier in the morning—and he was out of the office a good deal, working elsewhere, often abroad, anyway.

The MD to whom Abigail had previously spoken had said, regarding his move to Solihull, 'Gave it out that his wife was missing her family—as if we're in Outer Mongolia here! Still, no telling with women, after all. He did have to leave her on her own a good deal, must admit—all part of the job, though.' He admitted that he'd only met Mrs Ensor a few times, at social functions connected with the firm, but she'd obviously made a hit. He remembered her very well. 'Did him credit, damn good-looking woman,' he said admiringly.

He was elderly, white-haired. The sort to take it for granted that a man would have the sense to choose a wife who looked the part.

'Thanks very much.' Abigail finished her call and put the receiver back. 'Ensor *did* live in Milton Keynes.'

They looked at each other. 'So they both moved, Ensor and Voss. Why did Dermot Voss come here? I can see why he couldn't have carried on with his other job—it would've meant wishing his children on to relatives—not that he seems averse to that!—or sending them to boarding school, I suppose. If that's the reason he gave it up, then I'll hand it to him. But why buy that damned great house—he's surely got enough problems without that? I daresay it would work for somebody like that

259

Mrs Whatsername who used to run it—
somebody there on the spot, doing nothing
else, but—'

'He says it's a paying proposition. Pays his
mortgage and a bit over. Maybe he's strapped
for cash.'

'That wouldn't surprise me.'

Abigail said slowly, 'Avis Walker, Ensor's
sister-in-law, said something, when we were
talking about Ensor lending her husband
money, which has stuck in my mind. Folks don't
like to be beholden, she said. Assuming Ensor
and Voss did know one another, and say Voss
had been in difficulties and Ensor had bailed
him out—'

'And Ensor was dunning him to pay it back?
They met, had this argument, things got out of
hand, and Ensor ended up dead?'

'I was going to say maybe being obligated to
Ensor had stuck in Voss's craw to the point
where he'd grown to hate him—but yes, it's
more likely to be as you suggested.'

'Anyway, at this point we're not concerned
with why. Motivation's a slippery notion at the
best of times. Find out who and we'll know
why. But the night Ensor was killed,' Mayo
said, warming to his theme, 'Voss was staying at
the Saracen's. Twice he's gone out of his way to
mention that alleged food poisoning he got
there—which could have been an excuse to
leave Sarah because he had an appointment
with Ensor he didn't want her to know about,

260

for whatever reason. Colley Street is only round the corner from the Saracen's. Based on the assumption, of course, that Voss and Ensor did know each other. Whatever, Ensor is the key to all this. We have to find out more about him. When someone's life is so damned tidy, I worry about it. It's not natural. Abigail, I want you to get over to Solihull again. Have another talk with Judith Ensor. Put pressure on her, if needs be, bring her over here if necessary.'

'I'm not sure how she'd respond to pressure—she struck me as being very stubborn, the type just to dig her heels in more. But the softly-softly approach didn't get me anywhere last time, so it has to be worth a try.'

'Get her to talk, somehow.'

'OK, I'll take care of it. I'm due in court in an hour, and I'll be there most of the day, but I'll get over as soon as I can.'

*   *   *

Imogen had risen early, after a restless night. She buttered toast, poured herself another cup of tea, then let it go cold as she reread yet another accusing letter from Melissa.

It hadn't really been necessary to read it in the first place. It was the same as all the others—Mel, from her sixteen-year-old vantage point, offering criticism and telling her mother what she must do. They knew it all, today's children, potted psychology from television soaps. But not from experience. All very well for Mel to tell her she was being selfish, she *must* go back to Daddy, whatever was wrong wasn't wrong enough to split the family up. Imogen hadn't told her exactly what the rift was about, nor, presumably, had Tom— only that the marriage wasn't working. Which must have seemed patently untrue to Mel. She'd been home the weekend before Imogen had so precipitately left, and everything had been quite normal. Mel would have noticed if it hadn't been, she was sharp and very intuitive, possessive even, where her parents were concerned. Except that she seemed to have got it into her head somehow that she, Imogen, was following up some women's lib prescription, doing her own thing, making a menopausal bid for freedom. Yet Imogen shrank from telling her the truth . . . to a child of Mel's generation, it would surely seem a trivial reason for breaking up a marriage . . . most of the parents of her friends at that expensive school were in and out of bizarre relationships like jack rabbits. Perhaps Mel had seen the effect on their children . . .

She stared down at her toast, which appeared to have got itself cut into minute squares, scarcely big enough to feed a mouse. She scraped the lot into the bin. She wasn't hungry, anyway. Her appetite had disappeared halfway through that Chinese meal last night, when Dermot's heavy hints left no room for doubt as to how he was expecting the evening to end.

She couldn't blame him. She'd been expecting the same thing, which was why she'd accepted his invitation. Defiantly. Sauce for the goose, she'd thought. I can't go on living my life like this. I'm not like Hope. And Dermot Voss was a very attractive man. Free, what was more.

And then, for some inexplicable reason, she'd chickened out. She'd had no need to say anything, he'd sensed her change of mood immediately, and correctly guessed the reason for it. He hadn't bothered to hide how he felt; while keeping up a semblance of conversation for form's sake, he'd been incandescent with anger underneath. The waiters had impassively removed her half-eaten food, managing to convey intense Oriental disapproval without blinking an eyelid and then, as if to humiliate her further, Dermot had gone to ask Gil Mayo and the two women he was with to join them, without so much as asking her whether she would mind or not.

Not that she did. It was a relief at first, until the conversation had slid, inevitably, around to Patti Ryman's murder. Mayo, however, had skilfully avoided making comment on that. Professional etiquette or something, she supposed, but those watchful, slate-grey eyes were alert, she knew he'd missed nothing of what was said.

She suspected that he'd known right from

the beginning, when he'd first come to interview her, that she was keeping something back, and she knew, if he questioned her again, she wouldn't be as successful this time in avoiding him. They could do you for obstructing the police in their duty, that much she knew. Did that include lying by omission?

She was dodging the issue. Anyone with any sort of social conscience would have told them before now. It wasn't loyalty, or that she couldn't imagine something that had happened all those years ago not having any bearing now—all too easily she could imagine that. Human nature didn't change, human failings remained constant. You could keep the lid on a can of worms for half a lifetime but sooner or later it would burst open and the fat would be in the fire. God, her metaphors were as confused as her thoughts.

The truth was, she was frightened, thrown badly off balance by a fear she thought she'd conquered years ago . . . She'd wanted so desperately to believe that the past was over and done with, but that little girl, Patti, had made it impossible.

The awful loneliness that had rolled over her yesterday morning—fear as well, rearing its head from her childhood—grabbed her again. Feelings of hurt and injury, memories of being left out of their shared secrets. But more than that, much more. She'd been so frightened of them, of Francis especially, but of Hope as well. They'd been thoughtlessly cruel to her, terrifying her with their peculiar games and their closeness and their half-understood innuendoes, in that hateful old house, Heath Mount. She had thought, when it was pulled down, that its power would have been destroyed forever, but the past, like some frightful miasma, hung over this house and its occupants, too. Something terrible was happening here.

She was alone in the house. Hope was at school and Francis nowhere to be found—probably on one of his long walks, or shut up in his study with his icons and his books, and his holy pictures. Where she could not—dared not—disturb him.

She couldn't cope with this by herself. Her life hadn't equipped her to deal with this sort of situation, but there was no one else she could confide in, she'd lost touch with most of her old friends when she went away to live. She wanted, needed, Tom. But would Tom, after everything that had happened, want her?

CHAPTER SEVENTEEN

Lucy had been invited to tea with her new friend Jodie, and Jodie's mother had telephoned to say she would meet both children out of school, arranging to have Lucy at home by half past six.

Sarah could see that it would be no bad thing just now that Lucy should have the chance to do something on her own. She was being difficult, and it all had to do with the people at Simla, with Imogen and, to a certain extent, Francis. It was on Allie, for some reason, that their favour had especially fallen. Anyone else might have been in danger of becoming spoiled through all the attention being paid to her, but Allie, being Allie, accepted it without appearing to notice. Poor Lucy, who was used to being the one in the limelight and couldn't be blamed for not understanding what was going on, had her nose sadly out of joint.

Hope, despite the gift of the dolls, remained detached from all this, which Sarah had decided must be due to diffidence, in view of how she'd sent the children's presents over via Imogen, rather than giving them herself. 'I think she's basically a very shy person,' she'd told Fitz.

His reaction had been disconcerting. 'Don't let the children get too close to the Kendricks, Sarah. They're an odd bunch.' He wouldn't say anything more and she wondered what he meant. But Fitz had grown up in this area and had known the Kendricks all his life, he'd gone to school with Francis, they'd both been day boys at Lavenstock College. She sometimes forgot what a tight community this was, compared to a big, anonymous city like

266

London, how well known so many people were to each other.

She drove up to the school at home-time, parked in the long line of cars belonging to waiting mothers, and settled down until Allie should put in an appearance. The children came out, Lucy and her friend Jodie (hair *definitely* highlighted, ye Gods!) piled into Jodie's mother's car after she (*her* hair improbably auburn) had had a brief word with Sarah, and were driven away. Other children followed, until Sarah's car was the only one left. Lisa had often laughed about how she and an impatient Lucy had sat thus outside their former school, times without number, waiting for Allie to emerge. She was invariably one of the last, if not *the* last, trailing out, clutching her slipping possessions, dreamily unaware how long she'd taken.

Sarah sat staring through the windscreen at the pleasant grouping of the red-brick school buildings and, as seemed to happen every spare moment now, her own problems swam into focus.

She'd spoken to Simon last night. He was becoming increasingly irritated at her refusal to say when she was coming back. Fending him off had been just another cowardly excuse for not coming to grips with what she really ought to say to him—that this space between them had given her time to think, that she was now sure that her own future couldn't include him, not in any way meaningful to him. But, apart from the fact that she didn't want to ask herself why this decision was connected with Fitz, telling Simon the truth took more courage than she'd been able to summon up last night, after she'd at last remembered where she'd last seen the face in the photograph.

The knowledge lay like a heavy, indigestible lump in her stomach. She couldn't yet bring herself to do what she knew she must, eventually. She'd once despised others in the same situation, not seeing it as a viable choice. She understood better now. Yet there was no decision, not really. It was not a matter of if, but when. And not really even that—it must be now.

The last, lingering child had departed, and still no sign of Allie. She should have been out ten minutes ago. Sarah got out of the car and went to jolly her along.

Three minutes after that, she was on the telephone to the police.

*   *   *

Dermot was furious with the school. 'What the hell do they mean, they let her go with that woman? They're supposed to be responsible for the children in their charge, for God's sake!'

'*That woman*', DC Jenny Platt reminded him gently, was Hope Kendrick, a well-known and respected member of the community, another teacher, and although not of their school, known to most of the staff at Greymont JMI as well. Known also to live next door to Allie, her affection for Allie obviously returned. All the same, Sarah could see that she agreed with Dermot. The school was in serious dereliction of duty, they should have checked, there was simply no excuse for letting her go off with anyone, no matter how plausible the reason for taking Allie out of school. Allie's class teacher, now appalled at what she'd done, had been far too ready to accept that Hope had been asked by the child's father to pick Allie up for him that morning—a forgotten appointment, she'd said, with the orthodontist who was building up that chipped front tooth. Reasonable enough to be accepted by a busy teacher.

It was now nearly eight o'clock, and the house fully lit up, with a heavy police presence everywhere, doorbells ringing, people coming and going. In view, presumably, of what had happened to Patti Ryman, they were taking no chances, they'd sent this policewoman round to stay in the house, and they'd put out a search for Hope's car. But this must be a different matter to Patti's murder, entirely. Yet it seemed equally impossible to associate Hope with taking Allie away like that.

'She won't get far. We'll pick her up. It isn't as though we don't know who's taken her,' they'd said. Which made it all the worse in

Sarah's eyes. It was such an irrational thing to have done, and when reason went out of the window . . . She tried not to think what might be going on in Allie's mind, by now. Rigid-faced and making cups of tea for all as if her life depended on it, she couldn't make any sense of any of it.

With all her heart, she wished Fitz here. She'd telephoned him at his office, at the first available opportunity. 'What?' He'd listened without interruption until she'd blurted out the story, but when he answered seemed not anxious to prolong the conversation. 'Sarah, this is terrible. Don't worry, I'm sure she'll be all right. I'm sorry, but I can't come over straight away, I've made other plans for this evening. I'll try and get over later.'

It wasn't what she'd hoped for. She'd never spoken to him on the telephone before and hadn't realized how clipped and abrupt his voice would sound, more so than usual. Perhaps she'd rung at an inconvenient moment, but all the same, she'd expected concern and warm sympathy and felt depressingly let down.

They were all sitting in the cheerless drawing room with its incongruous furniture—why there, of all places, Sarah couldn't imagine, except that it was next to the hall and only a few strides from where the telephone was, and there was more room for all the people who were coming and going. Every time it rang, they all sat up, as if pulled up by wires attached to their shoulders, only to sag like puppets when one of the police answered it and there was no news.

Dermot sat with his head in his hands. Suddenly he looked up. 'What the hell are you all hanging around here for, doing nothing, when you should be out finding Allie?'

The policewoman, who said they should call her Jenny, had a clean-scrubbed appearance and well-polished shoes. She was young, but not afraid of showing her disapproval. All she said, however, was, 'There's still time for Miss Kendrick to bring her back. She may just have taken some misplaced notion into her head to take Allie out for the day.' She didn't look convinced. No one else did, either.

Doreen Bailey came downstairs at last from seeing Lucy calmed down and tucked up in bed. She'd insisted on staying with her, apparently thinking that someone was going to steal into the house and spirit her away, too. 'Asleep, poor lamb,' she said.

The doorbell rang. The lanky sergeant, Kite, looked round the door and summoned WDC Platt with a jerk of his head. A murmur of voices came from the hall and then Jenny Platt returned, shaking her head at their hopeful faces.

'Anyone fancy a cup of coffee?' Doreen asked.

'To hell with coffee, we're all awash with it,'

Dermot said, jumping up and beginning to pace the room. 'Sorry, Mrs B. In God's name, how much longer?'

Sarah, clutching Angel to her like a talisman, as if the doll could somehow summon Allie back, saw defeat traced on his features, defeat and something dark and deep in him that Sarah had never recognized before. Some realization of his inadequacy as a parent? At seeing the whole bright enterprise collapsing? A need for Lisa at this time—who could tell?

*   *   *

Abigail hadn't been able to leave for Solihull until the late afternoon, but a telephone call had established that by the time she got there, Judith Ensor would be home from work.

She was dressed in pale blue this time, in a matching dress and jacket that only needed a picture hat to make it suitable for a wedding. Her enamelled make-up was flawless as ever, colour-coordinated pink-frosted lips and nails, like strawberry sorbet, hair like dark candyfloss.

'Dermot and Lisa Voss?' At first it seemed as though she wasn't going to admit to having known them, but after a time it appeared to dawn on her that denial was pointless and she gave a grudging admission. 'We used to know them, once.'

'Used to?'

'They lived near us. Then we moved down here and we lost touch.'

'You mean you didn't see each other again? You didn't visit, or write?'

'No.'

'Not even a Christmas card?'

'No.'

'Had you quarrelled?'

She lifted one immaculate shoulder. 'These things happen.'

'Well. Did your husband ever lend Dermot Voss any money?'

'He may have done. He didn't tell me if he did.'

She crossed her legs and smoothed her skirt. Her expression was unyielding. It was going to be like drawing teeth. 'Mrs Ensor, don't you *want* to know who killed your husband?' Abigail asked gently.

For a moment, it seemed that might have got to her. Her colour came and went. Tears appeared at the corner of her eyes. Then she remembered her mascara. 'Would you like a glass of sherry?' she asked suddenly. 'I would.'

Why not, if it would get her to talk? After the first sip of the sweet, brown liquid Abigail left the little crystal glass to one side, waiting while Judith drank hers.

'How did you meet the Voss family? Were they near neighbours?' she prompted after a while, hoping the drink might have given Judith a bit of Dutch courage. Either it had, or she'd decided to give a little more. She began to speak, softly and quickly.

'Near enough. Philip met Dermot at some airport or other when their flight was held up for hours and hours. They got talking and found we lived in the same place, and that was how it started. We played bridge together. I used to babysit for them when Dermot was home. A faint smile momentarily softened the hard little face in its frame of cloudy dark hair. 'I liked the children. They were great.'

She sat elegantly on the settee, glass in hand, staring out of the window. 'This other murder you mentioned, this young girl,' she said suddenly. 'What's Dermot's involvement in that?'

'I can't say that, yet,' Abigail replied cautiously.

She didn't say anything for a while, then seemed to come to a decision. 'After you'd gone, the other day, I found something that might interest you. Excuse me while I get it, will you?'

When she came back, she silently handed over a packet of letters, enclosed with an elastic band. They were addressed to Philip Ensor, at his business address, handwritten in a stylish hand, with swooping loops and Greek Es. The ink was brown, the paper was thick, creamy-yellow, with a curlicued stylized flower in brown at the top right-hand corner.

Abigail skimmed through them. They were

love letters, not of the most steamy kind, but love letters, all the same, and all from Lisa Voss. The writing paper interested her.

'Very distinctive, this paper,' she said, putting the last letter back into the envelope.

'Dermot got it for her. He used to buy her lovely things all the time—a new supply of these every birthday, and once a special pen to go with it.'

'A fountain pen—with this same flower engraved on it?'

'It's not a flower—it was her monogram. She drew her initials like that!' Well, yes, Abigail saw that with the curved downstrokes of the V joining together at the bottom, and the L curling extravagantly around it, it did look exactly like a flower. 'He had the pen specially engraved to match. She didn't know when she was well off—a lot of women would've given their eye-teeth for a husband like that.'

Including Judith Ensor? She'd evidently liked Voss, which wasn't surprising. Good-looking, good-humoured, a good line in blarney. A way of talking to women that made them feel special . . . whereas her husband had been, to her at least, a very different proposition.

'She was like that, Lisa—always had to be different—her clothes, her house . . .' She glanced round in a dissatisfied way at the pristine, conventional room which had everything that money could buy. 'It was all right, if you didn't look beneath the surface—I mean, she wasn't too fussed about housework, for all she'd spend hours doing up old furniture and things.'

Her lips pursed together as if she'd been sucking a lemon. The female half of the Voss partnership, at least, had cut no ice with her.

Abigail snapped the elastic band round the letters Judith had conveniently 'found', while Judith drank her sherry and poured herself another, and stared at the carpet while tears gathered in her eyes. 'You see how it was,' she said. This time she didn't bother about her mascara.

'May I take these with me? I'll give you a receipt.'

'I don't want them back, I never want to see them again. You can keep them.' Her voice tinkled like icicles.

Abigail understood what she meant. In Judith's position she wouldn't have wanted them back, either. They explicitly charted the progress of Lisa Voss's affair with Philip Ensor, the secret meetings when Dermot had been away and Ensor supposedly on business elsewhere, the growing angst about not being able to be together permanently. Then the tone of the letters changed. Despite the care they'd taken to keep their affair secret, Dermot had somehow found out, and was taking it badly, refusing even to discuss a divorce, becoming abusive . . . it was in the last letter that Ensor was told that Lisa was pregnant.

'How did Dermot find out about Lisa and your husband, Mrs Ensor?'

She shrugged. 'How should I know that?' She avoided Abigail's eye.

Jealousy was an ugly word. An ugly emotion. Maybe it was an assumption on Abigail's part, though she didn't feel it was unjustified, that Judith Ensor was not childless from choice. How cruel then, to find out that her husband's mistress, with two children of her own already, was pregnant with her own husband's child. She said gently, 'Was it before or after Lisa Voss died that you moved here? Whose suggestion was it, yours or your husband's?'

'It was before, but does it matter? We both wanted to leave the place behind.'

That was understandable, on Judith's part, at least. Who would want to live within spitting distance of reminders of her husband's infidelities? But it also implied that she'd known what was going on, and that it was probably the cause of the split between the families.

Standing up, ready to leave, Abigail asked Judith Ensor, 'Why didn't you tell us this before?'

She sat in her baby-blue suit on her flowered settee, a sparkly little brooch in the form of an arch-backed cat with green eyes on her neat lapel, her beautiful grey eyes wide and unblinking. 'I always liked Dermot, he was good fun, and if he had killed Philip—well, it was only what Philip deserved, wasn't it?'

*   *   *

Down at Milford Road Police Station, Fitzallan was being shown into the nearest room, which happened to be one of the interview rooms. He'd appeared at the front desk with a curt request to see the senior officer on the Patti Ryman case, stating that he had something important to say. When the request came, Mayo shrugged on his jacket, adjusted his tie, drank the dregs of yet another coffee, and went downstairs. Summoning a PC to join them, he introduced himself, saying, 'I believe you've already answered the questions my officers put to you—is there something you've remembered?'

He spoke more impatiently than he knew. The whole station was alive with activity and tension, events were piling up, occupying his thoughts and his time—notably this latest worrying development, the disappearance of the little girl, Allie. He couldn't see how, yet, but if it was a coincidence, unconnected with the other happenings they were working on, then he was a Dutchman. He was in no mood to put up with time-wasting grumbles from the public, wherever they came from.

An abrupt man with deep-set eyes, not given to smiling easily at any time, now Fitzallan

278

positively glowered. Tall and broad-shouldered, in a casually expensive suit, he dominated the cheerlessly functional surroundings, throwing himself on to the hard chair offered without seeming to notice its comfort or otherwise. Then he startled Mayo by asking abruptly, 'First of all, do I need to go into my personal background? Are you familiar with what happened to my wife some years ago?' He added tersely, 'The officers who've already questioned me seemed to know all about it.'

'It's part of their job to know. I remember the case, too.'

'Yes. Well. I only mentioned it because I think it has some bearing on what I've come about.' He took a moment to organize his thoughts, and Mayo, beginning to be intrigued by the man and his purpose in coming here, didn't push him.

Fitz looked down at his hands, breathing deeply. He was fully aware that he wasn't one of the world's best communicators, and this was something he'd never yet been able to talk about freely, not to anyone: those reasons why it had been necessary for him to have the attic flat at Edwina Lodge as a bolt hole, where he could paint, and leave behind for a measure of time the woman who had been his wife, his responsibility, his burden but ultimately, as he'd continually reassured himself, his enduring love.

Elspeth, cool and beautiful when he'd married her, neurotic and unstable within a few years, bringing the structure of their lives crashing down. Her illness, a disturbing and little understood dysfunction with an unpronounceable name, had made her impossible to live with, impossible to abandon. It had resulted in a steady erosion of their marriage, problems with drink, drugs, suicide attempts. There were those who'd urged him to have her 'put in care' but, hellish though life had become, it would have shamed him not to cherish her as he had in the days before her illness, at least to try and love her and care for her as much as when she'd been well, and whole. All the same, when eventually she did manage to take her own life in that monstrous way, he blamed himself for not listening to the advice.

That day, she'd pumped into herself a cocktail of drugs and drink, taken her car out and driven it at speed along a busy road, with the inevitable conclusion: an appalling pile-up, with the people in the other car, an eight-year-old boy and the driver, his mother, being killed instantly.

'Mr Fitzallan?'

He blinked rapidly, then opened his briefcase and passed a sheet of grey drawing paper across the desk. 'I think you should look at this.' It was a child's drawing. There was a silence as Mayo studied it.

'Who drew this?'

'Allie, Voss's little girl. I'm doing a portrait of her, trying to, and she likes drawing, so I usually give her pencils and paper and let her draw while she sits for me. Can't expect a little girl to sit unoccupied for any length of time.'

It was a drawing in thick crayon, not remarkable for its talent. It was crude and childish, but it made the hairs on the back of Mayo's neck stand on end. The sheet of paper was large, and the simple outline filled it. A staircase in profile, with a man at the top, standing with arms outstretched. At the foot of the stairs lay a woman, flat out, arms and legs stretched out like a fly. Against the grey background, the crayoned lines were slashed on to the paper, heavy and thick, the chosen colours angry deep red and black. The circle that represented the man's face had been furiously scribbled over in black.

'Why did you bring this here? You said you thought it had some relevance?'

'You're familiar with art therapy? The theory that you get disturbed people to paint or draw, in the hopes that they'll bring out their anger, or fear, or whatever's hidden inside and troubling them. Something like that, anyway— a simplistic way of putting it, no doubt, but I'm no expert. My wife had years of therapy, it was one of the things they tried ... But it wasn't deliberate on my part when I gave Allie a paper and pencil, it was only for her to amuse herself while I painted her.' He paused, eyeing them from under his brows. 'I suppose you knew that Voss's wife died from a fall down the stairs?'

'She fell downstairs?' Mayo had known only that Lisa Voss had died during pregnancy, there'd been no reason to assume her death hadn't been caused by some condition arising from that. 'What are you suggesting?'

'I'm not suggesting anything. Only that Allie's apparently had a history of sleepwalking and nightmares since her mother died—and you must agree, it's a pretty morbid subject for a child to choose. And now that she's disappeared . . .' He left the rest of the sentence unsaid.

After a moment or two, Mayo said, 'Right, Mr Fitzallan. Thank you for bringing this to our attention. Leave it with me, if you would.'

Fitz stood up. He hadn't expected it to be any better received. He wasn't sure whether he ought to have spoken at all, whether he'd made a fool of himself or not, uneasily aware that this policeman might well think the picture nothing more than a childish scrawl, and himself some sort of crackpot amateur psychiatrist. He hesitated, then decided to say nothing more, took his leave and strode out.

*　　　*　　　*

When Fitzallan had gone, Mayo took the drawing back to his office and then stood in front of the window, staring out. The sky was a soft, heavy pearl-grey, one of those still, windless, moody evenings of late summer. It would be dark in an hour. A pigeon sat on the sill of one of the Town Hall windows opposite, listening to the grinding of gears at the traffic lights, the hiss of air brakes, looking too bored to move. The top of a red double-decker bus cruised past . . .

Rather than money, perhaps the source of the quarrel between Voss and Ensor had been Lisa Voss.

He turned his back on the window and went to look at the childish, disturbing drawing where it lay on his desk, depicting—what? Something Allie had actually witnessed? Was that scribbled-out face Ensor's, or was the whole thing something imaginary, an invented scene to explain to herself the deeply disturbing shock of her mother's death? Was it even possible that the child had seen it happening in reality? And told her father? Or had she done other similar drawings, which he'd seen, and drawn his own conclusions? If Voss had had reason to believe it possible that Ensor had pushed his wife downstairs, it was more than a motive for him to have killed the other man.

Yet why should Philip Ensor, if he *was* guilty of murdering Lisa Voss, have come to Lavenstock to meet her husband? It would surely have been more logical for him to have kept out of the way. Why should he have killed Lisa, anyway—unless they'd quarrelled—if they'd been having an affair? He picked up the phone. 'Somebody get me details of the inquest on a woman called Lisa Voss,' he requested, giving the necessary details. 'Get them to fax it through. I'll be in my office for a while yet.'

When it came, he read it through carefully. The inquest recorded a verdict of accidental death. She had apparently tripped over the loose belt of her dressing gown and fallen to the bottom of a flight of polished, open-tread stairs. Her neck had been broken. She'd been alone in the house, except for the children, who hadn't wakened. She'd been discovered the next morning by the cleaning lady when she let herself in. Dermot Voss had been expected home the following day, and had in fact arrived about four o'clock, to find his wife dead.

'Check out Voss's flight from Belgrade,' Mayo said to Farrar, slapping the details on to Farrar's desk in the CID room. 'See what time he actually arrived. I'm on my way up to Edwina Lodge. When Inspector Moon comes in, ask her to meet me there.'

*   *   *

The doorbell rang yet again. Voices sounded in the hall, then the Superintendent came into the drawing room. 'Nothing new, yet, I'm afraid,' he said gently. 'There's a call out for Miss

284

Kendrick's car, as you know, but it hasn't been seen yet.' His face was grim and set. 'We still don't seem to be able to contact anyone else at Simla.'

'*What?*' Dermot looked up, his eyes wild. 'What did you say?'

'We're finding difficulty getting hold of Mr Kendrick. He doesn't seem to be at home, nor does Mrs Loxley.'

'Imogen?' Sarah suddenly remembered that she and Imogen had tickets for an open lecture on William Morris in the Ferraby Hall, part of Lavenstock College. She looked for the hundredth time at the clock on the mantel. The lecture would be over, they'd be well into the cheese and wine which was to follow by now. She hadn't given anything else a thought since hearing about Allie, but she couldn't understand why Imogen hadn't let her know if there'd been a change of plan. The disappearance of everyone from whom she might have expected moral support suddenly took on a frightening aspect.

'*No one there at all?* Are you sure?' For a moment Dermot looked nonplussed, then his eyes narrowed. Sarah saw that his mind was working in that peculiarly fast and connective way it sometimes did. Then he said, coldly and deliberately, 'There's something you should know about Francis Kendrick.'

'*Francis* Kendrick?' Mayo's voice was sharp as a whip.

285

'There was an incident—when he was a young professor at Cambridge. He played the organ at one of the churches—there was a young choirboy . . . It was all hushed up, just a piece of gossip—I only came across it incidentally because we happened to be making a documentary about his college at the time. Several people thought the boy was being mischievous, because Kendrick had reprimanded him over something, but . . .' He shrugged his shoulders.

Mayo was staring at him in speechless disbelief which echoed Sarah's own. When he found words, he said, incredulously, 'A young girl's been murdered—you have two of your own, one's disappeared—and you kept all this to yourself?'

'This was *Francis* Kendrick, not his sister. Choirboys and little girls—hardly the same, are they?' But Dermot avoided his eyes.

Sarah stood up abruptly and left the room.

'Anyway, I reckoned you'd have found out,' Dermot was saying, cockily—that's your business, isn't it?'

'We've no reason to go into a man's past unless he's a suspect.'

'Well, you've plenty bloody reason to suspect him now—what are you going to do about it?'

'My men are effecting entry to the premises now.' It was the way people expected the police to speak. He often found it useful when he was stalling.

286

Sarah came back, holding a manila envelope. 'Can I have a word with you, in private, please?' she said to Mayo. 'Come into the small sitting room.'

When they emerged, the telephone was once more ringing in the hall. The shrill, insistent note of the old-fashioned instrument, unlike the present-day warble, made everyone jump. Jenny went to answer it. Everyone grew silent, listening to what she said. 'What? *What*? Yes, I'll tell him. I expect he'll be over immediately,'

CHAPTER EIGHTEEN

Mayo sprinted across the few intervening yards between Edwina Lodge and Simla, though he didn't know why he was running. It was far too late for that.

His thoughts were spinning, and in the space of those few seconds all the reasoning which had caused him to send Abigail off to Solihull again was overturned. He'd been so sure he'd had the right answer. But could he have been wrong—had he been dangerously guilty of manipulating the facts to fit a theory? Maybe Patti's murderer *had* been someone with a penchant for young bodies, little girls—or little boys, come to that—after all.

The dismal hall, its upper reaches dark with shadows that swooped down from the ceiling, was lit with one central light that barely made inroads into the gloom. It was enough, however, for Mayo to see everything that needed to be seen: a longer shadow depending from one of the newel posts, a Modigliani figure, grotesquely elongated, its own shadow dancing alongside as it gently swung, a heavy, carved-oak upright chair kicked away and lying on its back.

Ison had been sent for and since he was at home when the summons came, he covered the short distance within minutes and was there almost as soon as Mayo. The body was cut down, and after a brief examination Ison was able to estimate that Francis Kendrick had been dead for only a few hours.

'It appears to be a straightforward suicide. No note, you say? Unusual. They usually do, poor sods, don't they, if it's only to leave the blame with someone else?'

That was true, though Mayo had often suspected that more notes were ever destroyed than came to the notice of the police. 'Hardly been time to look, yet,' he said.

Kendrick was dressed in his old, baggy cotton trousers and a short-sleeved cotton shirt, with a complete absence of that self-absorbed vanity of some suicides—those who tidied their houses, wore clean clothes before they finished it all, concerned to the end with leaving behind a good impression of themselves, not even a thought of cruelty to the living. Anyone who'd seen the number of suicides he had couldn't fail to be struck by how much humanity clung to its vision of itself.

'What's that in his pockets?'

A piece of paper protruded very slightly from the pocket of Kendrick's shirt. Extracting it in the prescribed manner, Mayo read aloud the four words written on it. *'The book is finished.'* 'And what,' he asked the doctor, 'is that supposed to mean?'

'Some cryptic reference to his life having come an end?' suggested Ison imaginatively.

Mayo blew out his lips. He could imagine some people putting it like that, but not Kendrick. Surely too uncharacteristically dramatic a gesture for such an apparently unemotional man as Francis Kendrick. More likely it meant just what it said, that the book he was working on was finished, it was ready to be dealt with. He, like everyone else, had ultimately had his little vanities. He could not leave the world behind without making sure that something of him would live on after he'd gone.

A uniformed constable came into the room. 'There's an unsealed letter here, sir—it was on the kitchen table.'

Reading between the lines of the hastily scrawled note from Imogen, addressed to Hope and Francis, explaining that she had suddenly returned to Brussels, it wasn't difficult to guess at the state of mind which had

289

made her leave so precipitately. 'I shall be back in a few days, either to collect my belongings, or to return permanently. It will all depend on Tom,' she wrote sadly.

They were not a happy family, the Kendricks.

But there were no more notes, nothing from Hope to say why, or where, she had taken the child, and nothing more written by her brother Francis to indicate what had brought him to take this final step. Remembering the last time he'd seen him, the unexpected sympathy he'd aroused, Mayo felt he might hazard a guess. He hoped he was wrong, that the reason Francis Kendrick had taken his own life, in a way that Mayo always found particularly gruesome and horrible, was not because of the weight of his sins preying on his conscience. But either way, the conclusions were not particularly comfortable.

'Sir, they've found the little girl!'

'Found?' All Mayo's sense of dread was contained in the word as he turned to Jenny Platt, framed in the open doorway.

'She's all right, on her way home with Mr Fitzallan.'

'*Who* did you say?'

'Fitzallan, sir. DI Moon's just arrived, and she took a telephone call from him. He found Miss Kendrick and the little girl. At their country cottage in Shropshire. They're on their way back now.'

He knew the full story now, what had led up to Ensor's murder and why Patti's death had followed. He and Abigail had exchanged information and the whole sorry scene was clear. He could now act, but there was no hurry.

About eight o'clock, a car drew up outside Edwina Lodge. Fitzallan's Range Rover. Fitzallan, dark-browed, strode into the house with Allie in his arms, fast asleep, her head cradled against his shoulder. Her face was dirty, she had lost her hairslide but otherwise she seemed unharmed and opened her eyes for a moment, smiling sleepily when Sarah put Angel into her arms before following Fitz as he carried the child upstairs to her room.

Hope Kendrick was beyond questioning that night. Possibly overcome by the realization of what she'd done, she sat rigidly in the passenger seat of the Range Rover until she was requested to come into the house. She had to be told about her brother's death and it was done as gently as possible but, dazed and emotionally exhausted, she hardly seemed to take it in.

'You'll not get anything out of her tonight,' Ison said. 'I'll give her a sedative and you can question her in the morning. Is there anyone who can be with her? I wouldn't advise her being left on her own.'

'We've already contacted Imogen Loxley in Brussels. She and her husband are coming over. I should think Mrs Bailey can be persuaded to stay with her until they get here.'

Fitzallan, meanwhile, was ready to explain his reasons for charging up to Shropshire, when a call to the local police there would have simplified matters. Did he have some personal stake in the fortunes of this family? Mayo wondered, and saw from the way he and Sarah Wilmot looked at each other there wasn't much room for doubt what that was. 'I had this idea,' he said. 'I knew the Kendricks had a cottage in Shropshire, not exactly where, though I'd a fair idea, so I decided to go and have a look. I suspected,' he said gloweringly, 'that you wouldn't take my idea seriously, any more than you did the drawing. In any case,' he confessed with a smile that was all the more disarming for being unexpected, 'I wasn't all that convinced myself. I went, without giving it too much thought.'

Mayo cut short further explanations. Fitzallan would have to be dealt with later, Hope Kendrick, too, but both could wait. Now that the child was safe, there were other matters to be attended to. He turned to Allie's father.

'Dermot Voss, we'd like you to come down to the station and help us with our inquiries into the murder of Patricia Mary Ryman.'

CHAPTER NINETEEN

Mayo drove slowly back to the station. After the last few dry, sunless, still and cheerless days the weather had taken a turn. With the new moon, a wind had sprung up, bringing rain with it. It had become heavy by the time Mayo returned from Edwina Lodge, with clouds obscuring the moon. The station, with all its lights on, glowed like a lighted ship against the black surrounding hills as he made a dash for the door.

Abigail arrived just behind him. By the time they had finished setting out the line their questioning was to take, despite her resolve, she was drinking coffee, and making no excuses for herself.

'Those children,' she said softly. 'Didn't he give a thought to his children?'

'I don't for one minute imagine that Voss gives a thought to anybody but himself. There's nothing to him. He's one-dimensional. Come on, I think we've left him cooling his heels long enough.'

They went downstairs and Mayo stood in front of the table that separated them from Voss, leaning forward, his hands flat on the surface. He spoke to the man he'd once thought of as a pleasant acquaintance, with whom he'd shared social congress. 'OK, we're ready to start, and I want it straight. Don't give me any bull on this. You've already wasted enough of our time as it is.'

Dermot Voss lolled in the opposite chair, smoking, a faint amusement on his face, unperturbed by the presence of a detective superintendent, a detective inspector, a sergeant and a constable. 'Do I have the impression you're about to interrogate me?' he asked, his smile deepening.

'I don't know why else you think we've brought you down here. And I don't much care *what* impression you have. What matters is that you answer my questions.'

'Dear me. Well, fire ahead.'

Mayo settled himself into the chair next to Abigail, taking his time, spreading his papers out on the table in front of him. Voss had totally dismissed the idea of being represented by a solicitor.

'Interview commences eleven thirty. Those present are Superintendent Mayo, DI Moon, DS Kite and WDC Platt.' He nodded to Jenny Platt, ready to take back-up notes, then turned back to Voss. 'First of all, I'd like you to explain to me what you were doing between seven thirty a.m, and five past eight on Monday, eleventh September.'

'I told you, I stopped at Patel's to get cigarettes. There was a queue, and God knows how long it took me to get served. When I came out again my car had gone. Disappeared. Vanished. Into thin air.'

'What were you doing between that time and arriving back at Edwina Lodge at five past eight?'

'Well, I cast around for a bit, looking for the car. It took me some time to grasp what had happened. At first, I thought I must have left it down that street, what's it called?—Allegar Street—and forgotten—you know, the one that turns off Albert Road just past Patel's. Sometimes, if there's no parking space outside the shop, I do leave it there.'

'Must've taken you all of two minutes to find out you hadn't.'

'Plus more time, wandering a bit further, wondering if someone had moved it for a joke. It *has* happened to me before, you know,' he added, as their faces said what they thought of this as an excuse. 'It must have been about ten to eight when I got back to the house.'

'Mrs Baverstock has stated that it was five past eight when you arrived back at Edwina Lodge.'

'And who's to prove her word against mine? That nosy bitch would say anything against me.'

'Your sister-in-law, Sarah Wilmot, didn't leave the house until after eight o'clock.'

'All right, so I arrived a bit later than I thought. I wasn't checking my watch every five minutes! Now, suppose you tell me something—this is all to do with that girl, Patti,

295

being killed, right?' His good humour was slipping a bit. 'So give me one good reason why you think I should be concerned in that?'

'We'll come to that. First I'm going to put forward what we believe happened, then you can tell me where you think we're wrong. I think you called for cigarettes, yes, but I also think you intended to waylay Patti, which you did—you followed her into Ellington Close and then into the wood, and killed her there.'

'You lot—you really are something else!'

'I haven't finished yet. You must have had one hell of a shock when you came back and found your car missing. If it had still been there, you'd have been away and nobody the wiser. So you did the best you could—got out of sight as quick as possible, back to Edwina Lodge, where everyone would be out, as you thought. I don't suppose you knew Tina Baverstock was at home on Mondays.' He saw by the flicker of Voss's eyes that he'd hit the nail on the head.

'Well, naturally I came back—I had to sort myself out, report the car missing, get picked up and all that. And all right, I did see Patti. We met at the entrance to the Close, as a matter of fact, as I was going back to the house. She asked me if I could hear a noise. It sounded like an animal in pain, and it was coming from the direction of the wood. She ran in and I followed. I found her in tears, crouched beside a dead cat. It had been mutilated and she was

296

terribly upset, she said she'd have to tell the owners. I offered to do it for her but she wouldn't have that. In the end, I had to leave her and go home. I was due on an important assignment that morning, and I had to report my car missing and arrange for another to pick me up.'

'This is a substantially different version of your first story.'

'Since she was alive and well when I left her, I didn't see the need to complicate matters.'

'It complicates things a good deal more when people take it on themselves to lie to us.' Dermot looked pained. 'And that was the last you saw of her?'

'It was.'

Like all good liars, he was keeping to the truth as much as he could, but there wasn't enough of it to support his story. 'What you haven't given me,' he complained, 'is one plausible reason why I should have killed that girl?'

'It might become clearer to you if we went a bit further back, then—to the Saturday night Ensor was killed.'

Dermot frowned, puzzled. 'Ah yes, the man on the allotments.'

'The man who was your very good friend, Philip Ensor,' Mayo reminded him sharply.

'Oh, *Philip* Ensor,' he said, as though there were other Ensors who had met with the same unfortunate end.

'Don't pussyfoot around, Mr Voss, we've already established how far your acquaintance with him went.'

'I knew him at one time, yes. Slightly.'

'Rather more than that, I believe.'

Abigail bent over the briefcase which stood on the floor to extract a bundle of what looked like letters. She put them on the table, without saying what they were. Creamy yellow paper, brown ink. Dermot rocked back in his chair and stared at the ceiling.

'You were in fact very good friends,' she said.

'At one time, maybe. Not of late.'

'Why was that? Did you quarrel?'

'They moved house, we lost touch, you know how it is, it's the women who keep these things going, and Lisa didn't bother.'

'But the friendship was mainly between you and Philip Ensor, wasn't it? You'd known each other for several years, I think.' Her hand went out absently and touched the creamy yellow bundle. She slid out one of the letters and laid it flat, facing herself.

'Can I have another cigarette?' Voss asked, lowering the chair and leaning forward while it was lit for him.

'That's true,' he said eventually, 'to a point. I met Ensor when we were marooned in an airport—Athens, I think. We got talking and struck up a rapport. Then a few weeks later, by an amazing coincidence, we found ourselves in adjoining seats on another flight home from

Germany. Discovered we lived not far from each other, liked golf. One thing led to another . . .' He shrugged.

'And you did, in fact, become close friends.'

'We used to see quite a bit of each other. Our wives weren't all that keen. But they went along with it. I think Judith was inclined to be jealous of Lisa—she couldn't have a child, and we had two.'

'And maybe she began to have further cause for jealousy. Especially when your wife became pregnant again.'

Dermot raised an eyebrow, apparently not seeing fit to reply to that, so Mayo went on.

'By that time, they'd moved from Milton Keynes—at Mrs Ensor's insistence, since she didn't like the association that was growing between her husband and your wife.'

'I don't know anything about that.'

'That's not exactly true, is it?' Mayo tapped the letters. 'It's all here—what was going on between them, your reactions when you found out.' He let that sink in for a while, then suddenly changed tack. 'The night Ensor was killed, you were staying at the Saracen's Head, here in Lavenstock. You gave it out you had food poisoning.'

'I did have food poisoning.'

'If you say so. But your sister-in-law ate the same food and wasn't affected. It was nothing but a ploy to slip out and meet Ensor, wasn't it? At a place you'd sussed out when you'd previously stayed at the Saracen's, when you were house-hunting.'

'That's a load of rubbish. And I repeat, I did not go out and meet Ensor.'

'I must tell you that we have a witness who saw you.'

'Probably when I slipped out for a breath of air for a few minutes, after I'd thrown up.'

'The witness recognized you and will swear he saw you and Ensor fighting.'

'You can't witness something that didn't happen,' Voss said, but with much less conviction.

'There were, in fact, two separate witnesses. Perhaps you were too occupied to remember the car that drove away—but you did remember Patti, when you met her later, as being the girl who'd walked through the allotments when you and Ensor were fighting, which is why you killed her.'

'No. I'd as little reason to kill her as I had to kill Ensor.'

Mayo began sifting through the papers on the table and soon found what he was looking for. 'Do you recognize this?' He held up the polythene-encased photograph of Ensor that Sarah had found, then turned it over so that Voss could read what was written on the back, explaining what he was doing for the benefit of the tape recording.

Voss stared at it. 'Where the hell did you get this?'

'It was found in the bottom of your wife's jewel box, by Sarah Wilmot.'

'Sarah?' He sounded as though he'd had a blow, right where it hurt.

'She found it a couple of days ago but she'd never met Philip Ensor and knew nothing about him. She only connected it yesterday with the E-fit picture we'd issued of him— which wasn't all that good a likeness, but as near as we could get. Show him the other exhibit, Inspector Moon, if you will.'

Abigail held up the drawing that Allie had done. The colour drained from his face. 'What are you trying to do to me? Who drew that?'

'It's one of your daughter's drawings—Allie.'

For once he was silenced.

'The night your wife died, you took an earlier flight from Belgrade and arrived home a day sooner than you were expected. We've checked with the airline, and we've found a taxi that left you at your home at ten o'clock in the evening. The driver remembered you very well, on account of your photographic gear. I believe a quarrel blew up almost immediately between you and your wife about her association with Ensor, which ended with you pushing her down the stairs.'

'Your imagination's in overdrive, Mayo,' Voss said, stubbing out his cigarette. But his hand had begun to shake, and he avoided looking at anyone.

'But that's a substantially correct account of

301

what happened, isn't it? You must have woken your daughter with the noise, and she saw it happen. She's pushed it to the back of her mind, as children—and not only children—do with traumatic events that are too terrible to deal with. But it's been there in her subconscious ever since, manifesting itself in sleepwalking, drawings like this . . .'

'Stop it!'

Voss put his folded arms on the table, laid his head on them and began to weep. 'I didn't kill Lisa. And I never meant to kill the others,' he mumbled indistinctly.

'Will you raise your head, Mr Voss, and say that clearly for the benefit of the tape?'

There was no response, except for the sound of his weeping. Eventually he raised his congested face and after being prompted again, repeated what he'd said.

'Why don't you tell us exactly what happened?'

'What'll happen to me if I do?' he asked abjectly.

Mayo looked at him as he swiped the tears away with his hands. 'That's not for me to say. I've already cautioned you, and I must warn you that we have enough evidence to support a charge against you of murdering Patti Ryman.'

'What evidence?'

'We found this pen at the scene of the crime. Do you identify it as one belonging to your wife, which you'd occasionally used since her death?'

'It looks like the one I bought for Lisa, yes.'

'We've also found traces of burnt, bloodstained clothing in your garden incinerator, fibres of which match those found on Patti's school blazer, and—'

'I didn't push Lisa down the stairs! She tripped over that damned belt—she'd been warned often enough about leaving it unfastened. I did come home early, and yes, we did have a row—she'd been asking me for a divorce, she was pregnant, and I knew the child wasn't mine. The children were asleep, and she was already undressed, ready for bed. She said she wasn't going to argue any more and was going downstairs to make some tea. I followed her and grabbed at her at the top of the steps, but she twisted away from me and fell. I swear I didn't push her downstairs. If—if Allie saw it, it may have looked like that to her, but it was an accident. I tried to grab her but her dressing gown was satiny stuff and it slipped through my fingers . . . She was dead when I got to the bottom of the stairs. I didn't know what to do, so I just left, walked to the station and took a train to London, came back next day as if I'd just arrived. Nobody ever questioned me.'

There was a long silence.

'And on Monday the eleventh of September?'

'It's basically true what I told you. I stopped the car outside Patel's to get some cigarettes and saw Patti coming along with the papers. I'd recognized her a few days earlier, when that Baverstock bitch was bawling her out about leaving her bike outside the house. I went out to tell her it was my house and the paper girl could leave her bike where she damn well liked. God, I got a shock when I saw who the girl was! That hair, you know, impossible to mistake.' He was speaking fast, his words tumbling over each other, anxious to justify himself. 'I was pretty certain she'd recognized me, too, but I couldn't be sure. It happened as I told you on the Monday morning, I went with her into the wood, we saw the cat and all that, but then, as we were leaving, she suddenly burst out, "It was you, wasn't it, the other night by the allotments? You were fighting—I shall have to tell the police, but it'll be all right, Mr Voss. I looked back but he was standing up, so it couldn't have been you who killed him, could it?" She was so innocent, so naive. But if she'd told you what she'd seen, it would've been all up with me. She walked away and—I hardly remember how or why—I picked a piece of iron up that was lying around and hit her with it. Then I went back to pick my car up and found it had gone.'

He'd walked away, just as he'd walked away from Ensor—and his own wife. He'd gone into the wood with Patti, and emerged a few minutes later, without a soul having witnessed his entry or exit from the wood.

'I'm sorry I did it, I never would have killed her if I'd thought about it,' he said, beginning to weep again.

'And you wouldn't have killed Philip Ensor either, if you'd thought about it?'

'That was different. We were fighting. I knocked him down once and he got up. I picked a stone up and hit him with it. I left him lying in a puddle—I thought it would cool him off. How was I to know he'd die?'

'Tell me exactly what you were fighting about—how he came to be in Lavenstock that night.'

'He'd been threatening me. I'd had a letter from his wife, Judith, telling me what was going on. I found it hard to believe—I'd always thought Philip a decent sort, we'd always got on well, but he was hardly the sort a woman would die for.' Seeming not to have noticed his unfortunate choice of words, he went on, 'We'd been going through a bad patch, Lisa and I . . . she wanted me to get another job where I could spend more time with her and the children, for one thing. But I never thought things were that bad. It was hard to stomach the idea of her and Philip. I wrote her some rather strong letters, telling her she must give him up.'

'You mean threatening letters, don't you?'

'What do you think? She'd been playing around while I was in the thick of it in Bosnia. I wasn't exactly happy about that. I told her she'd better come to her senses, or else. She wrote and told Ensor—those letters, I suppose,' he said, gesturing to the pile on the table, 'telling him that I'd threatened to kill her. The baby was his, you know. He was abroad when she died, but when he came back and heard about it, he threatened to take the letters to the police, unless . . .' He couldn't finish the sentence but Mayo finished it for him.

'Unless you paid him back the money you owed him. Your wife mentioned the debt, several times, in her letters.'

'Yes, she would. She didn't like me not paying it back. I don't think he was bothered about it, he had a good job and never squandered his money—but I'd have paid it back if I could. Wouldn't you hate the idea of owing money to a man who'd been sleeping with your wife? When he began to pester me, I paid some of it back, but eventually I told him that was it. I'd no more to give him.'

'What was his reaction to that?'

'He said he had a proposition to put to me. He'd found out about my move to Lavenstock and demanded I met him that night, which I did.'

'Where?'

'Where? Oh, I didn't want him inside the hotel where Sarah might see us, so I arranged to meet him outside, in the car park. He was late.'

'He didn't park in the hotel car park.'

'No, it's not very big and there was a function on that night, and all the spaces round about were taken up, too. He said he'd had to shove his car up some back alley. He wasn't the sort to let things upset him, usually, but I think it had annoyed him that he couldn't find anywhere. At any rate, he became abusive with me over—over Lisa's death. I thought he meant to kill me, but I pushed him down and ran off—anywhere, I didn't know that road led to the allotments—but he followed me and— well, I've told you what happened then.'

There was silence when he'd finished.

'Thank you, Mr Voss. We'll take a break, and then go through all this once again. And I'd advise you to change your mind about getting a solicitor.'

EPILOGUE

Down a short, steep drive leading off the country lane, there is the house, a small, irregular brick-and-timber Elizabethan manor, tucked into a fold of the hill. Sarah sits curled in the window-seat, reading a letter.

The first time she saw Fitz's house was nearly three months ago, shortly after Dermot's arrest, on a warm October day. The front door and several windows had been wide open, and the sounds of a violin concerto floated across the garden.

'That's Mrs Mac's radio,' Fitz explained. 'She's tuned in to Classic FM all day.' But she'd evidently heard the car, and had come into the hall to greet them, a raw-boned, ginger-haired Scots woman with a soft, sibilant Highland accent. 'Och, I was not expecting you so soon! I'll be having your tea ready in half an hour,' she said. 'Maybe the wee girls would like to help me make some drop scones while you two make yourselves comfortable?' and bore the children away.

'She doesn't usually come over all stage-Scottish like that,' Fitz said. 'She's either embarrassed or wants you to get a good impression.'

'I'm impressed, all right,' Sarah said, following him as he led the way from the wide, stone-

flagged hall into a pleasant room with a big stone fireplace where now a huge log fire burns. The room was slightly shabby, the slipcovers faded, some of the rugs on the wide polished boards threadbare, but the furniture was old and beautiful and everything bore witness to Mrs McLaren's meticulous Scottish housekeeping, right down to the squarely placed cushions and the single pot plant on a mat, dead centre of a shining, gate-legged oak table. 'It's a lovely, lovely house,' Sarah said.

Fitz's shoulders relaxed. 'I've been hoping you'd say that. I didn't know how you'd react. It was a small farm at one time, with quite a bit of land round it when my parents bought it, but now there's only the house.'

'And the garden,' Sarah had said, looking out of the low-silled, latticed windows on to a stone flagged terrace with a garden beyond, glowing with dahlias, asters and chrysanthemums, beech trees at the bottom just turning gold. 'That's beautiful.'

'I'll take you round later, though it's no thanks to me it looks the way it does. My father moved into a cottage in the village with no garden to speak of when I married, so he's very happy to look after this. It was my mother who laid it out and we just try to keep it as she did.' He gave a gusty sigh. 'Like the rest of the house, I'm afraid. Nobody's done anything to it for years. Elspeth and I were always going to do it up, but somehow we never did.' He could mention her name now,

not yet easily, not entirely without pain, but without too much awkwardness. 'You can do what you want with it, when we're married.'

That was in October, and Sarah Wilmot is now Sarah Fitzallan. She looks up from her letter at the now familiar room. The changes she's made have been small—a few lamps and some of Fitz's skyscapes that she's persuaded him to let her hang, huge jars of leaves and berries, new loose covers, supplied by Lois French, but it's made all the difference . . . It has a heart, it's a home now, for her and Fitz, Lucy and Allie.

'A ready-made family, Fitz' she'd reminded him, gently. 'It's a lot to be taking on.' A lifetime's commitment, maybe.

Dermot had been kept in custody, awaiting trial. Superintendent Mayo refused to speculate about what would happen when the trial came to court. He'd had nasty surprises from juries before. Dermot refused to plead guilty, and the police might fail to secure a murder conviction—but whatever happened, there were huge difficulties regarding the children's future, and though there was no question for Sarah about where their immediate future lay, she could see Fitz might not feel the same about it. 'If it's a problem—'

'That's a bonus, not a problem,' he'd interrupted firmly. Straight down the line, Fitz. He'd had it all worked out, he wasn't under any illusions that it was all going to be plain sailing, but he'd accepted what it would mean and it hadn't made any difference. Why had she thought

311

it would? If anybody could cope, it was Fitz.

'I love both of them dearly,' he told her gruffly, 'but if they were the most horrible brats in Christendom, I'd still love them for your sake.'

'Fitz,' she'd said, laughing, close to tears, 'that's almost a romantic thing to say!'

'What I mean is—' But what he'd meant to say had been interrupted by the arrival of tea.

'I made them, I made the drop scones all by myself!' Lucy said, presenting a plate of rather odd-sized and misshapen scones, liberally spread with butter.

'No, you didn't! Angel and me helped,' said Allie.

'I put the batter on the griddle from the spoon!'
'I turned them over!'

'That's why they're such a yukky shape!' countered Lucy, getting in the last word, as usual.

'Well, it doesn't matter who did what, they're delicious,' Sarah said, placatingly. 'You'd better show me how to make them before Mrs Mac goes back to Scotland.'

It's now two months since Mrs Mac departed to live with her sister in Arisaig, the garden is winter-bare, the children are looking for cones from the Scots pine, to take to school and gild for Christmas decorations. Allie stands under the tree, looking up, reminding Sarah unbearably of the day she'd stood under the sequoia, the day of the welcome party at Simla, and the notes of 'Alice Where Art Thou?' sounding through the house.

'Do you think the children would like to have the Polyphon?' Hope had asked, when she was clearing out the house. Then, painfully, seeing Sarah's face, 'No, better not.'

Allie had talked constantly at first about the wonderful day when she was unexpectedly taken out of school by Hope, when they had the long ride in the car and she was given all sorts of treats and Hope was so kind to her. Everyone was so interested in what she had to tell them, but after a while they stopped questioning her and by now it's only a memory. Any scars left are Hope's.

Haltingly, at intervals, Hope had forced herself to tell Sarah everything, about Francis, and Sven, and the child which had never been born, and the unsatisfied longings which had built up over the years. The events surrounding Patti's death had brought it all back, and suddenly there had been a confusion in her head, a compulsion to take Allie away, to have her just to herself. The madness hadn't lasted long. If Fitz hadn't appeared that night, she would have brought Allie back the next day, she swore that.

Sarah believed her. The letter which she now rereads is from Hope. She has taken up a live-in teaching post at a school near Shrewsbury. It isn't far from her cottage on the Long Mynd, where she spends most weekends. Imogen is back in Brussels, Simla is empty, and up for sale. The Baverstocks have bought Edwina Lodge. 'Thank you for the invitation to spend Christmas with you,' Hope writes, 'but I've already arranged to

313

spend the holiday in Madeira, with a colleague from school.'

The tragedy has brought the two women together in a tenuous friendship, one that Sarah has deliberately worked on. Both of them have lost someone they loved very much as a direct consequence of what happened. Sarah has lost Lisa, and Hope has lost her brother, and this has formed a bond between them. Predictably, Hope found it nearly impossible to express her feelings about this, but Sarah, sensing the necessity for Hope to untangle her emotions about Francis, and what had caused him to take his life, wouldn't give up.

The inquest on Francis recorded a verdict of suicide while the balance of his mind was disturbed. By what, it was not stated. But later, when the first shock had worn off and, encouraged by Sarah, Hope was able to talk about it, she admitted, 'I know that it was Patti being killed that tipped him over the edge, being questioned about it. He knew that Dermot had recognized him that day at the party and felt it was bound to begin again ... the gossip, the persecution. That was what ruined his career, the first time. It was groundless, and cruel ... I was his twin, as close to him as his own self, and I know. There was never any room for anyone, or anything else, between us. Believe me, I know what he was capable of, what he himself was, and wasn't. It nearly broke him, the first time. He'd eventually made something of his life, but he couldn't have stood up to it a second time.'

'You might like to know,' she writes now, 'that I sent Francis's book to his publishers, and I heard this week that they've accepted it for publication. They think it's the best thing he's ever done.'

Sarah smiles and uncurls herself from the window seat. She goes into the room at the back of the house that Fitz now uses as a studio. It's empty but for the paraphernalia of painting. The completed picture of Allie is on the easel. The drawing, to be more accurate, in pastels.

Allie is shown kneeling on the floor, drawing, caught as she looks up at the painter with a glancing smile, her expression one of perfect trust.

It's the best thing Fitz has ever done, too.

We hope you have enjoyed this Large Print book. Other Chivers Press or G.K. Hall & Co. Large Print books are available at your library or directly from the publishers.

For more information about current and forthcoming titles, please call or write, without obligation, to:

Chivers Press Limited
Windsor Bridge Road
Bath BA2 3AX
England
Tel. (01225) 335336

OR

G.K. Hall & Co.
P.O. Box 159
Thorndike, Maine 04986
USA
Tel. (800) 223-2336

All our Large Print titles are designed for easy reading, and all our books are made to last.